COLLUSION

WINNER OF MAYHAVEN AWARD FOR FICTION

COLLUSION

WINNER OF MAYHAVEN AWARD FOR FICTION

ʃʃʃʃʃʃʃʃʃʃʃʃʃ

HARRY HAINES

Harry Haines 11/23/10

Mayhaven Publishing, Inc.

This novel does not depict any actual person or event.

Mayhaven Publishing, Inc
P O Box 557
Mahomet, IL 61853
USA

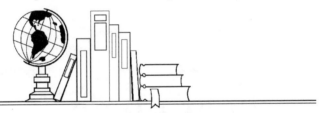

Cover Design: Steven L. Mayes
Copyright © 2010 Harry Haines
Library of Congress Control Number: 2010935545
First Edition—First Printing 2010
ISBN 13: 978 193227871-2
ISBN 10: 193227871-0

To the three musketeers:
Howard, Harvey, and Holly

CHAPTER 1

The Harvard Business School, Cambridge, Massachusetts

I teach white-collar crime.

Because—thanks to the crooks who commit embezzlement, do money laundering, take kickbacks, engage in financial statement fraud, and dozens of other illegal acts—society needs forensic accountants. Somebody has to train them.

I like the work. I get tired of explaining it to others. On October first, a bright, beautiful fall day, my new secretary Donna Woolbridge sat in the chair in front of my desk and popped the question.

"Dr. Hartman, could you give me a simplified definition of forensic accounting?"

"Who wants to know?" I smiled, knowingly. I'd gone through this many times with new employees.

"Me. My husband. Even the other associates I work with in the outer office."

At Harvard we call Donna an associate, not a secretary. She had started her job that morning in our clerical pool down the hall.

"Do you recognize the term, forensic pathologist?" I asked.

"I think so. Isn't that an M.D. who examines bodies to find the cause of death?"

I nodded. "Exactly. Well, a forensic accountant is—" I paused, hoping to lead her thinking.

She looked at me, her eyebrows pulled together.

I caved, and for the zillionth time recited my well-practiced, twenty-word spiel, "A CPA who examines financial records to find the cause of problems and determine if there has been any wrongdoing."

Donna smiled. "Sounds so simple when you say it." She got up to leave.

"You'll catch on. Just give it some time." I looked at my watch, alarmed to see that I had let so much of my class-preparation time slip away. "Hold my calls, please, Donna. I'll get back to them tomorrow morning after class."

She left the room, and I turned my attention to research for the next day's lecture. People who know anything about the Harvard Business School know that HBS is famous for teaching business practice through actual case studies. Tomorrow's case involved a telephone communications company that discovered customers were using their long distance services without paying. I'd just settled down to read the data and focus on how to present the most important facts when the damn phone rang, disrupting my concentration.

I thought about not answering.

The phone continued to ring.

"Hello." I said it loudly and let the frustration create an unmistakable edge in my voice.

"Dr. Hartman," Donna said, "it's Bryan Banks from Texas Energy, Incorporated. He says it's personal."

The name of my son-in-law took me by surprise. I couldn't remember his ever calling me at the office. "Okay, I'll take it." I pushed the button.

"Bryan, what an unexpected pleasure," the edge now gone.

"Grandpa Chris, sorry to interrupt, but I need to ask a favor." He paused.

When my daughter, Jennifer, Bryan's wife, gave birth to her first child almost ten years earlier, they started calling me Grandpa Chris and my wife Grandma Helen. Grandma was now gone, cancer two years ago, but Bryan still used the appellation in addressing me. "Sure," I answered.

"I . . . I wonder if you could fly to Houston for a luncheon meeting tomorrow?"

He sounded nervous. I sensed the need to offer immediate reassurance. "Probably. Who's the meeting with?"

"Me."

His one-word answer raised a red flag. Though he and I were both accountants, we'd never discussed his business nor my professional consulting. In fact, we made it an unwritten family rule to keep our relationship personal. "What's up? Is this something we can discuss on the phone?"

"No." He paused again, and I could hear his erratic breathing. The silence, though brief, created an awkward divisiveness—the last thing I wanted.

"Okay, I'll catch an early flight tomorrow morning. Where shall we meet?"

"My office at TEI How soon can you get here?" he asked.

"I'll try to book the Continental flight that leaves Logan at seven-thirty—arrives Houston at ten, central time. I think I can be at your office by eleven. Can you give me a clue? What's happening?"

Another pause, much longer, silently communicated my faux

pas. I had pushed too hard. But before I could get my apology out, Bryan unloaded. His bad news came in a rush.

"Chris, this is big, and it's probably going to take me down with it. I need an expert in forensic accounting to look at our corporate data and see if there is any way out. It has to be done *now*."

"I'll be there in the morning."

He left me holding a dial tone.

I returned the phone to its cradle and thought about a double Scotch on the rocks. Instinctively, my right hand reached into my pocket for the chip, a small, round, plastic, coin-like disc about the size of a silver dollar. A gift from George, my AA sponsor, it had the words "One Day at a Time" engraved on one side. I turned it over to read the date on the other side, the day of my last drink—one year, two months, one week, and three days ago.

It helped.

CHAPTER 2

Boston's Logan Airport

The next morning I caught the first plane to Houston, Continental's flight 683. For an outrageous price I booked a seat in first class where an attractive stewardess, wearing the nametag "Mitzi Miller," brought me a cheese omelet, large orange juice, fruit compote, and steaming hot coffee. I gave her a big smile and asked, "You like knock-knock jokes?"

"Sure," she answered.

"Knock, knock."

"Who's there?"

"Amos."

She grinned and shook her head. "I know, a mosquito bit me."

"No. A most lovely lady brought me breakfast."

Again she grinned and shook her head, obviously deprecating the level of my humor.

"Knock. Knock," I said.

She shook her head and gave me a wary look. "Who's there?"

"Andy."

This time she laughed out loud. "I know that one, too. And he

HARRY HAINES

bit me again."

"No, no," I said. "And he . . . *appreciated* it."

"You say that to all the girls?"

"No, of course not."

"Liar," she said, hand on her hip, smile at full width. "You said it to me on this very flight last spring." She turned and left to serve another passenger.

Mitzi Miller had boosted my spirits. I needed it. Bryan's brief information had me worried, and his inference to possible dire circumstances dominated my thoughts. After breakfast I wanted a diversion, so when Mitzi offered me a copy of the *Wall Street Journal,* I took it. The ride passed quickly and before I knew it we were in the terminal hiking with a mob of people toward an airport sign that read "Ground Transportation."

I walked out the door to the taxi queue at George Bush International Airport, and the infamous Houston humidity hit me like a bucket of steam. Thankfully, the cab had an air conditioner running at full blast. I gave the driver a simple address: "Texas Energy Incorporated, the TEI Building." He nodded, clicked the meter, and we entered morning traffic in America's fourth largest city. The twenty-mile trip took almost an hour.

A huge building directory listed Bryan Banks, Chief Accounting Officer, 4901. I searched for a way to get there and found the elevators in the first bank covered only floors one to twenty-five. Farther down a sign indicated express elevators, floors twenty-six to fifty. My ears popped on the ride up.

Room 4901 turned out to be the corner suite, an office befitting the CAO of a Fortune 500 company. I walked into a spacious reception area where thick, plush carpet, oak wall paneling, and the smell

12

COLLUSION

of rich leather chairs gave an unmistakable aura of corporate power. Two secretaries with worried faces stood between their desks engaged in conversation. Both glanced up. One turned away and left the room; the other flashed a big smile and extended her hand.

"Good morning, Dr. Hartman," she said. "I'm Elizabeth Garcia. Mr. Banks is on the phone, but I'm sure he'll be with you in just a moment. May I get you a cup of coffee?"

I'm poor at judging the age of women, but I guessed this beautifully coiffured Hispanic to be in the forty to fifty range. Her long black hair complemented a well-tailored gray business suit and created an immediate impression of personal assurance. I caught a whiff of expensive perfume as I shook her hand, declined the coffee, and took a chair by the window.

The window was not really a window, but in reality, a huge glass wall. It stretched from floor to ceiling and offered a magnificent view of the Houston ship channel. I scanned the panorama to find a row of tankers lined up alongside the oil refineries. The big ships looked like toys floating in a tiny sliver of blue liquid that stretched as far as the eye could see. I counted them. Twenty-six. I re-counted them several times while another inched its way up the waterway. Soon there would be twenty-seven. I glanced at my watch and noted I'd been waiting almost thirty minutes.

The second secretary returned and held the door for a man wearing blue coveralls. He pushed a two-wheel dolly toward Elizabeth Garcia's desk and asked, "Where are the papers you want shredded?" She frowned—looking at me to see if I'd heard. When I failed to register a response, she rose shaking her head, and without speaking, led him to a stack of boxes in the corner. I watched as he loaded and rolled them out the door.

As he left, another man entered. Tall and gray-haired, he wore a dark, pinstriped suit with red-and-gold striped tie. The so-called power tie brought to mind an Armani ad in *Esquire*. Elizabeth rose to greet him, and they exchanged a few words. I thought I heard my name mentioned and they both looked my way. When they walked toward me, I stood.

"Dr. Hartman," Elizabeth said, "this is Jerry Norton, our comptroller." She again offered coffee, and this time I accepted.

"You teach forensic accounting at Harvard?" Norton asked.

"Well, I try," I answered.

"I've read your book." We settled in with our coffee. "Bryan speaks highly of you."

I opened my mouth to respond, but, before I could get a word out, a loud noise exploded from the direction of Bryan's office. It sounded like a gunshot, and for a brief moment, the four of us—the two women, Norton, and I—sat transfixed in confused bewilderment. Then, as if choreographed by simultaneous thought, we all jumped up and ran to the door. Elizabeth got there first, jerked on the doorknob, but found it locked. Frantically, she turned to her desk and rustled through a couple of drawers until she found a set of keys.

During these ten seconds, I pounded on the door and called out to Bryan. No response.

Elizabeth returned to fumble with the lock, finally got the door open, and rushed into the room.

She let out an ear-piercing scream.

CHAPTER 3

Bryan Banks's Office, the TEI Building

I hurried into the room a step behind Elizabeth and almost knocked her over. She'd stopped just inside the doorway, staring at the blood-splattered body of my son-in-law. One couldn't blame her for screaming. My stomach churned at the horrific sight, and I rushed forward to check on him. Kneeling and placing my fingers on his throat, I felt for a pulse in his carotid artery. A feeble throb indicated he was still alive.

"Call 911," I said.

No one responded. I looked around to see the other secretary leaving the room. Norton was gagging and throwing up in the wastebasket, and Elizabeth stood behind me as if in a trance.

"Elizabeth!" I yelled.

She blinked. Stared at me. Didn't speak.

I looked her in the eye for a second and decided to try a different approach. "Bryan needs help," I said in an even, quiet tone of voice. "Call 911, now."

She seemed to comprehend. I nodded toward the phone on Bryan's desk.

"Speak in a slow, clear voice. Ask them to hurry."

She did what I asked.

And while she was making the call I turned my attention to Bryan. He was breathing, but the hole on the side of his head, at the temple just in front of his right ear, didn't offer much hope. Blood continued to gush. We needed to do something. I yanked off my tie, wadded it into a makeshift pad, and held it to the wound, trying to stanch the flow of blood.

"They're on their way." Elizabeth knelt beside me, apparently now able to cope with sight of all the blood. "How's he doing?"

"I have no idea."

"Is there anything I can do?"

"We need to make some plans."

"Yes."

"I'll go with Bryan in the ambulance. As soon as we find out where they're taking him, call Jennifer."

"All right," she said. "I can do that. What else?"

"I'm not sure Jennifer knows I'm here. Tell her I'll be at the hospital."

"I understand."

"You okay?" I asked.

"I . . . I think so." She neither looked nor sounded okay.

"You're going to be peppered with questions."

"What should I say?"

"Tell the truth. Don't try to shave the facts."

Norton moved to stand by us. He looked colorless and held a Kleenex to his mouth. "Have you called public relations?"

"No," Elizabeth answered.

"I'll go call them." Norton left the room.

COLLUSION

"Elizabeth, be careful," I warned. "You're going to be an important witness. But, remember, you'll never get in trouble if you stick to the truth."

"Why would I say anything else?"

"TEI may not want this to get out."

"Oh."

"It's certain to create a media frenzy."

"I understand."

I continued holding the pad against Bryan's wound, trying as best I could to stop the flow of blood, until the sound of loud voices came from the outer office. Then an EMS team rolled a gurney into the room. Elizabeth and I moved out of their way. Efficiency took over. Minutes later Bryan and I were riding in an ambulance, lights flashing and sirens wailing, on our way to Houston's Hermann Memorial Hospital.

They took Bryan into an operating room and asked me to meet with a young woman from the admissions office. I thought I probably looked terrible. Dried blood covered my hands, and I felt the tears running down my cheek.

"You want to wash up before we do this?" she asked.

"That's probably a good idea," I answered.

She led me to a nearby restroom. "I'll wait for you at the admissions counter."

"Thanks."

The image in the mirror shocked me. I had blood on my face, in my hair, everywhere. And my clothes looked like those of someone who worked in a slaughterhouse. It helped me to wash up. I took my time with my skin and hair, decided not to worry about clothes.

I went back to the admissions woman and tried to answer her

17

questions. We had just started down her list when two Houston policemen appeared. Spying the blood on my clothes, the two came right over.

"You a witness?" the first officer asked, extracting a notepad from his breast pocket.

"Well, I was in the room next door," I answered.

"Do you know the name of the injured?"

"Bryan Banks."

The officer scribbled the information down. "Your name?"

"Christopher Hartman."

"Address?"

"One twenty-five University Road, Cambridge, Massachusetts, 01121."

"Massachusetts?" His pencil paused, and he raised his eyebrows.

"I flew to Houston this morning for a luncheon with Bryan. He's my son-in-law."

The officer wrote this information. I waited. Then I heard a familiar voice, a voice in distress. I rushed to the adjoining room to find my daughter. We embraced, and she wrapped her arms tightly around me. For a moment this thirty-two-year-old woman was my little girl again. I patted her on the back and tried to give her comfort. She hugged me for a very long time. Finally, she relaxed her grasp. She held onto me with her right hand, using her left to dab at her face.

I pulled a small package of Kleenex from my shirt pocket and gave it to her.

"Thanks," she whispered. "I'm so glad you're here."

"Let's sit a minute." I gestured toward a couple of chairs in the corner.

COLLUSION

She held my arm as I led the way. We sat. She took my hand.

"Dad, give it to me straight. I . . . I want to know." Tears rolled down her cheeks. "Is he going to be okay?"

"I don't think anyone knows how badly he's hurt." I wasn't about to tell her about the hole in Bryan's temple.

"When will we find out?"

"The doctors are doing their best." I looked at my watch. "He's only been in there for thirty minutes."

"Thirty min . . . minutes." She started crying again.

I shifted to sit closer, reaching over, and putting my arm around her shoulder.

She sobbed, uncontrollably.

"Are the kids okay?" I asked.

"They're in sc . . . school."

"This may take a while."

She took a deep breath, struggled to compose herself, then looked at her watch. "I can call Diane Thornton. She lives across the street."

Talking about the safety of the children seemed to give her strength.

She looked again at her watch. "I could ask her to spend the night if need be."

I withdrew my arm, held her hand. "Tell me about the kids. What're they up to?"

"The usual for a ten-year-old and a seven-year-old. They keep me busy."

"Can you tell me about this morning."

"Luke is starting orchestra. Melissa's on the soccer team."

"I wish—" I was going to say I wish I could see them more often, but before I could get the words out, a woman in green hospital scrubs

19

interrupted.

"Bryan Banks family?"

I stood. "We're here."

She walked over to stand by us. "Come with me, please, to the conference room." She said it softly and with a respectful countenance. Reading an unspoken implication in her manner, a chill ran down my spine.

We followed her down the hall to a small room with a table and four chairs. "The doctors will be with you in just a minute."

As she opened the door to leave, two men in green surgical clothes entered. Both wore grim expressions.

"I'm Dr. Carter. This is Dr. McAfee."

"I'm Jennifer Banks. This is my father, Chris Hartman." We shook hands, a formality without greeting.

"Let's sit for a minute," Dr. Carter said. As we each took a chair at the table, I could tell by their body language—the slowness of their movements and the grimness in their faces—that the news was not good. Jennifer grasped my hand and held it firmly.

"We have your husband on a respirator," Dr. Carter said.

"Is . . . is . . . he going to be all right?" Jennifer almost choked as she tried to get the words out.

"Your husband has no cognitive functions," Dr. Carter said.

"No, no—" Jennifer whispered.

I moved closer, put my arm around her.

"The injury to his brain is irreparable," Dr. McAfee said. "The respirator is only sustaining his life in an artificial environment."

Dr. Carter heaved an audible sigh of resignation. "The layman's term for his condition is that he is brain dead."

Jennifer wailed, collapsing against my shoulder. I held her there to keep her from falling.

"As hard as it may sound, we think it better to let him go," Carter said.

Jennifer sobbed.

The doctors sat silently.

I patted Jennifer on the back. "It's okay. Cry it out."

"We'd like you to make some decisions about organ donation," Dr. Carter said.

"As you can see, she's in no condition to talk about this," I replied, appalled.

"Unfortunately, these decisions won't wait," Carter answered. "We don't have a lot of time."

"How much time *do* we have?" I asked.

"Difficult to say. Maybe. . . minutes."

"I know this isn't easy for either of you, but bear in mind," McAfee added, "these healthy organs could mean life for several people."

"May we see Bryan?" I asked.

The two doctors exchanged weary glances. "It's pretty grim," Dr. Carter said.

Jennifer seemed to stiffen with resolve. She lifted her head from my shoulder and wiped her eyes. "I want to see him," she whispered.

"Give us a few minutes, please," Carter replied.

The two doctors rose and left the room. I held my daughter. Gradually, her sobbing subsided.

"Take slow, deep breaths," I suggested.

She did.

"I think you should sign the release," I said.

She used the back of her hand to wipe both eyes.

"It's up to you." I kissed her on the forehead.

"Okay," she whispered.

The door opened. "Come with me," Dr. McAfee said.

We followed him a short way down the hall to an operating room where we found my son-in-law lying on a table. Death hung in the air as the sound of a respirator hissed in rhythmic pulses. The life-sustaining mask covered Bryan's face, but the side of his head lay exposed, and I could once again see the grisly hole in his temple.

Much to my surprise, Jennifer turned loose of me and walked, without assistance, to stand close to the table. She found Bryan's hand and clasped it with both of hers. The doctors, the nurses, and I watched for a long time as she stood there quietly. Then, very gently, she placed his hand back at his side, bent over to kiss him just above the respirator mask, and walked back to stand by me. The two doctors joined us.

"You're sure?" she asked, her stoic grief breaking my heart.

"Absolutely," Dr. Carter affirmed. His voice and expression conveyed a sincere empathy for Jennifer.

"There's no hope for cognitive functions," Dr. McAfee added, "I'm sorry."

A deathly hush fell over the room. Finally, Jennifer whispered, her words so soft I could barely understand them, "Where do I sign?"

"I'll make the arrangements," Carter murmured, and left the room.

"Let's go back to the conference room," McAfee suggested. He led the way, and we followed.

Jennifer and I again took chairs at the small table. Moments later, Dr. Carter returned with a police detective.

"I'd like you to meet Detective Joel Wilson, Houston PD,"

COLLUSION

Carter said.

We each shook his hand.

"Just routine," Wilson said. "An investigation is required when death is caused by gunshot."

I could see that this was upsetting to Jennifer and decided to intercede. "Look, we're just trying to do the right thing."

"Of course," replied the detective. "We all are. I have just a few questions."

I turned to the doctor. "Help us out. We're trying to cooperate."

"Officer, surely you can see that time is of the essence," Carter said.

"Of course," Wilson answered. "We're ruling it death by suicide unless the family has any questions."

At the word "suicide," Jennifer reacted. "Nooooo." she yelled, and started sobbing. I put my arms around her.

Dr. McAfee entered the room, a clipboard pressed to his chest. "If Mrs. Banks will sign here, we'll begin the procedures for transplant."

Jennifer, pulling herself together as best she could, signed the form, offering her husband's body for organ donations. And then, as I held her and steadied her, she signed a second form.

I took the form and handed it to the police. In so doing, I glanced at the document's heading—REQUEST TO WAIVE AUTOPSY.

23

CHAPTER 4

Hermann Memorial Hospital, Houston

A tall slender man, dressed in a suit, came into the crowded little room.

"Don," Jennifer said. "Thank you for coming." She stood to embrace him.

The doctors left. Detective Wilson moved to a back corner of the room, away from the door.

"Dad, this is our minister, Dr. Donald McIntyre. Don, I'd like you to meet my father, Christopher Hartman."

We shook hands.

The detective closed his notebook and excused himself.

"Jennifer, how can I help?" asked the minister.

"I . . . I don't know." She blotted her eyes, again.

"The children—" I started, then stopped.

"Patti is at the school, standing by." He pulled out his cellphone and turned to make eye contact with me. "Patricia Messer is our associate minister for the children's ministry."

"I think the children should get this news from their mother and me," I said.

COLLUSION

"Of course," he replied. "I just mention Patti and her location to indicate that we're available to help if you need us."

"Jennifer, we need to go to Luke and Melissa," I said.

She nodded, "I agree," she said, and wiped her eyes again. We stood. The minister offered a brief prayer.

We got into Jennifer's car for the thirty-mile drive to Sally Ride Elementary School. Jennifer and I sat in the back seat while the minister drove and talked on his cellphone. We could hear him making arrangements with the school and with the associate minister.

Upon our arrival, the school nurse and the school counselor quietly brought Luke and Melissa to meet with Jennifer and me in the principal's conference room. We hugged, and I let Jennifer do most of the talking. Luke teared up for a few minutes. Melissa didn't seem to have much reaction, or perhaps she didn't understand fully the implications of her daddy going to heaven. The result was that the four of us met briefly and then called in the two ministers for prayer.

We left the school and I took the wheel for the short drive to the house.

At home, Jennifer and I made phone calls. Patti Messer talked with the kids. Don McIntyre scheduled an appointment for us to meet with the Woodlands Funeral Home and then left to notify members of the church.

Diane Thornton, Jennifer's best friend who lived across the street, came over to man the door. This turned out to be one of the most important jobs, as a steady line of friends, neighbors, and co-workers came to bring food, condolences, and offers of assistance. And, of even greater help, Diane knew how to handle the media. Three TV stations sent camera crews. Diane went out to talk with each of them, to make a plea for family privacy. Shortly thereafter the news media

25

packed up and left.

Allen Ray, from the Woodlands Funeral Home, came and met with us. We arranged to have Bryan's remains cremated and to hold a memorial service at the Woodlands Presbyterian Church in two days at four PM. Gradually, darkness fell, people stopped coming, and a frantic day came to a close around the dining room table.

Diane offered to assemble a meal from the pile of food brought by churchwomen. The fried chicken, vegetables, and homemade bread, which would normally have been a feast, seemed unappetizing. I picked at my food, urged the children to try to eat theirs. It was good to have Diane with us. She led the conversation.

"You probably haven't heard about the stock market," she said.

"Diane," Jennifer groaned, "the stock market is the last thing I'm interested in."

"Is there something in the news about TEI's stock?" I asked.

"Can't we talk about something other than TEI?" Jennifer complained.

A thought suddenly occurred to me. "Jenny, did you know I was coming to Houston today?"

"No, but I'm so glad you did. Come to think about it, why *did* you come, Dad?"

"Bryan called me yesterday afternoon."

"Oh?"

"He didn't tell you why he called?"

"No—"

"He wanted me to look at TEI's finances."

An eerie silence fell over the room. No one ate. Finally, Melissa broke the silence.

"I'm not hungry," she said, pushing her plate away.

COLLUSION

"Mom, may Melissa and I go watch TV?" Luke asked.

"Okay," Jennifer said, hugging each before they scampered off.

"Bryan told me on the phone that something catastrophic was happening at TEI," I said. "He asked me to come and advise him as a forensic accountant."

"I can't believe Bryan would do that," Jennifer protested. "Over the years he went out of his way to avoid accounting talk with you."

"I know. His call surprised me, too."

"Maybe I have the answer," Diane interrupted.

We both stared at her. The room became so quiet I could hear air moving from the air conditioning vent.

"TEI dominated the evening news," Diane said.

"The stock price fell?"

"Cratered."

"They blamed it on Bryan's death?" I asked.

"Not exactly," Diane answered.

"So what did they say?"

"The sell-off started this morning," she answered. "The two news reports I saw, one national—one local, treated Bryan's death as a result. Not the cause."

"Dad, I don't want to talk about this," Jennifer pleaded, sinking her forehead into her palms.

"Sure." I made eye contact with Diane. She nodded, ever so slightly, and looked down at her food.

We sat at the table saying nothing more. Obviously, no one felt like eating. Jennifer stood. "I think I'll go back to be with the kids for a little while," she said, rubbing her temples. "Just leave the dishes. I'll clean up later." She left the room.

Diane and I, without speaking, began clearing the table and

27

loading the dishwasher.

"How much?" I asked.

"How much did the price of TEI fall?"

"Yes."

"I really don't know. Is there a limit to how much a stock can go down in one day?"

"That's for commodities."

"Oh." Diane continued to rinse the dishes, her facial expression indicating deep thought. "One thing I do remember, TEI was the most heavily traded stock."

"How many shares?"

"Sorry. I'm not really into stock talk. All I can recall is that it was a big number—in the millions."

"That's okay. We'll get the full report in tomorrow morning's newspapers."

"Chris, what's going on? None of this feels right at all."

"Wish I knew," I said, placing a coffee cup into the dishwasher rack.

"Is there some kind of scandal at TEI?"

"Sure looks that way."

"And Bryan's involved?"

"God, I hope not."

"He's the chief accounting officer. The CAO?"

"Yes."

"Then how could he *not* be involved?" she asked.

"That's the obvious question," I answered.

I had a sinking feeling in the pit of my stomach.

CHAPTER 5

44 Leisure Cove, The Woodlands
thirty miles north of downtown Houston

The next morning I woke early and went out to get the paper. The *Houston Chronicle* printed a story infinitely worse than I'd expected. TEI stock fell from $41.23 to $9.86, a record for the NASDAQ. With special interest I read a front-page sidebar titled "Free Fall Records." The newspaper reported three: the loss of $31.37 as the largest point decline, the exchange of more than 41,000,000 shares as the largest volume, and a number so huge I couldn't comprehend it, the loss of almost $1.3 trillion as the new record for any one stock on a single day.

Bryan's picture appeared on the front page. The heading and the story called his death a suicide, a result of the fall in the price of the corporate stock. While the story didn't spell it out, the circumstances certainly suggested guilt as probable motivation for him to take his life. It seemed so unfair. Without any opportunity for disclaimer, the newspaper had created a terrible inference, a massive burden for my daughter and my grandchildren.

The whole thing made me furious.

HARRY HAINES

I thought about trashing the paper and walked halfway to the dumpster—then decided against it. Without any rational judgment, I ended up taking it with me back to my room. The paper had me so rattled, my decision-making ability started bouncing around like a ping-pong ball. I took a long hot shower and, with the scalding water cascading over me, tried to sort out a plan for the day. My thoughts went back two days, to Bryan's phone call, to his words, which were etched forever into my memory. He'd said, "I need an expert to look at TEI's corporate data—"

By the time the water turned cold, I had a plan. I'd offer to retrieve Bryan's car, which was probably still downtown at the TEI parking garage. While there, I'd stop by Bryan's office and ask Elizabeth Garcia if I could look over the material Bryan had prepared for our meeting. It sounded simple.

At breakfast I told Jennifer I'd pick up Bryan's car. She found an extra set of keys for me. I called a cab and, during the forty-minute trip, used my cellphone to call Bryan's secretary.

Elizabeth Garcia offered to help me find the car, and, while she knew nothing about the corporate data Bryan had prepared for yesterday's meeting, she agreed to look for it. I had the distinct impression she was on my side, and that she, like me, wanted to find out what caused Bryan to take his life. I sensed that in the near future, a line would be drawn and people—all of us who were caught up in TEI's financial tragedy—would be forced to choose sides. While I hardly knew Elizabeth, I felt reasonably sure she was innocent of any wrongdoing, and as a result would end up on the side of the good guys.

Arrival at the notorious building thrust me into a media circus. Reporters, television crews, and print media photographers tussled with TEI Security while the Houston Police in huge numbers stood by to referee. Obviously, a visitor like me wasn't going to be allowed anywhere near the elevators. I called Elizabeth on my cell. She agreed to meet me on the south steps by the now infamous TEI sign.

I waited patiently and watched the media do battle with those who tried to restrain them. The confusion and turmoil caused me to face the building, to focus my attention toward the glass doors. I concentrated so intensely on the people, especially on those coming and going toward the elevators, that I didn't notice when someone came and stood next to me—until I got a whiff of an expensive perfume.

"Let's walk casually this way, toward the garage," Elizabeth said.

"Where'd you come from?" I was completely taken by surprise.

"I took the elevator to the basement and came out the back door by the loading dock."

"Pretty sneaky."

"If I'd tried the front door, I was afraid someone from the media would recognize me as Bryan's secretary."

"And we'd still be there," I said. "This place is crazy."

"It's worse on the inside," she answered.

"You mean worse than out here?" I grimaced, shaking my head. "Can't be."

"People are behaving like wild animals. It's worse than panic at the zoo."

"Give me an example."

"Upton called, asked me to run the CAO's weekly report."

"Reed Upton, the chief financial officer?"

"Yes, Bryan's boss."

"Sounds routine," I said.

"Are you kidding?" she huffed. "I've been here ten years, and that's the first time a corporate vice-president ever called and personally asked for our weekly report."

"So?" I let it linger, waiting for her to explain.

"So, five minutes later, he called again."

"And—"

"And cancelled the request."

"Upton called you twice?" I asked, for clarification.

"So did Zimmerman," she answered.

"Richard Zimmerman, the CEO?"

"Yes, personally," she said. "Not his secretary—the big man himself called me."

"Over the past ten years, how often have you spoken to Zimmerman?"

"Today was the first time. Ever."

I thought that over. "Okay, so what did he want?"

"Same as Upton, the CAO weekly report."

"And what did you tell him?"

"I said, "Yes, sir,'" she answered, emphatically. "The *first* time."

"The first time?"

"He called again."

"And cancelled?" I asked.

"Just like Upton," she replied. "And he wanted to know if Upton had called me."

"What'd you say?"

"The truth. I told him Reed had called twice."

"Good for you."

"I remembered your advice."

"My advice?"

"You said I'd never get into trouble if I just reported the truth."

COLLUSION

I smiled. By this time we'd walked halfway down the length of the garage and I could see at least a dozen Porsches, apparently the automobile of choice for TEI executives. Elizabeth stopped, next to a new, bright red, Porsche 911 Carrera.

"This is Bryan's," she said. "It has the special vanity plates."

I looked down to read it: ACC-1, the common abbreviation for accounting and the number "1." Just to be sure, I unlocked the door, climbed in, and tried the key. It worked.

"Thanks," I said, turning off the engine and stepping out.

"No problem," she answered.

"Have you thought about my other request?" I asked.

"The material Bryan had prepared for his meeting with you?"

I nodded.

"To be honest, I've not had much time to look. Want to go up to the office and help me search?"

"Sure. Is there a back way?"

"I'm afraid not."

"Yecht." I turned, and we started walking back in silence.

Arriving at the steps, we waded through enough lights to illuminate a football stadium. With cameras rolling and flash bulbs popping, Elizabeth talked me through security, and we took the express elevator to the forty-ninth floor. The police were just leaving. I recognized Detective Joel Wilson and greeted him.

"How's the family?" he asked.

"As well as can be expected," I answered. "Thanks for asking."

"Anything Houston PD can do to help?"

"Nothing I can think of. What's happening here?"

"Routine," he said. "We always take photographs and dust the scene, just in case."

"Find anything new?" I asked.

"No. But I'd like us to stay in touch, just in case either of us discovers something."

"You bet."

The detective turned to Elizabeth. "You, too." He handed each of us his card.

"Is it okay to clean up the office now?" she asked.

"Go ahead," he nodded. "We've pulled the yellow tape and signs." Wilson and the two uniformed policemen left.

Elizabeth and I walked into the blood-spattered room and, again, I felt my stomach roil. I noticed that Elizabeth parted her lips, breathing through her mouth to avoid the smell of death. We stood there silently for a brief moment.

"Bryan wanted me to look at corporate data."

Elizabeth sighed, shook her head. "Dr. Hartman, that could include almost anything."

"Would you prefer I called you Ms. Garcia?"

"No, please call me Elizabeth."

"Then you need to call me Chris."

"Okay, Chris. What are we looking for?"

"I can tell you, word for word, the last thing Bryan said to me."

"Okay," she answered.

"He said, 'Chris, this is big, and it's probably going to take me down with it. I need an expert forensic accountant to look at our corporate data and see if there's any way out. It has to be done now.'"

Silence prevailed as we thought about possibilities.

"Blackberry," she said.

"I don't understand." I said.

"Bryan kept key information like that on his Blackberry."

"But this is big," I argued. "It would be the essential corporate data. Probably hundreds of pages and mostly spreadsheets."

"I know. But Bryan would still keep it on his Blackberry and download it to his desktop computer for analysis, for printing, or for transfer to others."

"I don't understand. Why would he do that?"

"Security," she answered. "That way, only he would have access to the innermost corporate information, the basic raw data from which public information was derived."

"You're implying that this 'basic raw data' was sometimes massaged before TEI released it to the public?"

"Not sometimes—always."

"Oh, really." This startled me. "Who did the massaging?"

"Upton and his crew," she answered. "Bryan only kept track of the basic raw data."

We heard people in the outer office. Elizabeth and I started for the door. Halfway there we stopped as two men in dark, pinstriped suits came into the room. Elizabeth made the introductions.

"Dr. Hartman, I'd like you to meet our CEO, Richard Zimmerman, and our CFO, Reed Upton. This is Christopher Hartman, Bryan's father-in-law."

We shook hands with somber faces.

"We're extremely sorry for your loss," Zimmerman said. His tone of voice carried a sense of personal concern.

"As you can see, this has come at a bad time," Upton said, his words clipped, even harsh. "Why are you here in Bryan's office?"

Upton's question flustered me. I hesitated before answering.

"He has come for Bryan's car." Elizabeth came to my rescue.

"Were you able to help him?" Upton asked.

35

"Yes," I answered, for her. "I have the keys, and Ms. Garcia has helped me locate the car."

"And you'd like Bryan's personal things?" Upton asked.

"Yes, of course."

"I'll have TEI Security assist Elizabeth in collecting them," Upton said. "We'll send them to the house. No need for you or any other family members to come to the office."

"I appreciate your help," I said, struggling to bite my tongue.

"Elizabeth, would you help Dr. Hartman through security downstairs?" Upton gestured toward the door.

He said it smoothly, even politely, but it came at me like a command. I thought it extremely rude. Obviously, he wanted to get rid of me. We locked eyes for a moment, neither of us blinking, then, without a word, Elizabeth led the way and I quietly followed.

In the elevator, on the way down, I asked a question. "Did you notice Upton took the lead in our conversation? Zimmerman just stood there."

"That's the way it always is," Elizabeth replied. "Most of us think that Upton runs the corporation. Zimmerman stands aside and lets him do it."

"But Zimmerman is taking the hit," I argued. "TEI is in a free fall, and everyone blames him."

"Amazing, isn't it?"

The doors opened and we looked out into a lobby filled with people. The sound level, approaching a roar, ended our conversation. I exited the elevator and glanced back at her. Our eyes met for a moment, the doors closed, and she was gone.

The possibility of finding Bryan's information seemed more remote than ever.

CHAPTER 6

Houston, driving north on I-45

Early afternoon and already Houston traffic filled the interstate. I judged it worse than Boston, but maybe the circumstances, especially my apparent inability to learn anything about the free fall of my son-in-law's corporation, colored my evaluation of the traffic. A big pickup swerved to change lanes in front of me and caused me to brake suddenly. My spastic, uneven response caused a domino effect, and I heard the squeal of tires. Drivers behind me honked their displeasure.

I needed a drink.

My problem with alcohol, marginal throughout my adult years, became serious in the last year of Helen's life. As her cancer symptoms escalated, my refuge in the bottle grew. However, no one blamed me for drinking to excess because "poor Chris" had the perfect justification and, in effect, the blessing of society.

The year following my wife's death, circumstances changed. I became known as "the lush," the guy no one wanted to be around. Students withdrew from my classes. Friends and neighbors avoided me. My downward spiral increased to the point that everyone left

37

me alone, both in metaphor and in reality, with my bottle.

Then one morning I called Alcoholics Anonymous, and a guy named George offered to meet with me. That was the day that changed my life. Since then, dozens of times, temptation visited me. However, never so strongly as now, driving toward the grief in my daughter's home.

But, I made it. And once there, the associations with a seven-year-old and a ten-year-old trumped any thoughts of booze. Love of family brings a compelling diversion, and the needs of youth elicit the strongest possible concern. So, the kids and I sat on the back steps and talked about life cycles. It brought us together, and I relished the opportunity to lead them in conversation about the elusiveness of religion, coping with life and death, and the intangibles of the human spirit. The blind faith of grandchildren is one of life's greatest blessings.

However, life goes on, and children can only take a limited amount of philosophy. So, after an hour of "heavy" talk, we adjourned to the family room and played cards until dinnertime. When Jennifer called the kids to wash up, I took a minute to catch the lead story on the evening news. As expected, TEI continued its fall. What was astonishing was the price per share—now down to twenty-six cents.

After the meal, Jennifer asked me to go with her upstairs to their little home office to talk.

"Dad, I'm worried about money," she said.

"Of course," I answered. "Bryan was the breadwinner."

"I'd like your help in going over our finances."

"Sure. Let's see what you have."

"We keep all our papers in here." She pulled open the door to a small safe in the credenza behind Bryan's desk.

"Why don't we make an inventory?"

COLLUSION

She emptied the safe's contents and heaped everything on the desk, a pile of papers about ten inches high. I made a quick pass, rearranging the documents into stacks of insurance policies, deeds, mortgages, and general information. I placed Bryan's will on top and his financial statement second.

"Bryan took care of the finances," Jennifer said. "I've never, ever looked at this stuff."

"I understand," I answered. "He was the CPA, and he probably wanted you to concentrate on other things."

"I took care of the children, the house, our social activities."

"Jenny. You don't have to justify."

"It's just that I feel so ignorant. I don't even know how much money we have."

"Let's start with the will," I said. "We'll read it together."

So, we did. Only two pages long, we read it in a couple of minutes and found it was exactly what I expected. Very standard, Bryan left everything to Jennifer. Without discussion, we moved on to the financial statement.

"Wow, you have a lot of TEI stock," I said.

"Bryan used to say that it would take care of Luke, Melissa, and me, if anything ever happened to him."

"He lists 150,000 shares at $41.27, for a total of $6,190,500. That was your major asset."

"Was?"

"You know the price per share has dropped."

She sighed. "I guess I haven't been paying attention."

"On the news tonight, they reported it at twenty-six cents a share," I said.

"You'll have to translate. Give me the total."

HARRY HAINES

I punched in the numbers on my pocket calculator. "That's $39,000."

"Dad! How could that be?" Blanching, she slumped into the desk chair as if her bones couldn't hold her up.

"Jenny. Stocks go down as well as up."

"But six million to thirty-nine thousand?"

I thought she might break down. Most people would. But, she didn't. My daughter just sat there and shook her head, a near life-less form that could no longer comprehend bad news.

I struggled to find words of encouragement. "Let's look at your other assets," I said.

"There's the house and the cars," she whispered.

"Of course." I looked at the financial statement to see that the house and the two cars all carried heavy loans. Little or no equity there. "Let's come back to this," I said, careful to keep my expression noncommittal.

"And life insurance. Bryan told me he had taken out a million-dollar policy."

I looked through the pile and found a big, thick Prudential document. "You're right," I said, leafing through the pages. "The amount is one million dollars."

"Well, at least that's something."

Like all policies, this one contained paragraph after paragraph of special provisions. I found the header for suicide on page six:

In the case of death by suicide, this policy remains in force whether the insured is sane or insane. However, if death by suicide of the insured occurs within two years from the date of issue, the liability of the company shall be waived and all coverage becomes void.

COLLUSION

I Immediately looked for the date on the policy and found that it had been purchased a year earlier. With a heavy heart, I showed it to my daughter.

Jennifer sagged. I tried desperately to think of something to say. I couldn't. So, we silently continued through the stack: birth certificates, marriage license, an inventory of their household belongings . . . but no other significant assets. Bryan had placed all his hopes on Texas Energy, Incorporated.

And like so many others, the sudden and unexplained TEI collapse had wiped him out. The realization hit me harder than ever. I stood, held out my arms, and embraced my daughter. My concern for her, the single most important thing in my life, now carried a new motivation.

While I held her I made a silent vow. To her and to my grandchildren, I promised myself I would not rest until I found out what caused the fall of this giant corporation.

CHAPTER 7

Woodlands Presbyterian Church

The next day we went to the funeral. An usher led the family to the reserved seats near the front, and I did my best to provide support for Jennifer, Luke, and Melissa.

All of Bryan's family came, his parents, his brother—a Chicago newscaster—with his wife and four children, a total of eight. But, as small as this might seem, it doubled the Hartmans. Our only living relative, my father's elderly brother, in a nursing home in Boston, was unable to attend, so our three generations numbered only four people. Virtually all of Bryan's living relatives totaled only twelve people at the service.

Presbyterians, at this church at least, referred to the service as a memorial, not a funeral. To me it seemed unbearably long, and for my family, a burden rather than support for their grief. But, we endured. And after the service we made our way to the church's fellowship hall to receive the condolences of hundreds of people, the majority of whom were strangers to me. We stood in a receiving line as people shook hands or embraced Jennifer, tried to give comfort to the children, and introduced themselves to me and to Bryan's family. It didn't take long to see that Jennifer needed relief. I found the associate minister, Patricia Messer, and she arranged for Jennifer and the children to go back to the house in one of the funeral home's white limousines.

I returned to the hall and stood with other members of the family as the reception gradually wound down. Finally, at the end of the receiving line, I found a familiar face—Elizabeth Garcia.

"Thanks for coming," I said.

"He was my boss," she answered, a touch of umbrage in her voice. "And one of my closest friends."

"Of course," I replied.

I tried to think of a way to change the subject. Glancing around the room, the crowd rapidly thinning, I asked, "Could you give me a ride home?"

Her face softened and she shrugged. "Sure, I'll wait for you in the parking lot. A white Toyota Camry."

"Give me a few minutes."

She left. I completed my obligations and walked to the parking lot. The only Camry I saw was parked in the last slot on the back row. I climbed in and sniffed a faint remnant of a familiar perfume.

"Thanks for waiting."

"No problem."

"I'd like to visit a minute. There's a coffee shop two blocks south, in the village."

"Sounds good."

She drove the short distance in silence, parked, and we walked inside to the table in the corner.

"Any luck on the Blackberry?" I asked.

"No," she answered, giving her head a little shake. "Have you looked at home?"

"Yes. And searched the car. It's not there."

The waitress brought our coffee.

Elizabeth restarted the conversation. "I've noticed something unusual."

"Unusual? What?"

"No one at the office has asked about it."

I thought about that for a moment. "I wonder why?"

We sipped our coffee for a few moments, each of us alone with our thoughts.

"Who would know about Bryan's use of his Blackberry?"

"Everyone," she answered. "Everyone who knew Bryan or worked with him. He always carried it."

"Surely not *everyone*."

"Well, the executive board. The finance committee. Everyone in the accounting office."

"Sounds like quite a few people."

"Dozens. Maybe a hundred. I really can't tell you for sure."

"Upton?" I asked.

"Absolutely," she answered. "Upton was Bryan's boss. Bryan took the Blackberry to every meeting he ever had with him."

"Zimmerman?"

"Of course. But in a different way."

"How's that?"

"Zimmerman tends to be oblivious of details."

"Oh? Give me a for instance."

She gave me a wry smile. "For instance, he has no idea whether or not I wear a wedding ring."

Immediately, I looked. But she had her left hand in her lap, below the table.

COLLUSION

"Guilty. I admit I've not looked, either."

She pulled her hand up. No ring. "You're like Zimmerman. You see the big picture."

"I think I would have noticed if Bryan carried a Blackberry."

"Because you're an accountant," she answered. "Zimmerman would notice the price of energy in Northern India or Western Samoa."

"But not the equipment used by his chief accounting officer."

"He wouldn't care how Bryan did it, only about the results."

"So, who would care?"

"Upton, for sure." She thought for a moment and shook her head. "And probably a dozen others of the people I mentioned."

I heaved a big sigh. Nothing seemed easy. "So, we've got to keep looking." I glanced at my watch.

"Ready?" she asked.

"Yeah. Grandpa's needed at home."

She dropped me at Jenny's driveway. Inside, I found Bryan's family saying their goodbyes, and I walked them to the door. Then, after a quiet dinner, Jennifer took a sedative and went to bed early.

Melissa and I played "Go Fish," for a while, but soon, she began to yawn. We put the cards away. She gave me a kiss and slipped off to bed.

Luke fell asleep in front of the TV. I carried him to his bedroom, pulled off his shoes, and laid him on his bed, fully clothed, with a light cover.

The end of another day—one filled with the rituals of death, heartache, and uncertainty for my family—finally dragged to an end. I tried to sleep. Couldn't. Wished for a glass of ice and a jigger of pale, golden-hued, seven-year-old, Scotch whisky. I tossed,

45

turned, and finally dropped off.

The next thing I knew it was morning, and Jennifer was gently shaking my shoulder. "Dad, it's Elizabeth Garcia." She handed me the cordless telephone. I looked at my wrist, amazed to see that it was after eight o'clock, the latest I had slept in years.

"Hello," I said, my voice husky with sleep.

"Chris, it's here," she said. "I walked in and found it on Bryan's desk."

"Found what?"

"The Blackberry."

I bolted up. Swung my feet to the floor. "I'll be right there."

"And I have Bryan's password."

"Great." Adrenaline surged through me like electricity as I thought of the implications. Then, before I could express my feelings of elation, her next six words hit me like an ice storm.

"I checked. Someone wiped it clean."

CHAPTER 8

44 Leisure Cove, The Woodlands

One week after the funeral, Jennifer and I approached the subject of my return to Boston. With the children settled back into their school routines, I could see her gradually coming to accept the reality of Bryan's death. Each day started a bit easier. On the seventh morning, we lingered over breakfast coffee at the kitchen table and talked about the days ahead.

"You need to quit worrying about us," she said.

"I can't help it. I feel it's my job to worry about you and the kids."

"We're going to find a way out of this."

"Sure. I know."

"Harvard needs you more than we do."

"Jenny!"

"You know what I mean. Your students—"

"I can stay as long as I'm needed."

She sipped her coffee, looked out the window.

I studied her profile and tried to think of what to say that would be supportive.

"You need a little time to let things settle?" I asked.

"Yeah."

"How about I book a flight back to Boston tomorrow morning?"

"Seems like it's time."

"And we'll get together for Thanksgiving?"

"Of course."

"You and the kids want to come to Boston?"

"That would be nice." She perked up, and for a fleeting moment I could see a sparkle in her eyes—the Jennifer I remembered. "Could we spend a few days in my favorite cottage in Hyannisport?"

"You bet," I answered.

"I think getting away from Houston would help," she said.

"The smell of the ocean, walking on the beach."

"Oh, Dad—" She started to cry again, but swiped her eyes with her fingers. "I'm so damn tired of crying."

"You need to be in a place with happy memories."

She picked up her napkin.

"So, I'll go book my flight," I said.

She nodded, dabbing at her eyes with the corner of her napkin.

"But I've got one more thing I'd like to do while I'm still here in Houston."

"Okay."

"I'd like to visit with TEI's accounting firm, Stephen Svensen."

"Whatever. You need my help to do that?"

"No," I answered. "I'll drive downtown, and be back in time for dinner."

I called and made an appointment with Dennis Johnston, the head of Stephen Svensen's Houston Office. Apparently, he knew me by reputation. He seemed pleased to receive my call, eager to talk with me, and agreed to meet for lunch at the Petroleum Club, a pri-

COLLUSION

vate restaurant on the top floor of the Exxon Building.

When I stepped off the elevator, a tall, slender, gray-headed man with black horn-rimmed glasses walked toward me. Navy blue blazer, khaki slacks, striped blue-and-brown tie—if accountants had a uniform, he was wearing it.

"Dr. Hartman, I'm Dennis Johnston."

"I'd prefer first names," I said. "Please call me Chris."

"Sure, Chris. Everyone calls me Denny."

The maître d' seated us at a table by the window. I could see the TEI Building just a few blocks to the west. It loomed like a black cloud over our conversation.

"I understand Bryan Banks was your son-in-law," he said.

"That's right."

"My condolences for your loss."

"Thank you," I responded. "How well did you know Bryan?"

"Not well. Most of my TEI dealings are with Upton, the CFO."

"That's understandable. From what I hear, he practically runs the show."

Denny chuckled. "You know I can't comment on the internal politics of one of our major clients. Especially one that's under fire."

I shrugged. "I don't expect you to."

"How're my former colleagues?" He named three Harvard professors who taught accounting, all of whom had started their careers as CPAs with Stephen Svensen.

"Fine, I think. I've been gone two weeks, for most of the time that TEI's been in the headlines."

"Those lucky bastards," Denny said with a smile. "They knew when to get out."

"You looking for a spot in academia?" I asked.

49

"If I survive."

I shook my head. "No question about that."

"Thanks. I appreciate the vote of confidence. But how much do you know about what's happening on the inside?"

I smiled. "Just what I've read in the papers."

His face turned serious. "When I sit here with the country's leading expert in forensic accounting and he tells me his son-in-law didn't give him any inside info, I get nervous."

"It happens to be the truth."

Dennis Johnston didn't answer. He looked out the window, toward the TEI Building. I could see the wheels turning as he considered my denial. Then, abruptly, he changed the direction of our conversation. "Will you be acting as consultant for the government's investigation?" he asked.

"Not that I know of."

"Jeez, Chris, I've always heard you're a straight shooter."

"And I've worked hard to earn that reputation."

"Then why is it I feel like I'm being sandbagged?"

"I'm not sure I know how to answer that."

He stared at me for several moments. Then he threw down his fork and slumped back in his chair.

I studied him as his gaze returned to the window and and at the well-known building to the west. He looked whipped. It was a persona I had seen before, but in a different setting. Usually, I found it in a courtroom—the look of a man convicted as a white-collar felon.

"Denny, I'm mainly interested in learning the extent of my son-in-law's involvement in this mess. Can you help me?"

He heaved a big sigh, squirmed in his chair, and leaned forward with his elbows on the table. "How do I know you're not lying through your teeth, setting me up for an SEC investigation?"

"So help me God, I'm just trying to ease my daughter's loss, and to find out what happened. But, I understand. You must treat your client's corporate information as confidential."

"Glad we see eye to eye on that."

"But—" I let my one-word answer linger.

"No 'buts' about professional regard for one's clients."

"Yes, but some of this must be public information," I said.

"Of course. And you have all the public information."

"That's the problem," I responded. "I don't."

"Look, everyone's paranoid," he pleaded. "We're scared."

"I know that, and I empathize."

"The government's looking for someone to place blame."

I narrowed my eyes. "Such as my son-in-law."

"Bryan Banks is the last person to whom any of these problems can be traced."

"That's comforting to hear."

"If anything, he was a bit too much of a purist."

"How so?"

"Bryan wouldn't cut corners."

"How do you know this?"

"I witnessed several occasions when people asked him to adjust the figures, to make corporate accounting reports look better."

"And?"

"And Bryan wouldn't do it," Denny answered. "It surprised me that he kept his job as CAO."

"Really?"

"I saw the pressure to get rid of him."

"Is that public information?"

"Probably not. But—"

"But eventually these things all come out?"

"You probably know better than I."

I sensed that Denny Johnston had gone as far as he felt he could go. I couldn't help him with any information about government inquiry. In return, he couldn't, or wouldn't, help me with my informal attempts to gain inside knowledge about the TEI collapse.

"What do you think about the weather?" I.

"It's too damn hot." I saw his persona snap back. "Especially for October." The fear in his face evaporated.

"Thanks for meeting with me," I said.

"My pleasure."

We shook hands at the elevator. He excused himself to visit with someone, and I took the long ride down, alone with my thoughts. I had found that people were scared, that a government investigation loomed closer, and that at least one person thought Bryan had no part in the scandal.

The reassurance about Bryan's integrity helped. None of the rest did. I really hadn't learned anything new.

Then, in the car, driving north to Jennifer's house, something wormed its way out of my subconscious. What was new was what I *didn't* learn. Stephen Svensen did the audits for TEI. They were the watchdogs. They were the guys whose job it was, or was supposed to be, to blow the whistle if anyone tried to, using Denny's words, "cut corners." So why was Johnston so worried about the government inquiry and about me? I could think of only one plausible answer. When auditors get caught playing footsy with those who are being audited, an ugly word comes to mind.

Collusion.

CHAPTER 9

Room 209, Hawes Classroom Building
The Harvard Business School

The students seemed glad to see me. And, for sure, I was happy
to see them. After a brief apology for my absence and an expression
of my thanks for their patience and understanding, we jumped into
a case study of Montgomery and Ward, the giant retail firm that had
recently gone belly-up. Well-prepared students make it easy for me
to lead the discussion, and today, after a two-week delay, this class
tore after the subject like ravenous wolves hungry for fresh game. I
had to rein in the discussion in order to close with my PowerPoint
presentation, which summarized the leading causes of the failure.
No white-collar crime here—just poor management.

Class ended. Most students hurried off while I powered down
the projector and unhooked my laptop computer. Two students
joined me at the teacher's console, obviously waiting to chat.

"How've you been?" I asked.

"We're glad you're back," the first student answered.

"Really glad," the second added.

"But we understand," the first said.

"Please accept our condolences," the second said.

"Thank you," I said.

Then they left. Nothing big, just two human beings trying to empathize with my family problems. It helped. And once again I was reminded of the primary reason I loved this job—the students. At this point in my life, in my professional career as a forensic accountant, I could make many times my university salary working as a professional consultant, or better yet, going into private practice. But, I wouldn't have contact with students. They charged my batteries.

I went back to my office to tackle the work and found at least a hundred e-mails. Many were university or professional announcements, information I could scan and quickly delete. Others concerned routine matters that needed only a brief answer or a delayed response. If it could be handled in a minute or less, I responded and deleted. If it couldn't, and this left only a few, perhaps a dozen or so, which required serious attention, I saved. One jumped out at me for an immediate answer. I printed a copy.

TO: Chartman@harvard.edu
FROM: JWilson@HoustonPD.gov
RE: New developments

Good Morning Dr. Hartman,
I have some additional information about the circumstances associated with the death of Bryan Banks. Elizabeth Garcia called me about the Blackberry. I reviewed the photographs of Banks's desk and found some interesting inconsistencies. I need to talk with you about my findings and would appreciate a call at your earliest convenience.

COLLUSION

Joel Wilson
Houston PD
713-555-5012

I called him immediately.

"Good morning, Joel. Chris Hartman. I've just read your e-mail."

"Dr. Hartman. Thanks for calling."

" Detective Wilson, I thought we had agreed to use first names."

"Fine with me, Chris," he laughed.

"So, Joel, what's up?" I asked.

"You recall that the crime lab always takes photographs when a death involves gunshots?" he said. "It's routine."

"Yes, you told me that on the day of Bryan's death."

"Well, after Elizabeth called me about the Blackberry, I pulled the photographs to study them more carefully."

"What did you find?"

"We have three photographs of the desk. All show a rectangle three inches by five and one-half inches where there is no blood spatter."

"What are the dimensions of the Blackberry?"

"Exactly the same."

"So, are you telling me the Blackberry was on Bryan's desk at the time of his suicide?"

"There's no other logical explanation."

"And that, at some time between the shooting and the taking of the photographs, someone took the Blackberry?"

"It sure looks that way."

"Can you pinpoint the time the photographs were taken?"

"Yes, 12:43 pm he replied. "The CSI camera automatically records the date and time of every photo."

"I'm a little fuzzy about the time of the gunshot," I said. "Seems to me it happened around 11:30."

"We have the exact time of the 911 call, 11:39 a.m. Elizabeth tells me she called immediately after the shooting."

"She's right. I was there. She dialed the number within one or two minutes of the gunshot."

"That gives us a window of slightly more than an hour," Wilson said.

"So, the Blackberry was taken from the desk between 11:37 and 12:43."

"Exactly."

"However, we were there with Bryan until the EMS crew arrived," I cautioned. "That narrows the window. Probably only 12:00 to 12:43."

"There's another possibility," he said.

"What's that?"

"That the Blackberry was taken *before* you and Elizabeth entered the room."

I thought about that. And, as one thought led to another, I felt my pulse quicken.

"Chris. You still there?" he asked.

"Yeah—"

CHAPTER 10

Harvard Business School, Morgan Hall, Office 223

My thoughts swirled. I felt lightheaded, confused. I gripped the phone, harder, until my hand ached as I tried to sort out the ramifications. Finally, after what seemed an inordinately long pause, I formed the question.

"How could that be?" I asked. "We entered the room just seconds after the sound of the gunshot."

"Two possibilities," Joel replied.

"I'm all ears."

"This person could have hidden in the small closet in the southwest corner of the office, then slipped out during the confusion."

"Seems unlikely," I said. "What's the other?"

"A secret entrance—a back door to Bryan's office."

"How could that be?" I asked. "Surely the likelihood of a back door would have been checked out by your CSI lab team, by Elizabeth, or by someone from TEI."

"I agree."

Silence. What I've heard referred to as a pregnant pause. At the risk of offending him, I broke the stillness and voiced the implication.

"Sloppy police work?"

"It happens."

Another pause ensued, much longer. I thought about how drastically this would change the nature of the circumstances. For starters, it could mean Bryan was murdered, that he did not take his own life. And while I wished with every cell in my being that this were so, it just didn't seem likely.

"Joel, I think this is only wishful thinking."

"We're checking out both possibilities," he answered.

"I wish you well."

"Actually, this may be the most likely answer to the disappearance of the Blackberry," he said. "It's less probable that someone entered during the time period after the EMS team's departure and before the arrival of the CSI lab crew, from 12:00 to 12:43."

"Meanwhile, everything's on hold?"

"Yes. But I thought you'd like to know about these developments."

"I appreciate it more than I can say. Thanks for calling."

"I'll be in touch."

Just as we were about to disconnect, I had another thought. "Joel?"

"Yes?" he answered.

"Does Jennifer know about this?"

"No, I haven't contacted her."

"What would you think about holding off?" I asked. "I wish you wouldn't give her false hopes."

"I could do that, but she's probably going to find out soon anyway," Joel answered. "Stuff like this always leaks. Three seconds after the media smells something, it's all over the front page."

COLLUSION

"Uh, could we talk about it for a minute?"

"Sure."

"Just suppose," I hesitated, "that you've found something, that someone was there."

"I admit, it's a long shot."

"Yes, but—" I let my thought linger.

"But?"

"How do you give yourself the best hope of resolving this question?" I asked. "Would it be easier if you tip your hand, if you let this person know you're looking?" I paused. "Or if—"

"Or, if we keep our suspicions quiet," he responded.

"Yes."

He didn't think about it long. In two seconds he gave me his answer. "Obviously, the latter." His three-word answer came with firmness and a Texas drawl.

"So?"

"I agree. We need to put the lid on."

"Might help." I said it quietly, not wanting to sound like I was trying to run his show.

"You professors," he said. "Sometimes you think you're smarter than the rest of us. All the same, I appreciate your suggestion about keeping it quiet," he said. "This won't be easy, and I can't promise we can do it."

"As I said before, I wish you well."

He signed off and I went for coffee.

At the Harvard Business School, almost all faculty have their offices in Morgan Hall, a beautiful and well-designed building next to the Baker Library. However, one of the little things the architect overlooked when he planned the building was the essential faculty coffee break. So, we overcame. The faculty and staff set up coffee and all the extras in the hallway. I selected a blueberry scone—with a large cup of decaffeinated hazelnut cream—and carried them back to my office to attack the mail.

My new secretary, oops, *associate,* had arranged the envelopes neatly on my desk. For the next hour I plowed through it. Envelope after envelope, much of it junk mail. The task was one of my least favorite things . . . but the coffee and the scone helped. Near the bottom, with current mail, I found an odd-looking, plain, white envelope. No return address. No clue about its source or its contents. I started to throw it in the trash, but for some reason, providence perhaps, I happened to glance at the postmark.

Houston, Texas.

I ripped it open and scanned it.

Dr. Hartman:

Hope you'll look at the partnership corporations formed by TEI. A good one to start with is Cayman Energy Limited. Reed Upton sold his CEL stock and pocketed over 30 million.

A Friend

Someone was obviously playing a Texas version of "Deep Throat." Again, I thought about trashing it. But I didn't. At this point in the TEI scandal, any clue was better than nothing.

CHAPTER 11

The Anderson Bridge over the Charles River, Cambridge

When the weather's nice, I like to walk to work. The mile and a half hike from my condo to the Harvard Business School runs through my residential neighborhood, across Harvard Square, down JFK Avenue, over the Anderson Bridge to the HBS campus, and ends at my office building, Morgan Hall. While the brisk morning stroll invigorates my senses, and would be, in and of itself, sufficient reason to choose to walk, the real payoff is the return home. Nothing surpasses a Friday afternoon in late October and the panorama offered by a view from the Anderson Bridge.

Crewing, the quintessential Ivy League sport, finds its home on the Charles. What Yankee Stadium is to baseball, or the Rose Bowl is to football, the bay on the Charles River, located just to the east of Anderson Bridge, is to scull racing. On Friday afternoons, boats fill the water. On this beautiful autumnal afternoon, as the sun inched low in the west, hundreds of people watched as two teams practiced.

Some of the boats, called shells, were manned by a single person, others by two. For these, each rower pulled two oars. And they west fast, skimming over the water with indescribable grace and smoothness. But as fascinating as these two-oared shells appeared, they paled in comparison to watching one pulled by a crew of eight.

The skill and coordination required to race a long, paper-thin shell pulled by eight oars has few peers in the world of team sports. "Crewing," as the sport is most commonly called, actually requires nine people. Eight, strong husky athletes, each pull one oar, while the ninth member of the team, usually a small, light-weight person, often a woman, sits in the stern and calls the tempo of the strokes. When done well, the shell skims over the water like a bullet. I leaned on the bridge railing and waited for the inevitable. As the sun fell lower and lower, the two crews maneuvered their shells and came to a parallel position just east of the bridge. I could hear words exchanged, then laughter, followed by jeers, and then the two crews began, rowing at moderate speed to a starting point. Suddenly, by some prearranged signal, the race was on.

As the two crews pulled away from my view, they appeared to be neck and neck. I watched as long as I could until, as the sun sank below the western horizon and dusk began to fall, they passed from sight around the bend in the river. I started north for the thirty-minute walk home. Harvard Square, as expected, bustled with people. I stopped at China Inn, a really great Asian restaurant on the west side of the Square, for takeout.

Home felt good. And the end of the week added to the feeling of respite. I flipped on a local news program and settled in front of the tube to enjoy Szechwan Beef. After only two bites, the phone rang. A familiar voice addressed me by title.

"Grandpa," said a seven-year-old female.

"Who is this?" I asked.

"Guess."

COLLUSION

"Is it Betsy Ross?"

"Grandpa!"

"Is it Melissa?"

"Of course."

"When are you coming to see me?" I asked.

"Thanksgiving."

"That sounds so far away."

"It's four weeks from next Thursday."

"You have it figured exactly?"

"Yes, but if you talked to Mom, maybe we could come sooner.

"Okay, let me talk to her."

"May I ask you a question, first?"

"Sure, ask away."

"Why do we have to move?"

"I'm not sure." I answered. "Want me to try to find out?"

"Yes, please."

"Okay," I said. "Now, may I speak with your mom?"

"Here she is."

"Melissa?"

"Yes?"

"I love you."

"And I love you, too, Grandpa."

I could hear the rustle of the phone, and then a loud crack almost took my ear off. A faint voice said, "Sorry, it slipped." Then the exasperated voice of my daughter came on the line.

"Dad?"

"How's my favorite daughter?"

"Sorry, Melissa dropped the phone."

"Hey, that's not the first time a seven-year-old dropped a phone."

I could hear the sound of her breath as she heaved a long sigh.

"Can you talk?" I asked.

"Yes, the kids have gone into the other room to watch TV."

"I'd like a straight answer, no hedging."

"What's the question?"

"How're things?"

Silence. I could hear her breathing, long deep breaths, like she was fighting to maintain control.

"Let me rephrase the question," I said. "Tell me about the kids. How're they doing?"

"Fine, I think," she answered. "I probably made a mistake."

"Tell me."

"I mentioned last night at dinner that we're going to have to move."

"And?"

"Luke hardly noticed, but Melissa took it hard. She wanted to call you immediately. I told her wait until tonight to ask you."

"Well, she just did."

Another long pause. I thought I could hear her crying, softly.

"Jenny, life goes on," I said.

"I know, but—"

"You've got two great kids."

"And no money. I can't pay the bills on the first of the month."

"Yes, *we* can. I'll help you. You know that." I silently cursed myself for not working this out before I left Houston.

"Oh, Dad, we can't sponge off you."

"You're not sponging. You and the kids are going to inherit everything I've got, sooner or later."

"I . . . I'm just so worried, so flustered."

64

"I have a suggestion."

"Okay. Excuse me a minute."

I heard her blow her nose.

"Ready for the suggestion," she said.

"Remember the TEI stock certificates you found in the upstairs safe?" I asked.

"Yeah. Those amazing, twenty-six cent certificates."

"Call your broker and sell them."

My instructions took her by surprise. She paused.

"I don't know how," she said. "I've never sold stocks."

"Call the broker. His sticker, with name and phone number, is on the certificates. I saw it."

Again, a long pause. This time I waited for her to respond.

"Dad, you still there?"

"Yup."

"Okay, I'll call him on Monday."

"And go over your bills. Make a list. Call me on the first of the month and give me your total."

"Oh, Dad—"

"Hey, this is what accountants do."

"Yeah, I can see that it helps to have a plan," she said. "I just feel so helpless sometimes."

"Speaking of plans, if you're moving you need to start thinking about options."

"Yeah, I know."

"I have one to suggest."

"Okay, lay it on me."

"Suppose I give you the house out on the Cape. How would you and the kids like to live in Hyannisport?"

Silence.

"Like I said, you're going to inherit it sooner or later. Why not sooner?"

Silence.

"Jenny?"

"May I think about it?" she asked.

"Of course," I answered.

"I don't want to sound ungrateful, but—"

"It would be a big change."

"I'd love it. But, they're three of us that would have to live with such a decision."

"Like I said, you need to have some ideas. Probably be good to have several."

"I agree."

"So, before you come, why not contact a realtor?" I asked. "Look at some possibilities for smaller homes in Houston? If you find something you like, you could sell the house in Hyannisport, use the money to buy a house there. Or maybe you could use this money to partially pay for 44 Leisure Cove."

"Dad, we know that's not a option. We can't afford this house."

"Just a thought."

"But I agree," she said. "It's time to start a list."

"It'll be good for you."

Then, a surprise, she laughed.

"What's so funny?"

"You accountants. You're so organized."

"Well . . . yes."

She laughed again. "I think, growing up, I rebelled. And then when I married Bryan, I tried to be deliberately disorganized."

"A way of expressing yourself as an individual?" I asked with a chuckle.

"It's overwhelming, sometimes. First my father, then my husband, all these lists, everything so planned."

"Want me to number the hangers in your closet?"

"Sure. When can you start?"

Then we both had a long laugh.

"Bought your airline tickets for Thanksgiving?" I asked, thrilled to have the old Jennifer back, even if temporarily.

"Hey. There you go again, trying to organize my life." She sounded more than a little testy.

"Sorry."

"But, you're right," she said. "I need to get going with the planning." She chuckled. "The list."

"And selling the stock certificates."

"Yeah. Yeah. We've spent all our time talking about me. How's life in Boston?"

"Same old, same old."

"Dad."

"My big thing is Thanksgiving, and I can't make any plans until I know your schedule."

"I hear you."

"E-mail is good."

"Quit pushing!"

"I love you, Daughter."

"I love you, Father. You'll probably never know how much."

She hung up. I looked at the cold Szechwan Beef, thought about warming it in the microwave. It didn't seem worth the effort.

CHAPTER 12

One week later, Friday morning at the Spangler Center
Harvard Business School

I felt good. The crisp, November morning invigorated my brain, and the thirty-minute hike to campus, with New England leaves changing color, and a beautiful, blue cloudless sky providing an unencumbered stage for the brilliant sunrise, created a buoyant expectation. Today felt like a great day, and I owed at least some of this anticipation to the HBS's newest Building.

Opened in January 2001, and named in honor of Dick Spangler and his family (MBA '56, former president of the University of North Carolina), the Spangler Building was a 121,050 square-foot student center. It housed all the typical "student union" facilities, dining rooms, meeting rooms, bookstore, post office, etc., and it did so at the most luxurious level I'd ever found. The breakfast offerings, especially, were outstanding—the best in Boston, in my opinion.

I picked up a *Boston Globe* and carried it with my briefcase to my favorite table in the southeast corner of the big, beautiful first-floor dining room. A quick trip through the line for a Belgian waffle, fresh blueberries with hot blueberry syrup, and hazelnut cream cof-

COLLUSION

fee, completed my arrangements for beginning the day. As I removed the food from my tray and placed it on the table, the aroma of the coffee heightened my ebullience. I sat, savored the first bite, and unfolded the paper. The headline soured everything. It read:

TEI FILES FOR BANKRUPTCY

Not that I hadn't expected it. As I read the gloomy details, I realized this result had been inevitable. The story recounted the losses and listed a blow-by-blow chronology. The story's history peaked when the corporation issued a reduction of shareholders' equity of $1.2 billion. That was when, as everyone remembers, the stock price plummeted from forty dollars per share to its all-time low of twenty-five cents. The only surprise, and the reason this was headline news, was the speed with which it happened.

Obviously, the bankruptcy halted all trading. I wondered if Jennifer had managed to sell her shares. While twenty-five or twenty-six cents wasn't much, anything was better than nothing. The story continued on page three. I half-heartedly scanned the inside page for the remainder of the details. I found a zinger in the last paragraph.

Congressional hearings, scheduled for next week in Washington, would be open to the public. With that sober thought, I bused my tray and went to work. It took all of five minutes to walk the short distance to Morgan Hall, pick up my mail, and settle into my office.

Then came the surprise of the morning—in the stack I found an "Express Mail" letter from Texas Energy, Incorporated. I held it for a few seconds, incredulous that anyone from the renowned company would be writing to me, and tried to interpret the return address. It read, "Board of Directors." I opened it and read the letter slowly.

HARRY HAINES

Dr. Christopher Hartman
Professor of Accounting
Harvard Business School
Cambridge, MA 02163

Dear Dr. Hartman:

The Board of Directors of Texas Energy, Incorporated
has established a Special Investigative Committee and
appointed me to serve as its chairman. Our mandate is to
conduct a comprehensive review of the events and transactions of our recent financial history that have led to the
unfortunate current status of our corporation.

The committee has authorized me to contact you and ask
if you would serve as our Chief Forensic Accountant and
lead this investigation. The parameters of the appointment
state that you would have free reign to conduct your inves-
tigations and make your report. We want it clearly understood that, should you find any wrongdoing by any members
of our board or by any employees, you would have complete, unrestricted autonomy for disclosure. We ask only
that your findings be thorough, factual, and as comprehensive as circumstances allow.

Obviously, time is of the essence. I would appreciate your
immediate response to the phone number on this letterhead.

Sincerely,
William R. Powell, Jr.
Member of the TEI Board of Directors and
Chairman, Special Investigation Committee

70

COLLUSION

Might as well do it now. I dialed the number, asked to speak with Mr. Powell. I gave the secretary my name.

In a few moments, he came on the line. "Dr. Hartman?" he asked.

"Yes, sir."

"You received my letter?" He spoke with a slow southern drawl, what I've heard characterized as a Texas accent.

"Yes."

"Thank you for your prompt response."

"I understand the need to avoid delay."

"I hope you have good news for me."

"Well, I'm interested," I replied, cautiously.

"I'll be in Washington on Wednesday for the hearings," he said. "Could you come, observe, and then meet with me that evening?"

I thought for a minute about clearing my schedule. "Yes, I could do that."

"Assuming we can come to terms, we'd like you to sign a contract."

"I understand."

"What's your usual fee for this sort of thing?"

"An hourly fee of $1200 plus expenses."

"How many hours do you anticipate?"

"Impossible to say."

"Would you be interested in a flat fee, say $100,000 for the report?"

"No."

Neither of us said anything for a few seconds. The brevity of my answer must have thrown him off balance. I decided to wait.

"We're under a lot of pressure," he said. "And scrutiny. Whatever your fee, it's going to end up as public information."

"I understand," I answered.

"I'm a little skittish about an open-ended check. If your bill is several hundred hours, this could add up to hundreds of thousands of dollars."

"I've heard that one of your corporate officers, a member of your board of directors, sold his shares in one of your partnership corporations for thirty million."

"Good God!" He sounded genuinely appalled, as if this was new information. Either that, or he was reacting to the fact that I knew about it.

"I'm perfectly willing," I continued, "to have my name on the front page of the *Washington Post* with his, and my fee—whatever it is—to be published alongside his profit."

"Do you know this for a fact?"

"No, but if you hire me, I can trace the sale of stocks."

He didn't respond for a long moment. I could almost hear his mind whirring as he weighed his options. "Dr. Hartman," he said, finally, "sounds to me like we can negotiate a fee."

"Good. However, I have two issues to run by you before we sign off."

"All right. If you have any concerns, I certainly want to hear them."

"I like to be on a first-name basis with people," I said. "How would you feel about calling me Chris?"

"That's how we do it in Texas." He chuckled, sounding surprised I hadn't laid another heavy on him. "And you call me Billy Ray."

"Thanks, Billy Ray. And there's one more thing. Your chief accounting officer was my son-in-law."

COLLUSION

"Yes, we all know that."

"Any problems?" I asked.

"That's up to you," he answered. "It's not a problem unless you shade the facts to favor him."

"I've been through this before with friends and professional colleagues."

"So I've been told."

"I just let the chips fall. Facts always speak for themselves more eloquently when unencumbered by an interpretation from the investigator."

"Exactly what we want."

"Uh . . . Wednesday evening, where would we meet for dinner?"

"How about the Willard Hotel Coffee Shop, seven o'clock?"

"See you there."

We rang off. I slouched back in my chair. This could be a biggie—the most important case of my career as a forensic accountant. I needed to see the dean to ask for a leave of absence.

I felt my heart pounding, and if there was such a thing, a sense of blood rushing through my ears. Powell had just offered me the key to their closet, the authorization to open the door that held all the TEI secrets. The bloodhound in me could smell the trail. I loved it.

CHAPTER 13

The Caucus Room, The Russell Senate Office Building,
Washington, D.C.

I'd been to congressional hearings before, in this very room, but never with such a crowd. Luckily, I'd arrived early and got a seat. Even the media struggled to find a tiny space. Instead of the usual C-SPAN crew, representatives from the major networks, and several others I'd never heard of, showed up. On the side of one camera I recognized the big letters, KHOU, and drew the conclusion that even Houston stations had sent their own people to cover the event. I looked around the room to see how many people I could recognize.

At the front of the room I found the "hot seats," a large rectangular table with chairs reserved for those who testify. Of the dozen or so people seated at that special place, I recognized only three, all TEI corporate executives. Front and center sat CEO Richard Zimmerman. On his right, I recognized CFO Reed Upton beside Jerry Norton, the corporation's comptroller. On Zimmerman's left sat a woman whose name I couldn't remember, but whose face I recognized from television newscasts. She had apparently been among the first to warn

COLLUSION

Zimmerman of the coming disaster, and her now famous letter had been published on the front page of the *Houston Chronicle*.

I started a list. If they hired me to lead their investigative committee, these would be the people I'd need to interview first. My list looked like a pitiful start. I counted fifteen people in the hot seats and, of the four on my list, I only had three identified by name. But, in our litigious society, I guessed that at least half of the remaining people clustered around the front table were lawyers.

The chairman, a Republican senator from a New England state, rapped his gavel and called the hearing to order. The room quieted. Video operators started their cameras. I settled back in my chair, expecting that much of the verbiage filling the room in the next few hours would be smoke and mirrors.

While the chairman went through the customary ritual of opening the hearing, thanking those who had come to testify, and setting the time limits for questions, I searched the audience, looking for someone I might know. My seat, the last one on the far side of the front row, selected with care and for this very purpose, allowed me to inspect the sea of faces without drawing attention. I found one. Dennis Johnston, the head of Houston's Stephen Svensen office, sat on the far side. Apparently, he was also scanning the room, searching for faces. He looked straight at me.

I tipped my head, acknowledging his glance.

He returned the gesture.

I added his name to my list and shifted to face the senators, the members of the committee lined up at their special tiered desks that rose well above the level of the witness table. It was intimidating enough to be testifying; looking up at those in judgment made it even more daunting.

75

The chairman called on Richard Zimmerman for his opening statement.

TEI's CEO began reading his prepared remarks. This was the part of congressional hearings that I hate. I wish someone would invent a way to bypass the reading of "opening statements." It seems to me, in the two-hundred-plus years of our great democracy, someone could come up with a way to avoid the reading of long, tedious, self-serving remarks by those suspected of wrongdoing. But, they hadn't, so we endured. Trapped, along with the four hundred or so miserable souls crowded into this room, I half listened while Zimmerman droned on, trying to excuse his actions and those of his minions who had gobbled up billions of dollars. Finally, he finished. I sensed an air of expectation filling the room as we waited for the fireworks to begin.

During the next hour, the fireworks fizzled.

The proceedings reminded me of a firing squad in a third-world banana republic. There were some good questions—direct aims that hit the target. Some. But much of what transpired was, in my opinion, politicians taking potshots in the dark. They suspected wrongdoing, that the people seated at the table had hoodwinked the rest of us and made off with the contents of TEI's multi-billion-dollar cookie jar. As best I could, I tried to write down their questions and summarize TEI's answers.

When it became obvious to the committee, and to everyone in the world, that questions were becoming repetitious, the chairman called for a break.

With a collective sense of relief, the crowd gradually emptied the room. My seat on the front row grouped me with those last to exit. When I finally made it to the hallway, I looked for Dennis

COLLUSION

Johnston and found him coming out of the men's room. He didn't greet me, but said, "I remember someone who told me his questions were personal," Johnston said. His eyes flashed with anger, and the corners of his mouth turned down, transmitting an unmistakable feeling of contempt toward me.

"I'll stand by my statement," I answered. "At that time, I had no other motivation to seek information."

"At that time?"

"Two weeks ago," I said. "Then, day before yesterday, Billy Ray Powell called me, and asked me to meet him tonight."

"So, you *are* involved."

"Not yet."

"But you will be," Johnston's voice was accusatory.

"Dennis, you and I had lunch, that's all."

"But you approached me, knowing you would likely become involved in the investigation." His voice became louder.

People stared at us.

"Wrong," I answered. I spoke softly, with sincerity. "I had no idea I would become involved. Quite the contrary, I believed my son-in-law's involvement would disqualify me. And I'm still not involved, officially."

"Humph!" Johnston shook his head, obviously trying to think of another way to express his anger.

"Dennis, one day in the not-too-distant future, you and I may be sitting at that table, and one of these senators will ask about our luncheon at the Petroleum Club."

"I can hardly wait to see you squirm, trying to answer questions about sandbagging me."

"No need to squirm," I answered. "If we had a tape recording of everything said, we could give it to the *Washington Post* and let them print it on the front page."

"You've got guts," he said, shaking his head.

"No, just a clear conscience," I answered.

I held out my hand. Reluctantly, he accepted it.

"Thanks for meeting with me," I said.

"Chris, stay out of this," he warned.

Before I could respond, he turned and walked away. His advice gave me pause. I thought about it for a few minutes as I walked back to my seat in the hearing room. Dennis Johnston knew most, if not all, of the inside information. And for the next few seconds I could hear a small voice in my subconscious saying, *maybe I should take his advice.* But that's all it lasted, a few seconds, and then I listened as Reed Upton, TEI's CFO, began reading his boring statement.

The hearing ground on like a marathon race. And at the end, like a bunch of tired runners, we staggered out of the room, exhausted. I looked around for William R. Powell. Having never met him, and unsure of how to identify him if I saw him, I quickly gave up the search, wandered outside, found a cab, and headed for the Willard Hotel. I stopped briefly at my room to freshen up, then made my way to the dining room. A portly, bald-headed gentleman walked up to me wearing a big smile. The cowboy boots gave him away.

"Howdy, Chris." He held out his hand.

"Billy Ray, a pleasure to meet you," I answered. His handshake was firm. A bit too firm for comfort, but it certainly gave the impression of sincere cordiality. I didn't doubt that he was glad to meet me.

We ordered, and then he started the conversation.

"Let's get our business out of the way first." He handed me two copies of a contract.

Without reading it, I signed one copy, handed it back, put the other in my coat pocket.

"CPAs don't read contracts?"

"I trust you," I replied.

He smiled, shaking his head. "What'd you think about the hearing?"

"The usual," I answered. "What'd you think?"

"No surprises for me."

"What were you expecting?"

"Hell, I was hoping the bastard who stole our money would stand up and confess."

I laughed. "Billy Ray, I don't think that's the way congressional hearings work."

He joined my laughter, a big, raucous Texas sound that filled the room. I laughed at his reaction. People at nearby tables looked at us. The thought crossed my mind that if these restaurant customers knew the subject of our laughter, they would be offended. White-collar crime at the multi-billion level should not be a laughing matter.

Our steaks came and we settled down.

"So, what is your plan of attack?" he asked.

"Follow the money trail," I answered. "See where it leads."

"What do you need from me?"

"Access to your corporate financial records."

"No problem."

"You'll need to communicate this to all employees," I said.

"Of course," he replied. "I'll send a memo over my signature tomorrow."

"I'd like to hire a small accounting firm to do the grunt work,"

I said.

"How much?"

"Only a hundred dollars an hour—a bargain."

"Another blank check?"

I grinned, but only briefly. "You could estimate the total," I told him, offering a sort of compromise.

"Okay, how about $500,000 as a cap," Powell said. "No more than a million in any case."

I could see we needed to clear the air. I thought a few seconds about how to phrase my words.

"Look, no one can predict what kind of timeframe and effort this will take. You could spend half that for little or no result, and your money would be wasted. On the other hand, if it takes ten times your figures, and we indict all those who embezzled, did money laundering, took kickbacks, engaged in financial statement fraud, and all of the other illegal acts, you would have the best forensic accounting contract of the century."

He didn't like my answer. He frowned while silently working on his dinner.

I decided to wait him out. Several minutes went by.

"I guess you've got us by the short hairs," he said. He didn't look at me, and the tone of his voice reflected a sense of resignation—of defeat.

"You don't have to select me," I said. "There are plenty of other CPAs who would love to do this work for you."

"I have a question."

"Sure."

"You said one of our board members sold his shares in Cayman Energy Limited for thirty million."

"Yes," I nodded.

"How do you know that?"

"I *don't* know it for sure," I answered. "But I suspect it to be the case and, in the very near future, I'll be able to confirm it one way or the other."

"What causes you to be suspicious of this?"

"A tip."

"From whom?"

"If I knew, I'd tell you."

"An anonymous tip?"

"Yes."

He threw his napkin down on his plate, pushed his chair back from the table, and stared at me with a look of supreme dissatisfaction. "Christopher Hartman, you son-of-a-bitch." We locked eyes for several seconds before he turned away and signaled the waiter for the check.

While the waiter came and took his credit card, I thought about calling it quits. For sure, there would never be a better time to sever the relationship before I embroiled myself in one of the greatest frauds in financial history. William R. Powell sat there with his arms crossed, eyes blazing.

I considered the pros and cons, pushed my own plate aside, and decided to make one more pass.

"Ever play a hunch?" I asked.

"What kind of a question is that?"

"I have a hunch that some TEI insiders have crossed the line."

"Well—" His belligerence softened, visibly. As he thought about my question, I could sense that he agreed.

"I talked with a reporter from the *Houston Chronicle* and asked her what she thought brought about the downfall of the corporation."

"And?" he asked.

"Hubris."

"Come again?"

"The excessive pride and ambition that usually leads to the downfall of the protagonist in a classical tragedy," I said.

"I agree, we have a classic tragedy."

"And, obviously, it's rife with contemporary white-collar crime."

The check came. He signed and moved forward in his chair, ready to stand and leave.

"Wish you'd just call it quits right now if you don't think I'm the man for the job," I said.

"You're not the only one with a hunch," he said. And then, as though angry with himself, he added, "I have a hunch you're just the person we need."

He stood to leave. I rose, and held out my hand.

He clasped my hand, but again our eyes met with confrontation.

"I've stuck out my neck for you," he said, "and signed a blank check against the advice of the board."

"I understand."

"Sure as hell hope you come through."

Before I could answer, he turned and left.

I had hoped for a better start.

CHAPTER 14

Office number 223, Morgan Hall, Harvard Business School

The next day, the investigation started. And once initiated, it took off like a stampede. On Thursday, I negotiated a six-month leave of absence from Harvard. By Friday, I had engaged three of my former students from a small Boston accounting firm to start collecting data. During the next ten days I made dozens of phone calls to Houston.

On Monday, the tenth day after I signed the contract, I again boarded Continental Flight 683. Mitzi, the stewardess in first class recognized me. We chatted about my being a steady customer. When she brought coffee, she lingered and asked about my photo on the front page of the *Houston Chronicle*, something in connection with TEI. I smiled, asked if she would do a favor and not talk about it. She smiled back, placed a hand over her mouth, and winked. I took it as a signal, and I thought about it over breakfast. If everyday people, people who did not live in Houston, recognized me and knew of my role in the investigation, my life was changing. The contemplation of public status caused me to think about my problem with alcohol and the fact that I hadn't been to an A.A. meeting since Bryan's death. I lingered over breakfast, took a third cup of coffee, and pulled out my TEI data sheets.

I tried to concentrate on the reports of some of TEI's partnerships. Thirty minutes after reading the material, I couldn't remember what I'd read. Thankfully, the plane started its descent, and the flight attendants asked us to put away our laptop computers.

The plane landed. I walked to the outside and found Jennifer waiting at the curb. We took off for the lengthy drive downtown to the TEI Building.

"How long will you be here this time?" she asked.

"Hard to tell, probably only a week," I replied.

"Want to change plans for Thanksgiving?"

"Not on your life."

"Good. Luke and Melissa are really looking forward to the trip."

"Me, too."

I left my bag in the car and promised to be at her house for dinner. Then I picked up a visitor's pass at the security desk, took the elevator to the fiftieth floor, and looked for Richard Zimmerman's office. At the door I paused and thought, for a few fleeting seconds, about Daniel's entrance into the lion's den.

The secretary received me like someone carrying the bubonic plague. With no hint of cordiality, she "parked" me in big leather chair while she scurried around from room to room, talking on the phone, occasionally glancing at me with a frown. About ten minutes later she walked over to where I was seated and gave me a command.

"Mr. Zimmerman will see you now in our conference room."

Dutifully, I followed her through the doorway.

I've seen beautiful conference rooms before, but none that could top this one. It was huge. The high ceiling gave a sense of spaciousness, and one whole wall was floor-to-ceiling glass, offering a magnificent view of the Houston skyline. A massive table with a dozen or more large leather conference chairs provided the room's centerpiece. Three ornate chandeliers over the conference table glittered with refracted light.

Seated around the table was TEI's Board of Directors. Billy Ray Powell rose, walked over, shook my hand. and directed me to an empty chair at the end of the table. Then came the ritual of introductions. I stood there as Powell went around the table, giving each person's name and, in some cases a corporate position or special board title or office. No one spoke. No one smiled. I sat and waited.

The next fifteen minutes moved along in agonizingly slow motion. Obviously, many of those seated at the table viewed me as the enemy. Their acrimony came through loud and clear in their faces and voices. Even the members of the investigative committee—Billy Ray Powell and two others, the board members who selected and employed me—reacted to my presence with reserved hostility. While they read and discussed my contract, I took the opportunity to observe their reaction to me, to the details of my appointment, and to the overall concept of a forensic accountant conducting a search for trouble.

The most surprising response, I thought, was that of Richard Zimmerman. He seemed personally oblivious. Either he didn't realize the threat my appointment represented, or he was giving an academy award performance. Insensitive? Unconcerned? It baffled me.

The second most interesting reaction came from Reed Upton. I've seen cool, and, in some cases, responses that were cold, but never anything like his.

"Mr. Chairman, I want to go on record as opposing the employment of Chris Hartman," Upton said. His persona came across as frigid and his eyes cut through me like laser beams.

I expected Billy Ray Powell, or some other member of the investigative committee to say a word in my defense. No one did.

"In my opinion," Upton continued, "this is a blatant example of how our corporation's money is being wasted." His few words came at me like rifle shots—clear, crisp, and combative.

Discussion ended. The chairman moved on to the next agenda item.

It was a relief to leave the room. I took the elevator to the lobby, found a pay phone, and called Elizabeth Garcia.

"How about lunch?" I asked.

"I don't think it's a good idea for me to be seen with the enemy," she answered.

"Okay, let's go somewhere where you'll not be noticed."

She hesitated, then asked, "Do you know Frank's Pizza, across from the *Houston Chronicle* building, on Travis Street?"

"No, but I'll bet I can find it."

"Thirty minutes." She hung up.

I took a cab and, as a precaution, looked to see if anyone followed. No one did, but just to be sure, I went into the newspaper building, sat in the lobby for fifteen minutes, then found my way out the back door and across the street to the restaurant.

Elizabeth sat in the last booth, and I had to scan the room twice to find her. As I slipped onto the bench seat across from her, I got a whiff of the unusual perfume. Even in a pizza place, it cut through with a distinctive, feminine scent.

She smiled. "Good to see you," she said.

"Yours is the first smile I've seen since I entered the TEI

COLLUSION

Building this morning," I replied.

"What did you expect?"

I dodged her question. "I've run into hostility before. It's S.O.P. for a forensic accountant, but—"

"But what?"

"This is the coldest response, ever."

"From—"

"Those on the fiftieth floor."

"I think you'll find, as you contact those at lower echelons, the response from folks will be more favorable. Most of us lost our retirement funds. We want to know what happened, and if there was any monkey business. We want to see that the bad guys get what's coming to them."

I thought of Jennifer and her enormous loss. I was hoping what Elizabeth just said would be the case. Only time would tell.

"I'm with you, at any rate," she said. She reached over, and patted my arm.

"Thanks. I appreciate your help."

"But, there's a problem." She withdrew her hand and her eyebrows wrinkled with concern.

"Not good to be seen dancing with the enemy?"

"Or eating pizza, or even talking with him."

I gave her my best smile and tried to speak in a reassuring way. "Circumspect is the word for the day."

"I could very easily lose my job."

"I understand."

"So, given my circumstances, how can I help you?"

"Just do your job."

"Look, Chris, if we're careful, I can do more. I'd *like* to do more."

I shook my head. "Thanks for the offer, but it's not needed."

"All the same, I want you to know I'm pulling for you."

"I know." And I gave her my best smile, hoping it would reassure her.

"And I can tell you something that may be helpful to you."

"Okay." I sat forward slightly. Any information she could give me would be helpful.

"The reaction to Powell's memo generated quite a response from the Stephen Svensen people," she said.

"How so?"

"More paper shredding."

Her words jolted my memory, and I thought back to that first day I met Elizabeth in her office, when a man in blue coveralls had asked about the papers to be shredded. "An increase?"

"I've never seen so much."

"Thanks for the tip," I said. "We'll look into it."

She changed her facial expression, a coy look with an unmistakable signal that her next words would be special. "And I have another tip."

"Ears."

She nodded, her grin widening. "In my office, I made photocopies before the shredders came."

"You did?" Her admission had me suddenly grinning, too.

"So did a lot of other people."

"Really!"

"You'll have to be careful how you handle this," she said. "But I know if you approach folks the right way, you can reel in a lot of useful information. Apparently, Stephen Svensen has done you a favor. A huge, gigantic favor—they've identified the documents for

COLLUSION

you. If you can get a copy of the shredding list, you've found the most incriminating records."

"Thanks, Elizabeth," I said. "You're the best."

"No problem," she answered. "I just wish you could find some way to get my 401K money returned."

"Welcome to the club. Bryan's family is in the same boat."

"Yeah, everyone I know got wiped out. We're no longer one big happy family." She looked at her watch. "Guess I'd better go. May I give you a lift?"

"Where are you parked?" I asked.

"Across the street. The *Chronicle's* parking lot."

"Would you mind dropping me off at Hertz?"

"Not at all."

We drove the short distance with almost no conversation. The silence seemed awkward. As we pulled up in front of the car rental, I tried to find a way to sign off.

"I'd like to see you again before I go back to Boston," I said, then added in case she thought I was asking for a date. "We need to compare notes."

"Sure. I told you I want to help," she answered.

"Probably best not to do it at work."

"Thanks. I appreciate your understanding of my position."

"How about meeting for dinner on Friday evening?"

"Sure. Where and when?"

"You pick it. I'll meet you there."

She thought for a few moments. "Let's try Macaroni Grill on Westheimer, just a few blocks west of I-610. I've eaten there dozens of times and never seen anyone from TEI."

"Okay," I said. "Friday. What time?"

"Seven?"

"Macaroni Grill on Westheimer, Friday at seven. See you there."

She drove off and I rented a car.

I didn't specify a brand, a color, anything. Hertz randomly handed me the keys, and it turned out to be a white Toyota Camry, exactly like Elizabeth's. I thought at the time, it might be useful to have identical cars in case we needed to do some cloak-and-dagger stuff, to try to shake off someone who might try to follow. Silly? I mentally chastised myself for the thought.

Back at the TEI Building, I met with three young CPAs from Cohen, Curtis, and Berns, the accounting firm I had engaged to help prepare the financial records for my review. Two were Harvard graduates—my former students. They already had our room set up: two big copy machines, desks, computers, file cabinets—the works.

We closed the door and I related to them the tip about paper shredding. And I lectured them about using a cautious approach.

"The last thing we want to do is to endanger anyone's job," I told them. "We'll need to go slow at first, just leave the door open. I suggest we try to provide opportunities for anyone who wishes to do so, to slip photocopies to us informally."

Then, as we were finishing our conference, I received a phone call from Jennifer. She was at the emergency room at Hermann Memorial Hospital. Luke had broken his arm.

I immediately drove to the hospital—finding her and Melissa in the waiting room.

"How is he?" I asked.

"Okay," Jennifer replied, looking every bit the worried, hassled mom. "The doctor said we can be with him while they build the cast."

COLLUSION

Melissa came over and hugged me. I found a chair and sat with her on my lap.

"What happened?" I asked.

"A strange accident. He fell off his bike and broke his arm," Jennifer said.

"Strange, how?"

"We can't figure out how it happened."

"Start at the beginning."

"A little after school, about four o'clock—Melissa was already home—a neighbor down the street phoned me. Her two kids found Luke lying in the street—out cold. She could see that his arm was broken, so she called 911. Then, she called me."

"You must have been frantic. What did you do?"

"Melissa and I ran down to the corner and got there just as the ambulance arrived."

"How was Luke?"

"Groggy, crying."

"What happened next?"

"The EMS crew put a splint on his arm, we all got in the ambulance, and here we are."

"It sounds like Luke just took a bad tumble off his bike. What's so strange about that?"

"The EMS guys smelled chloroform."

"Chloroform? It's an anesthetic?"

"Yes. And Luke has a big bruise on his arm, on the opposite side of the fracture."

"Did he get the bruise during the fall?" Dumb question, I thought the moment the words passed through my lips.

A nurse interrupted. "Are you the family of Luke Banks?"

"Yes, I'm his mother," Jennifer said, rising to her feet.

"We're putting the cast on now. Would you like to join us in the E.R.?"

We followed the nurse to the emergency room and found a brave ten-year-old getting a cast on his left forearm. The doctor assured us that things would be fine, and in six to eight weeks, Luke would be good as new. He didn't mention Chloroform, nor did we. Perhaps the EMS crew was mistaken.

When Luke was released, the three of us—mother, sister, and grandfather—took our patient to McDonald for hamburgers. By the time we got home it was bedtime for the kids. I read a story to Melissa, Jennifer gave Luke some warm milk, she and I talked for a few minutes, then I fell into bed, exhausted.

The bicycle accident worried me. I decided to give Detective Joel Wilson a call . . . in the morning.

CHAPTER 15

The Coffee Room, Houston PD

I felt out of place. Most of the men and women in the room wore uniforms, and the few who didn't, like Detective Joel Wilson, definitely had a police aura. These people all knew each other, and obviously, didn't know me. I was the only civilian in the room—the only person without a sidearm. I made sure I stood close to Joel as he poured coffee into two large, Styrofoam cups.

"Cream or sugar?" he asked.

"Thanks, just black."

He led the way to a small table in the corner. We sat and I took a sip. The coffee tasted terrible, and I guess my reaction showed.

"I apologize for the coffee," he said. "They make it strong, and, after working here a few years, we get used to it. Want some hot water to dilute it?"

"No thanks, this is fine," I lied.

"I've been working on the suicide ruling," he said.

"Any progress?"

"Nothing definite. No major breakthrough. But I'm taking it slow, trying not to make waves."

"Anything you can tell me?"

He paused, rubbed his neck, and appeared to be thinking. Then he leaned forward, elbows on the table, and spoke in a low voice. "Chris, we're talking about a member of your family. I want to share some information with you, but you've got to assure me that you're going to keep this strictly confidential."

"I understand."

"If it gets back to the high brass that I'm digging around in a closed case, and I'm passing all the details—my unproved suppositions—to you . . ."

" . . . it puts you in a bad light."

"Bad light, hell. I could lose my detective's badge."

"Joel, you don't have to tell me a thing."

"But, I need to," he continued. "I think it's essential to the case that I have your help. But you have to understand the politics, what's at stake, and promise me you'll watch what you say."

"Where's the Bible?" I asked. "I'm ready to swear."

"Sorry, I didn't mean to make a federal case out of this."

"All right, then. What do you want to tell me?"

"I've run into some resistance."

"Go on," I said.

"We have the photograph showing the Blackberry was gone and the absence of blood spatter in the small spot on the desk," he said. "The factual evidence speaks for itself. The tricky part is the explanation. That's where I have to be careful."

"It lends itself to several different interpretations?"

He nodded. "The first, the one I'd hoped for, was a back door."

"You've checked?"

"Yes," he said, "and ruled it out. It's obvious. There's no back door to Bryan's office."

I tried some more coffee. It wasn't so bad if taken in small sips. And the hot liquid helped me concentrate.

"The second," he continued, "the possibility that someone hid in the closet, then sneaked out, is going to be much harder to confirm."

"I can see the problem," I empathized. "So, how are you handling it?"

"I went over to Herman Memorial Hospital and interviewed the EMS team—the two men and a woman who picked up Bryan on the morning he was shot."

"How'd it go?"

"They weren't much help," he said. "When an EMS team comes into a gunshot scene, they focus on the victim. A stadium full of people could walk by, and they'd hardly notice."

"But you did ask?"

"Of course, and they all tried their best to give me a head count. They remembered you, Elizabeth, the other secretary, and the guy in the spiffy suit whom I've identified as Jerry Norton, the comptroller. Two of the three EMS crew have a vague recollection of a fifth person, but no description."

"Have you interviewed Norton and the two secretaries?"

"Yes, and that's where I picked up some resistance."

"Go on," I urged. "This is getting interesting."

"The two secretaries are like the EMS crew. They have vague recollections. Both say that someone else could have walked through the room. The second secretary, the one other than Elizabeth, even suggested a guy wearing blue coveralls, like the TEI maintenance crew wears."

"You said resistance?" I asked.

"From Norton," Joel said. "Of the six people, his recollection was remarkably different."

"How so?"

"The other five were hesitant, but consistent. Each individual's answer to the major question about whether or not someone else could have been present in the vicinity of the shooting was that they didn't think so."

"And Norton said what?"

"No. Absolutely not."

"Hmm,"

"So, I went back and questioned him a second time."

"Good for you," I said.

"Maybe not so good for me," he paused, taking a long sip of his bitter coffee. "Next day, the captain called me in, said he'd had a complaint from TEI."

"Really! What was the complaint?"

"Harassment. The captain said Reed Upton called him, complaining that some TEI employees felt I was trying to stir up trouble, to make this suicide into something to feed the tabloids, to sensationalize the death of a good employee."

"Does the captain know about the photograph?"

"No. And I didn't think it a good time to tell him."

"Joel, you're walking on eggshells here."

He laughed. "That's the understatement of the year."

I didn't think it funny. I leaned forward, using body language to emphasize the intensity of my response. "You need to tell him. After all, he is your boss."

"Of course, but I know how information leaks."

"When are you going to tell the captain?"

COLLUSION

"As soon as I have some corroborating evidence."

"For your sake, I hope it's soon. Who else knows about the photograph?"

"About the discrepancies? About the removal of the Blackberry?"

"Yes." I nodded.

"I think only three people. You, me, and Elizabeth Garcia."

I took another sip of industrial-strength coffee, grimacing, but it jarred my thoughts in a different direction.

"How long have you been with HPD?" I asked.

"Fifteen, almost sixteen years."

"How often have you tried to withhold details from your boss—information like this that could blow open a big murder?"

"This is the one and only time."

I shook my head and looked away, double gestures of disapproval. "I thought you were a smart detective."

"Hey, you were the one who suggested I keep it quiet."

"Yes, but it's your job that's on the line," I said. "Suppose this blows up in your face?"

"I'm committed. All the high brass are going to be pissed when they find out about details in the photo. My best bet is to ride it out and hope, when we find corroborating evidence, they'll understand."

We sat silently for a few moments, each with our separate thoughts. Finally, Joel broke the spell, grabbed his cup, and stood.

"More coffee?"

"No, thanks. One cup of this stuff is all I can take. But, I have something else I need to ask you."

"Okay, I'll be right back."

He walked over to the coffee pot, speaking to several colleagues as he made the round trip. He sat, made eye contact, and sipped.

"All right, what is it you need to ask?"

"My grandson Luke broke his arm yesterday.

"I'm sorry to hear that. Is he okay?"

"Doctor says he'll be good as new in six to eight weeks."

"Young bones are resilient. They heal quickly."

"Yes, but—"

"But what?"

"When the EMS team first found Luke, they said they smelled chloroform."

"Chloroform? On Luke's face? Clothing? What?"

"On his face. And Luke's details of how the accident happened are strange. They don't add up."

Wilson frowned. "You want me to look into it?"

"Please."

"Okay, let's start with some details. What happened, where?"

"A bicycle accident on his way home from school."

"In The Woodlands?"

"Yes."

"That's outside my jurisdiction, but I have friends at Woodlands PD. I could bring one of them with me to talk with Luke."

"How do you want to do this?"

"Let's set it up to interview Luke at home. Tonight, about five-thirty, six?"

"Okay, I'll let Jennifer and Luke know. Thanks, Joel."

We said our goodbyes, and I drove to the TEI parking garage. I walked into the office to find my crew, the three young CPAs, gathered around the conference table with stacks of paper. All three were smiling. Big smiles.

CHAPTER 16

Room 423, The TEI Building, Houston

"Okay, who ate the canary?" I asked.

"Come again?" asked Caitlin Cunningham, the young woman with the biggest grin, one of my crew from Boston.

"What's with the goofy smiles?" I asked.

"Dr. Christopher Hartman, you're not gonna believe this," said Jack Ward, another of my three aides. He shoved a stack of paper toward me. "Take a look at what came out of the woodwork."

I sat and started reading. It didn't take long to see that this particular mass of paper contained the financial records of Cayman Energy Limited, a corporation chartered in the Cayman Islands. I knew very little about CEL, except it was a corporate partnership that had spun off from TEI.

In the stack I found a memo. Someone had written some telling data on CEL, Inc., listing a number of illegalities in the corporate charter. This was the kind of information a forensic accountant only dreams of finding. Typically, I would rummage around for months and—if lucky, *extremely* lucky—might find something illegal in a corporation's charter. Stuff like this was akin to the proverbial needle in the haystack. I scanned it again.

Now I understood the smiles. We'd been on this job less than a week and had found the needle.

"Incredible," I said.

"Yeah, and there's more." The third young CPA, Bartholomew "Bart" Nichols, gestured to at least ten more stacks on the table.

"Where'd all this come from?" I asked.

"We don't know," said Caitlin, breaking out into the biggest smile of the morning.

As Elizabeth had predicted, TEI employees wanted to help us find proof of wrongdoing. The clerks, secretaries, and other clerical workers—the day-to-day employees who had lost their retirement funds—were leaking Xerox copies to us. These people were pointing us to the insider problems.

"We'll have to check this out," I cautioned.

"Of course," Jack said.

"Seriously, where'd you get this?"

"No names." Bart replied. "We promised."

"We don't have to have names, just credibility," I turned to face all three. "But I have to know. Is this for real?"

"I'd stake my life on it," Caitlin answered. Jack and Bart nodded in agreement.

"Maybe we need to talk about specifics. Tell me what you know about the illegalities in CEL's charter."

The three young CPAs looked at each other for a moment. Then Jack answered. "Caitlin, you probably know more details."

She nodded, opened her notebook, and arranged her notes. I remembered her from class, articulate voice, unusually strong vocabulary. Caitlin was at her best when reciting specifics of a case.

COLLUSION

"TEI created a number of partnership corporations called Special Purpose Entities, commonly referred to as SPEs," she said. "These SPEs were used to hide debt and to make TEI's balance sheet look better."

"And Cayman Energy Limited was one of TEI's SPEs?" I asked.

Again she nodded. "One of the biggest, and as it now turns out, one of the best for hiding sticky financial problems." She paused for a moment to study her notes.

"Go on," I prompted.

"As you know, in order for TEI to create a partnership corporation—an SPE, they must rally outside investors to put up the money," Caitlin continued.

"Yes," I answered. "The SEC, the Securities and Exchange Commission, requires that ten percent of the capital be new money. And this capital has to be at risk. As a rule it comes from those who are named as corporate officers, the principal investors."

"Exactly," Caitlin said. "And in the case of Cayman Energy Limited, the principal investors were Reed Upton and Jerry Norton. Together, they put up one million in TEI stock."

"Wait a minute," I interjected. "That's illegal. You can't use shares from the parent company. It has to be new money, investment capital that is at risk."

"Yup," Caitlin smiled. "But they used TEI stock. And when TEI's stock went down, so did Cayman Energy Limited. A classic example of the domino effect."

"Illegal as hell," I added. "That's what the SEC rule was designed to protect against.

"How could they do this?" asked Jack.

"Where were the auditors?" asked Bart.

Caitlin sat silently and smiled bigger than ever.

"I think the word is . . ." I cupped my hand to my ear, a gesture I use in class when asking for whoever had the answer to speak. They responded in unison.

"Collusion!"

I smiled. They smiled. We all smelled the trail.

"You realize what we have here is theoretical," I said. "Until we come up with the documents that prove they broke the law, this is just an interesting story."

"Shouldn't be hard to do," Jack said. "It's all a matter of public record."

"The hard part is knowing *what* to look for," Caitlin added.

"And we have a map to that," Bart said, "thanks to the folks who gave us this paper trail."

"Be careful how you handle this," I warned.

I lectured them for the next half hour about not tipping our hand. I emphasized the need to proceed in a general way.

"Don't ask for just the CEL charter," I said. "Instead, request all the charters for all the SPEs. Don't ask for records on the ten percent investment rule. Make it routine. Compile records on all investors and their amounts listed on the original charter applications. Upton, Norton, and all the other bad guys are going to be watching us like hawks. We have to make them think we're searching through tons of documents."

Smiles gone, no one took this assignment as a lark. We closed our meeting in a serious demeanor, and I felt really good about my three assistants. They were capable, intelligent, and most importantly, totally honest. We spent the rest of the day preparing to do what forensic accountants are supposed to do, examine financial records. We divided our list. I participated, making dozens of phone calls requesting the records needed.

At the close of a tough but satisfying afternoon, I took my rented Toyota and joined the bumper-to-bumper traffic headed north on I-45 to The Woodlands. After an hour of fighting the afternoon rush, I pulled into the driveway at 44 Leisure Cove to find my daughter in a wild emotional state. She was ecstatic.

Jennifer threw her arms around me and danced a jig. I dropped my briefcase and tried to keep from falling as she twirled me around.

"Whoa," I said. "What's happening?" After a few moments, I stopped. Jennifer continued to whoop and holler—incoherent words of joy.

Through excited, nonsensical phrases, she held up a deposit slip with a check stub. I read the amount: $3,094,500. The deposit slip was from a Swiss bank account in the name of Bryan and Jennifer Banks.

"What is this?" I asked.

She fanned her face, tried to compose herself.

"Let's sit," I suggested and we plopped down together on the nearby sofa. "Now, take a couple of slow deep breaths," I said. "Relax. We're in no hurry. Drink of water?" I asked.

She nodded. I went to the kitchen, filled a glass, and brought it back. She sipped, and I waited as her breathing returned to normal.

"The TEI stock," she said. "Bryan sold half of the shares."

I looked at the two documents from Bryan's stockbroker and saw the note on the bottom left side of the check stub. I read it aloud. "It says 75,000 shares sold at $41.26 four weeks ago. That was the day before Bryan's death."

"Yes," she replied.

"How did you find this?" I asked.

"Last week, the day before TEI went into bankruptcy? You suggested I sell all the TEI stock."

"That's right."

"I expected there would be 150,000 shares," she said, taking another gulp of water.

"Yes, I remember," I said. "That was the number Bryan had listed on the financial statement we found in the safe."

"Right, but when I called our stockbroker, he told me we only had 75,000 shares."

"And you argued?"

"Of course," she smiled. "That's when he told me about this." She waved the deposit slip. "The sale a month ago." She glowed. "Isn't this wonderful?"

"No."

"No?"

"Jenny," I said. "This is insider trading."

"Wha . . . what does that mean?" she asked.

"It means it is illegal," I answered. "You'll have to give it back."

CHAPTER 17

44 Leisure Cove, The Woodlands

Jennifer was in agony. Unbridled joy had quickly became tears of anguish. I put my arms around her, trying words of comfort.

"Jenny, it's okay," I said. "We hadn't counted on the money."

She sobbed.

Luke came into the room. A frightened ten-year-old with his arm in a sling, he stood there, looking at his mother with concern. "What's wrong?" he asked.

"Your mother's upset," I said. The obvious understatement of the day. Even a ten-year-old could see and understand.

"Mama?" Luke asked with concern. He put his good arm around his mother's waist, and as he did, Jennifer responded. The sobbing eased. She slipped away from me and embraced Luke.

"Mama, what's wrong?"

Jennifer held him with one hand, and with the other, tried to wipe her eyes. I handed her a Kleenex.

Melissa, like her brother, must have heard all the commotion. She burst into the room. "Mama, why're you crying?" She ran over and threw her arms around her mother.

Jennifer held her children close. "I'm so lucky to have you two," she said, pressing kisses to the tops of their heads.

"And when you have them, money doesn't matter," I added.

Luke, always quick to pick up on clues, looked at me. "Grandpa," he asked. "Is Mama crying about money?"

The doorbell rang, saving me from having to answer.

"I'll get it."

I opened the front door to find two policemen. Detective Joel Wilson of the Houston PD introduced officer Robert Neal of the Woodlands Police Department. Officer Neal wore a uniform and looked very young. I would have guessed him to be in his late teens or early twenties.

"Thanks for coming. Let's go back to the kitchen. I want you to meet my grandson, Luke Banks."

At the kitchen table, Jennifer met us, looking much more composed. I introduced her and the two children. There were only five chairs at the table, so Melissa sat on my lap.

"May I get you something—coffee or iced tea?" Jennifer offered.

The two policemen shook their heads. "Thanks, we can only stay a minute," Wilson said.

"Nothing for me," I said, turning in my chair to make eye contact with my grandson. I tried to speak in a calm, reassuring voice, "Luke, I've asked Detective Wilson to investigate your bicycle accident."

"Oh?" His eyes got big. I could see anxiety in his face.

"It's okay, Luke," said the detective. "We're here to help you."

The look on Luke's face changed from apprehension to puzzlement. "Grandpa, why do I need help from the police?"

I smiled and thought about how quickly a child can cut through social rhetoric, making it difficult for adults to hide their actual intent. "Luke, I don't know if we need help, but it doesn't hurt to have experts like Detective Wilson look at traffic accidents. You don't mind, do you?"

Luke shook his head. "I guess not."

"Good," I said. "Now do your best to answer his questions. Try to remember all the details, and don't fudge."

"Fudge?"

"Tell the absolute truth," I said. "Don't try to make the story better. Just tell him the details as honestly as you can."

"Grandpa, that's what I always do," Luke answered, a bit miffed. "Daddy always told me I'd never get into trouble by telling the truth."

"I know." I reached over and patted him on the shoulder. Then I made eye contact with Wilson and nodded.

"Luke, tell me about yesterday after school," Wilson said. "Tell me about your bike, where you park it. What route do you take to ride home? Was anyone with you? All the details."

"I have a Schwinn ten-speed," Luke said. "It's blue. I got it for Christmas last year, and I always park it at the big bike rack on the east side of the school. I always lock it."

"Tell me what happened after school," Wilson continued.

"I'm enrolled in honors math," Luke said. "Once a week my teacher meets with me after school and gives me special problems to take home. It usually takes about fifteen minutes."

"Yesterday was math day?" Wilson asked.

"Yeah. My friends were all gone, so I had to ride home by myself. I took the usual way, down Woodrush Street to the corner at Jerry's house, then around the corner to a short block to my street,

Leisure Cove. Then I always turn onto my street."

"You turned on Leisure Cove, and what happened?" Wilson asked.

"Yesterday, the street was crowded. There were a couple of cars parked at the curb, and I had to pull out toward the center of the street to pass them. So, I did. But, as I was passing the first car, I heard another car coming behind me. I didn't want to be out in the street, in his way, so I looked back for just a second."

"Is that when the accident happened?"

"Yeah."

"Luke, this is very important," Wilson said. "Go slow. Try to remember exactly how it happened. Don't leave anything out, no matter how small or unimportant you think it might be."

"Yes, sir."

"So you looked back?"

"For just a second. Like this." Luke twisted his head and shoulder. I did it quickly.

"Then what happened?" Wilson asked.

"When I turned back, there was a man standing there. I don't know where he came from. I hadn't seen him when I was riding toward the cars."

"You were close to a man?"

"I tried to stop."

"What happened?"

"I sorta ran into him. I didn't really hit him—my handlebars just grazed him—but it caused my bike to lurch and me to lose my balance. I fell over toward the curb."

"So, you took a spill?"

"Yes, sir."

COLLUSION

"Tell me about the man. What did he look like?"

Luke thought. He has a way of looking far off when he concentrates. Then his eyes returned to the detective. "Sorry. It happened so fast. Guess I didn't really look at him."

"Tall, short. Fat, thin. Anything?" Wilson coached.

"Black," Luke answered. "I think he had black skin. I know he was wearing black-colored clothing." He shook his head, as in apology. "Sorry."

"That's okay. Go on with the accident."

"I put my arm out to break the fall." He held up his right arm, encased in the cast.

"And what happened next?"

"And I guess I blacked out," Luke said. "I woke up in the ambulance, with Mom and Melissa, on the way to the hospital. My arm felt like it was on fire. I guess I cried—a little."

"He cried a lot," Melissa added. "And real loud."

"Shush," I said. "The detective wants Luke to tell it." I patted her on the arm.

"Luke, I'd like you to think back to the fall," the detective said. "Can you remember how you landed?"

Luke made a face, like he was trying hard to remember an unpleasant experience, and again I could see the faraway look in his eyes "I guess I was going sideways and down," he answered. "I remember seeing the curb and sticking out my right hand."

"The man. Where was the man?"

"Right there," Luke said. "I remember him bending over me."

"Do you remember a cloth over your face?" Wilson asked.

"Hm—" Luke lingered with his answer. "Yeah. Maybe. I don't know."

"And you hurt?" Wilson asked. "You felt pain. You remember that?"

"Yeah. But it all happened so fast, it's really hard to remember the details."

"Thank you, Luke," Wilson said. "You've done a good job reporting the accident." He leaned back and smiled. "Is it okay if I ask your mom some questions now?"

"Sure." Luke relaxed into his chair. For the first time I realized he had been tense, leaning forward, trying hard to recall everything.

"Good job," I said. I reached out and squeezed his good hand. I nodded a gesture of approval. I felt really proud of him and tried my best to communicate it.

"Mrs. Banks, just a few questions?" asked Wilson.

"Of course," Jennifer answered.

"Can you describe the man?"

"No," she answered. "He was gone by the time I got there."

"That's strange," Wilson said. "Usually the person responsible for an incident such as this will stick around to see what happens. Especially when a child's involved."

"At the time I was so concerned about Luke, I hardly noticed," she said.

"Who was there? Who did you notice?"

"My neighbor and her two children. And then the ambulance came."

"Did you ask your neighbor about the man?"

"No," Jennifer answered. "I only had a few words with her as the EMS team was treating Luke and loading him into the ambulance. Mostly, I thanked her for calling me."

"I'd like to speak with your neighbor and her two children,"

Wilson said. "To see if we can get a description of this man. She might help us find out why he left the scene of the accident."

"Sure," Jennifer said. She wrote out the neighbor's name, address, and phone number.

At the end of the interview I walked the two policemen to the front door. We stood on the front step for a moment.

"What'd you think?" I asked.

"Something fishy's going on," Wilson said.

"Absolutely," the young uniformed officer agreed. "Suppose you were there when a ten-year-old boy falls off his bike and breaks his arm. Would you leave, or would you stay and try to help?"

"Stay, obviously," I answered.

"Something's wrong," the officer said. He shook his head decisively.

"We'll look into it," Wilson said. "I'll get back to you."

I watched as they drove away in the Woodlands Police cruiser. Then I walked back into the house just as the phone rang.

"Hello," I said.

"Your grandson's arm is a warning," said a voice.

Immediately, Adrenaline surged through me and my heart began to race. "Who is this?" I said it loudly—with anger.

"You're going to do a small job for us. We broke his arm to get your attention."

"Who is this?" This time I yelled, much louder.

"You need to listen. Pay attention." The voice laughed. "We could have killed the boy. It would have been easier than breaking his arm. We didn't want to. And we won't if you'll cooperate. Help us . . . so we don't have to kill him."

I felt sweat break out on my forehead. I clenched the telephone.

"What is it you want?"

"Just a small job," the voice said. "Something you can do easily."

"I don't do anything for anonymous voices that threaten my family."

"Have it your way," the voice said. "We'll start looking for a way to kill him. Maybe the girl, too."

Panic shot through my body. "Wait!" I couldn't think what to say.

"Yes?"

"Why do you want to harm an innocent child?"

"Because we're in a jam," the voice said.

"That's not his fault," I yelled. "And it's not my fault."

"No, but you could help us out of this jam we're in."

"You have that wrong. I can't help you."

"You don't even know what we're asking. You'd better shut up and listen."

"I don't like being threatened."

"Fine. We understand."

"Then leave us alone."

"Sorry, we got no other way to handle our problem."

"So you threaten innocent children."

"This . . . is . . . no . . . threat!" The deliberate delivery of each word added a chilling, sinister effect to the message.

My anger boiled and I lost control. "The hell it's not," I shouted.

My words had no effect. He responded with seven ominous words. "We didn't want to kill Bryan Banks."

His statement took the wind out of my lungs. I couldn't breathe. I tried to speak. Nothing came out.

"Don't make us kill the boy . . . and the girl, too."

The click from the other end tore through me like a gunshot.

CHAPTER 18

44 Leisure Cove, The Woodlands

Paralyzed with fear and unable to move, I gripped the receiver with its incessant beep-beep-beep. My heart pounded.

"Grandpa," Melissa said.

Beads of moisture rolled off my forehead.

"Grandpa, supper's ready," she repeated.

I stood a long while, squeezing the phone in my hand.

"Grandpa, come on!" Melissa grabbed my hand and jerked, insistently.

I hung up. My first rational awareness, after the threats on my grandchildren from the mysterious voice on the telephone, was the high-pitched female voice and the tugging on my arm.

"Grandpa," Melissa whined.

I love my granddaughter dearly, but she is the most impatient human I know. She wants things to happen immediately, and she wanted me to join her at the dinner table—right then.

Good thing. This seven-year-old's perseverance brought me out of my stupor. With her pulling on hand, I felt my brain gradually begin to thaw and my cognitive functions return.

"Okay," I said. "I'm coming, Melissa."

"We've been waiting," she said, tugging me along toward the kitchen. "And Mama's mad because the food's getting cold."

I followed her to the table and took my chair.

"Dad, what's wrong? You look white as a sheet."

"I . . . I'm okay," I tried to speak normally, but my words came out in a raspy whisper.

"You're perspiring," my daughter continued. "Do you feel faint? Do you need to lie down?"

"I—I think I'll be all right." I took my napkin, wiped my brow, reached for my glass of water, and knocked it over. The spill stopped our meal. Everyone stood. Luke and Melissa went for dishtowels. Jennifer hovered.

"Come, lie down on the sofa." My daughter pulled me away from the table and into the den.

Staggering to the nearby sofa, I plopped down. Jennifer held my hand, reassuring me, and I felt my anxiety begin to ease.

"You seem to be having a panic attack," she said. "Is this about the money?" She knelt beside me, using a tissue to wipe my brow.

"No."

"Take a big, slow breath. Try to relax, Dad."

Her compassion helped, and I sensed my heart rate slowing.

"You were the one who said the money didn't matter," she said. "And you were right—we weren't counting on it."

Luke and Melissa joined us. They stood by their mother and looked at me with concern.

"We've mopped up the water," Melissa said.

"Grandpa, are you okay?" Luke asked.

I took a big breath, releasing it slowly. "I'm fine." For the first time, my voice sounded almost normal. I looked at my grandson and smiled. Then I reached up and tousled his hair. "And you're fine, too, aren't you?"

"Yes, sir," he answered. "I didn't spill my water."

I sat up, swung my feet to the floor. And then, with as much determination as I could muster, said, "Let's go eat."

Luke and Melissa led the way back to the table. Jennifer walked with her arm around me. "You sure you're okay? You still look awfully pale."

"I'm fine. Let's forget our problems for the moment and try to enjoy our meal with the kids. They need to feel our reassurance."

Jennifer released her grip on my arm, and we took our chairs at the table. Someone had refilled my water glass.

"Everybody watch," I commanded. I reached out, picked up the glass, and took a long, steady drink. "See? Nothing to it."

"Grandpa, I like you better when you're not so nervous."

"I like me that way better, too." I smiled. "Thank you for cleaning up my mess."

"That's okay. You want to play a game after supper?"

"Sure," I said. "What would you like to play?"

"Go Fish."

"Okay," I answered. "Shall we invite Luke to play, too?"

"I don't think he can," she said. "He only has one hand."

"I can hold cards with one hand," Luke said.

Their typical sibling rivalry was returning. I looked at Jennifer, and smiled. She nodded her head ever so slightly. For the moment, it seemed as if our little family had found its way back to normalcy.

We ate Jennifer's famous tuna noodle casserole. The meal passed without further incident.

After dinner, we played cards. Then the kids went off to bed. After they settled in, my daughter and I sat at the kitchen table, she with a glass of wine, and me with a Coke as we tried to recap the events of the day.

"How are we going to return the money?" she asked.

"Not sure," I said. "Give me a few days to work it out?"

"I just want to do the right thing."

"Of course."

"I'll wait for you to tell me what to do."

"Fine," I said. "And we need to talk about something else."

"Sure," she said. "What's up?"

"The cottage at Hyannisport."

"What about it?"

"Have you discussed it with anyone other than the kids and me?"

She shook her head. "No, why?"

"If you and the kids moved into it, how many people would know where to find you?"

"That's a strange question. What are you getting at?"

"Humor me, please."

"Okay, what is it you want to know?"

"If you and the kids were to slip away, to go someplace where no one could find you—"

"Is this about the money? I thought we decided—"

Then I lost it. "Jenny, answer the damned question. How many people know about our cottage on the beach?"

"Wow."

She looked hurt. Suddenly I felt like an ass. "Sorry, I didn't mean to yell."

Jennifer gave me an odd glare. Silence passed between us until she asked, "This isn't about the money, is it?"

"No."

"You going to tell me?"

"If I have to, But I'd rather not. How about a little trust?"

Jennifer backed off. She sipped her wine, and sat quietly for a few moments. "You know I trust you, always have . . . always will."

"This is very important," I said. "If you and the kids moved out to our cottage on Cape Cod, who would know—who would think— to look for you there?"

For the first time, I sensed that she gave my question her complete and undivided attention. Her expression changed. I could almost see her brain switching gears.

"I can't think of anyone who knows about it," she answered. "Truly, not a soul."

"Have the kids talked about it with their friends?"

"No. We just haven't had a chance yet to talk about plans for Thanksgiving. And it's been ages since they were last there."

For the next few moments, I sat quietly. My turn to analyze.

"Wish you'd tell me what's going on," Jennifer said.

"If you'll trust me for just a few days, I promise I'll tell you everything I know." I reached over and squeezed her hand. "Maybe I can work this out without upsetting you."

"Too late," she said. "My curiosity and that little uncharacteristic episode of yours at the dinner table already has me rattled."

"Trust me, please."

"I've just told you I will. But I want to know what has you so upset. I want to do something."

"Okay," I said. "I have something you can do."

"Finally."

"Help me with the kids," I said. "We've got to keep them from talking about the property in Hyannisport."

"Sure, no problem."

"Jenny, I'm serious. How can we get Luke and Melissa to refrain from talking with anyone about the cottage—especially, where it's located?"

"Simple," she answered. "We'll just tell them not to talk about it."

I caved. Her simple answer didn't sound like a good one, but I could see that further conversation would be counterproductive. "Okay, let's tell them at breakfast in the morning."

She finished her wine, and went to bed.

I tossed and turned, trying to think what to do. I dozed a little. Thought of a dozen different ways to protect my family. None of the alternatives seemed good. But I felt like I had to do something. It seemed certain I'd go crazy without some action. At about two a.m., I finally decided to call the only law enforcement person I knew personally, the one policeman I knew I could trust—Joel Wilson.

He answered the phone with an angry, sleepy voice.

"Who is this?" he mumbled.

"Chris Hartman." I answered.

"God, Chris. What time is it?"

"A little after two. I'm sorry to wake you."

"What's up?"

"I need to talk with you," I said. "I had a phone call this evening. A man called and threatened to kill Luke."

"Jeez, Chris," he said. The sleepiness left his voice. He spoke with no hesitation.

"The caller said that they had killed Bryan."

"*Who* said this?"

COLLUSION

"The voice on the phone. He said that they didn't want to kill Bryan, but they'd had to. And then he said they don't want to kill Luke, but they will if I don't help them. He said they might kill my granddaughter, too."

"Help them do what?"

"He didn't say, but I can guess."

"Okay, what do you guess they want you to do?"

"Whitewash the TEI report."

"Hmm," he answered. "Maybe we'd better get together?"

"That's why I called."

"Early Breakfast?"

"Sure. You name the place."

He thought for a minute. "Let's meet at the Greenspoint Coffee Shop—at the Wyndham."

"I have no idea where that is."

"On your way south on I-45, do you know the turnoff to George Bush Airport?"

"Yes."

"Okay, that's Highway #8 East." He gave me the directions from there. "Is seven okay?"

"Fine," I said. "Thanks, Joel. I'm sorry to have called you in the middle of the night."

"You had a damn good reason. See you in a few hours."

Turning the light out, I tried to go to sleep, but couldn't. Three hours later, I got up, showered, dressed, and left the house. At five-thirty a.m. I-45 was already busy. I joined the rat race south and found the turnoff on Highway 8-East.

Arriving at the hotel slightly before six, an hour before time to meet Joe, I sat in the car and waited.

CHAPTER 19

Wyndham Hotel Coffee Shop

The Wyndham Greenspoint Lobby was the biggest I'd ever seen in a hotel. Two stories high, almost as long as a football field and nearly as wide, with glass everywhere, it reminded me of a giant greenhouse. Dozens of full-grown ficus trees and numerous other green-leafed plants grew everywhere. I found the coffee shop among the trees in the northeast corner.

I waited some more—and worried.

Maybe this was a mistake, bringing in the police. I thought about movies where kidnapping or hostages were involved and villains gave strict instructions not to include the authorities. Almost all of the stories I could remember included dire threats. The bad guys stated that they would kill the hostages. While, I had not received specific instructions or specific threats, the voice on the phone had implied both were real possibilities, and there was the frightening incident with Luke.

Moot point. It was probably too late to back out, and Joel Wilson's arrival settled it. At about ten minutes till seven, he pulled out a chair and sat down across from me.

"You're early," I said.

"You, too," he responded.

I didn't tell him I'd been there for an hour.

"After you called, I couldn't sleep," he said as he surreptitiously gave the huge room a visual sweep. "Anyone follow you?"

"I don't think so."

"Okay, let's hear it. Take your time. Try to remember all the details." He pulled out a small notebook and started writing.

I recounted the phone call and gave it to him pretty much word for word. Joel made several pages of notes. When I finished, he sat silently, rereading his material, flipping pages, and occasionally shaking his head.

After several minutes of watching his page turning and head shaking, I broke the silence. "You don't believe me?"

"Of course I believe you."

"Well?"

"Let's go through the line." He tucked away his notebook.

Breakfast at the Wyndham was a monstrous buffet. We each chose something and returned to our table. I picked at my food, and waited for him to restart the conversation. Several minutes went by. I struggled to suppress my impatience.

Finally, he spoke, "I think you have good news and bad news."

At last, Joel Wilson had processed my ordeal and was about to give me his assessment. I set down my fork.

"Sounds to me like your family is safe for the moment," he said.

Hearing him say those words, a feeling of relief rippled throughout my body. "For the moment? That's the good news?"

"Yeah. The bad guys have not yet spelled out their demands, so there's probably no reason to escalate the terror."

"The threat to kill Luke or Melissa is just a threat?"

"Chris, this is serious. Really serious. I do think they'd kill you, and your entire family if it suits them."

"Well, thanks," I answered, appalled that he would be so blunt. "That's not exactly what I was hoping you'd say."

"With the information I have, I was already pretty sure they murdered Bryan," he said. "This phone call just confirms it."

I didn't know what to say. A cold chill rippled down my spine as I thought about the implications.

"These guys are good," Wilson continued. "They made it look like a suicide, and they did it so well they fooled everyone, including you, me, and the HPD Crime Scene Unit."

I took a deep breath. Clearly Wilson had concluded that Bryan had been murdered. While his conclusion was important news, the implications terrified me.

"And your grandson's bike accident—I talked to the doctor at the E.R."

"When did you do that?"

"Last night, on the drive back from The Woodlands. I called the hospital and found him on duty, so I drove by and had a cup of coffee with him."

"What'd he think?"

"He was suspicious. His theory was that the boy was rendered unconscious, then someone took a pipe and gave him a whack on the arm."

I sat, stunned by this confirmation of the attack on Luke.

"There's no other way to explain the smell of chloroform or the peculiar nature of the massive bruise on Luke's forearm."

"You said . . . " Wilson looked through his notes, then read my quote from the phone call, ". . . we could have killed the boy, it would have been easier than breaking his arm."

"That's the way I remember it, word for word," I answered.

"Stop and think about the veracity of that statement and its implications."

"I don't follow you."

"And the phone caller's characterization of the incident, that it would have been easier to kill Luke than to break his arm—"

"What a bizarre, ruthless thing to say." Just the thought turned my stomach.

"They went to a lot of trouble to stage this as an accident. They wanted to send you a message."

"Haven't they done that?"

He paused, looking me directly in the eye. Then he delivered four words with an ominous tone, "Chris. They're after you."

I believe that, like other forms of human reaction, the nervous system builds up resistance to fear. Last night, my reaction to the threat left me powerless. This morning, the threat to my family, to myself, scared the hell out of me, but I could manage to function.

"What . . . what do I do?" My voice had a raspy, whisper-like sound.

"Play along," Wilson answered. "Plan ahead."

"Help me out," I said. "How in the world can we plan ahead?"

"For starters, try to think about what it is they're going to ask you to do."

"No need to think about it. I already know.

"Tell me," he said.

"They'll want me to suppress any evidence of their wrongdoing in my report to the TEI Board of Directors. That's what this is all about."

He considered my conclusion for a moment, then surprised me when he said, "You don't know this for sure."

"Isn't it obvious?" I asked, a bit more sharply than I'd intended.

He shrugged. "All the same, I think you have to wait until they make their move, until they put pressure on you to do certain things."

I forced myself to calm down. "Okay," I said with resignation. "Then what?"

"Play along."

I shook my head, revolted by the suggestion, "Joel, I can't do that."

"This isn't a game," he said. "You have to."

"You don't know what you're asking."

"No, Chris. You're the one who doesn't understand. You have to string them along. And while you're doing that, you have to help us gather enough evidence to find out who they are and apprehend them. If you refuse, they'll do exactly what they've said."

I shuddered at the thought. "You said, 'until you have enough evidence.' How much is enough?"

"I think you'll know it when you see it."

I stopped to think, to ponder the future. It looked so grim I could only think of one possible way for me to handle it. Alcohol. At that moment I felt an overpowering urge to get rip-roaring drunk.

Joel Wilson sensed my apprehension. "Let's talk about details," he said. "About some positive ways you could handle this."

CHAPTER 20

Driving South on I-45, Houston

Bumper-to-bumper, rush-hour traffic—the bane of city life.

Creeping along, stopping, starting, jockeying for position with thousands of other cars, Houston's morning drive from northern suburbs into the downtown, tall-building area, was an experience guaranteed to bring out the worst in human behavior. And, as if to prove that things could escalate to an even higher point on the scale of urban frustration, this morning a fender bender blocked two of the four lanes. Ahead, I could see cars shifting to the left. Inch by inch, the poor souls in my lane and the lane on my right, worked to nudge their way into the two free lanes. Irritated, aggravated drivers elevated the game of chicken to a new art.

For me, however, this morning's Houston traffic was a blessing. It took my mind off *the* problem.

For a short while.

But, as soon as I parked, Wilson's advice again dominated my rational thoughts. His admonitions loomed like a giant, black cloud and shut out all other mental activity. Walking to my office, I reviewed his directives over and over.

He wanted me to proceed full speed ahead with the audit, all the while doing two other things. First, he insisted I not tell anyone about the phone call or the threat against my grandson. Second, he wanted me to keep my radar at maximum sensitivity, screening for likely suspects.

Easier said than done.

Somehow, I got through the day.

And the next.

By Friday my life settled into a semblance of routine. Each day started with family time, breakfast with Jennifer and my two grandchildren. Then an hour-long drive to work followed by twelve hours at the office and a thirty-minute drive home. Long, hard days. I usually arrived back at Leisure Cove around nine or ten in the evening.

The last hour of the day, I plopped down at the kitchen table for a light meal with my daughter. I looked forward to our time together. Inevitably, we got around to plans for the future.

"Suppose you and the kids need to disappear. Could you do it?" I asked, keeping my voice even and calm.

"I guess—if we had to," she replied, carefully. "Why?"

"Let's talk about how you'd do it."

She thought for a moment. "How long are we going to be gone?"

"No telling," I said. "But, let's plan for a worst-case scenario, a year or more."

"Wow," she replied. "That's more than disappearing. You're talking about a permanent move."

"For planning, it's better to think maximum time. Then, if it's shorter, the adjustment is easier."

"Well, I suppose we'd take as many clothes as possible."

"Toys for the kids?"

COLLUSION

"Some," she answered. "I could promise them we'd go shopping at Toys-R-Us as a reward for moving."

"This will probably happen on short notice," I said. "Could you handle that?"

She shook her head, obviously dreading the possibility. "Like I said, if we have to, we can do it."

I smiled and gave her a wink. "That's my girl. After you're gone, I'll call a moving company to pack everything that's left and put it in storage."

"You want us to fly to Boston?" she asked.

"I suggest you fly to a neutral city—Los Angeles, for example—then take a bus to San Francisco or Las Vegas. From there, it should be safe to book a flight to Boston."

"Trying to disappear is harder than it seems."

"Trust me, we won't be going to all this trouble unless it becomes absolutely necessary."

"You keep saying, 'trust you.' When are you going to open up and tell me what's going on?"

"I could tell you now, but the fewer who know, the safer we all are, especially, the kids."

"God, I hope you're right," she said. "My mind's been inventing all sorts of terrifying scenarios. I'm sorry, Dad, I can't help it."

I reached over and squeezed her hand. "Actually, I hope these precautions are unnecessary and that I'm wrong about everything," I said, attempting to soothe her worries.

"When will we know?"

"That I'm wrong?"

"Yes."

"Six months to a year. When the audit is finished and the criminals have been indicted."

"And if you're right?"

"Sooner."

"Dad, please," she said, sharply. "I need a better answer than that."

"Could happen tomorrow. I'd come home, say 'pack your bags,' and take you to the airport."

"I think I know what's going on," she said. "Someone's threatening our family to force you to falsify your audit report."

"Let's not talk about it." The fewer details you know, the less likely you'll let something slip."

"And any slip is a danger to the kids?"

I didn't reply. Obviously, we needed to move on. I searched for a way to change the subject. "What's the weather for tomorrow?"

With a frown of disapproval and a huge sigh of exasperation, Jennifer started clearing the table and loading the dishwasher. I gave her a hug and headed off to bed, the end of another long, tiring day.

The next morning started as usual—a hurried breakfast with the family. We said our goodbyes and I joined the hour-long battle of rush-hour traffic. While driving, my thoughts turned to the meeting with Elizabeth, which was scheduled for that evening. It seemed like years since our luncheon at Frank's Pizza. I hoped she remembered our plans and, for a few moments, I debated contacting her to reconfirm. But that seemed like a lack of trust, and I decided against it. We had a date. I'd do my part and expect her to do the same.

The day rushed by. My three young CPAs met with me individually to go over their data. As I reviewed their material, it became more and more apparent that our investigation was progressing well. Stephen Svensen's ill-fated plan for shredding had given us the clues to build an excellent case. The filing cabinets filled with hard copy, and our computer files grew proportionately. Best of all, the documents all held generic, fact-based data, nothing directed at any individual person. I could see that, at this rate, we'd soon be able to assemble a report which could expose the reasons behind the downfall of the TEI Corporation. We had not yet documented an indictment strong enough for legal action, but we were getting close. And when the time came, we could use our data to hunt down the names.

Late afternoon came, and people started preparing for their weekend. I tried to figure a timeline for my dinner with Elizabeth.

Driving times vary enormously in Houston traffic. During rush hour, the five-mile trip from downtown to the restaurant on Westheimer could take an hour or more. In late evening, with no congestion, I could probably drive it in ten minutes. I decided to play it safe and left the office at six-fifteen, allowing myself forty-five minutes for the trip. As it turned out, I made it in half that time and decided to drive around. In so doing, I noticed a white pickup that seemed to be following me.

I drove back to the Galleria Mall on I-610, parked near Macy's Department Store, and walked inside. The two guys in the white Ford pickup followed me, their cover now blown.

I found a congested area in the Mall and easily lost them; then walked to the Wyndham Hotel and took a taxi. I asked the driver to head west on Westheimer and watched carefully to see if we were followed. One block past the Macaroni Grill, I asked the cab driver to turn north and let me out. After checking to be absolutely sure no one followed, I walked back to the restaurant and arrived about five minutes late. I found Elizabeth at a secluded corner table.

"Elizabeth, it's so good to see you," I said, feeling a smile light my face.

She returned my smile, and then looked at her watch. "I was beginning to get worried."

"Sorry."

"That's okay," she said. "It's just that we set the time and place a long time ago, and I wondered—."

"My thoughts exactly," I said as I slid into my chair.

"So, how's it going?"

"Good. Your prediction about the shredding was right on target."

"You've received some Xerox copies?"

"A filing cabinet full."

"Helpful?"

"Elizabeth, this material is like gold in Fort Knox in terms of its value to the investigation."

"I'm glad."

"How're you doing?"

"I . . . I'm not sure."

"Oh? What do you mean?"

Her smile disappeared. "Looks like they're getting ready to fire me."

The waiter came. Elizabeth ordered lasagna with a spinach salad. It sounded good. I ordered the same.

"Why do you think that?" I asked.

"As you've probably surmised by now, Bryan was not on the best of terms with Upton and his bunch."

"Yes, I've picked up those signals."

"And, I think . . . *they* think I'm guilty by association."

"They see you as the enemy?"

"Absolutely."

"The only thing you've done is tell me about the Xerox copies."

"Well," she hesitated, "yes."

I wondered if I missed something. "And we would have gotten those without your help."

"Yes—" She lingered with her answer.

"What else have you done to cause trouble for Upton and his cronies?"

"Well . . . nothing." Again, she hesitated.

"I have a question."

Before I could reply, the waiter brought our salads. We waited while he sprinkled fresh ground pepper.

"You keep referring to 'Upton and his bunch.' Who're the people in his bunch?"

"His secretary., most of the clerical people in the CFO's office."

"Any of the corporate executives?"

She thought about it for a moment. "Well, Jerry Norton, the comptroller. He and Upton are thick as thieves."

"And Norton's secretary?"

"Probably."

"If you wanted to leak something and make sure it got back to Upton, who would you leak it to?"

"Norton. They're joined at the hip."

"How's your relationship with Norton and his secretary?"

"Well, okay," she said. "I think I see what you're getting at."

"Find something in Bryan's material that would be damaging to Upton—"

"And leak it to Jerry Norton or his secretary," she said. "Offer to bury it, to give them the impression that I'm trying to help them?"

"They'll want to keep you around." I took a bite of salad.

She thought about it for a few moments. "I'm new at stuff like this, the cloak-and-dagger world of misinformation. But your suggestion sounds like it might help me keep my job."

"It's worth a try," I said.

"My job's already on the line. So, I have nothing to lose."

I thought about her answer, and the fact that I knew Bryan's death was murder and she did not. I ate sparingly, silently.

She reached over, placed her hand on mine. "Chris, you look like you're a thousand miles away."

I tried to smile, to give her a look of reassurance. My attempt failed completely.

"Something's wrong?" she asked.

I nodded.

"Want to share it with me?"

I looked at her eyes. "You know what, Elizabeth? I really do."

She squeezed my hand, and then withdrew hers. She took a bite of salad and waited for me to carry the conversation.

"I think there's a lot more at stake than your job," I said.

She stopped eating and stared at me. I felt an emotional connection, something between us, a sensation of communication about the common concerns we shared. It had a tinge of sexual tension about it, and I struggled to think of something to say. Before I could get it out, she looked down, and took another bite of food. The silence increased the electricity.

Eventually she spoke, "You think there's more at stake?"

"The reason I was late tonight—"

She looked at me expectantly.

". . . Is that two men in a white pickup were following me."

Her eyes grew big. She looked at me with fear in her face.

CHAPTER 21

The TEI Building, Office of the Special Investigation

Another week whizzed by. Twelve-hour workdays didn't leave time for much else, which was fine with me. I wanted to get the report over with. On Friday morning, I phoned Billy Ray Powell and asked for a conference with the Investigation Committee. He surprised me with the immediacy of his response.

"Okay, let's do it," he said.

"Where and when?" I asked.

"This afternoon in the Board Room."

"This afternoon?"

"Yes, four o'clock."

"What about the other two members on your committee?" I asked. "I thought they lived out of town."

"You're right, James Wright lives in Austin, Dwight Young in Dallas."

"We could meet next week, give them time to make travel arrangements."

"Hell, they both have Lear Jets," Powell replied. "If I call them now, they'll be here this afternoon."

"Okay, four o'clock," I answered. He signed off. I rounded up my three CPAs to give them the news.

"We're going to make a preliminary report today." I told them about the meeting upstairs at four o'clock. They reacted with shock.

"Whoa," Caitlin Cunningham said. "We're not ready."

"I thought we had until Monday, at least," Jack Ward echoed.

"Yeah, I'm in the middle of rewriting our summary of the CEL Corporation," Bart Nichols grumbled, holding up a big, fat file.

"Pre-lim-in-ary," I answered, saying it slowly, emphasizing the syllables, trying to reassure them. I expanded the thought and said it again. "This is only a preliminary presentation. No names, no accusations directed at individuals."

"I wish we had until next week," Caitlin said, looking worried.

"If we could schedule the report for Monday morning," Jack added, "I'd work this weekend and—"

"Include a few names?" Bart asked. Jack and Caitlin nodded in agreement.

"Wait a minute, guys. It's too early to start listing names and going for indictments. And Powell is already contacting his committee members. I've committed us. We're on for four o'clock."

"If we had just a little more time," Caitlin muttered stubbornly.

"But, we don't," I said with finality. "Now, tell me what you know about the illegalities in CEL's charter."

They looked at each other for a moment. Jack shrugged. "Bart, give him the details."

He did. And it was terrific.

As Bart read a list of illegal acts he'd found in the corporation's charter, I started thinking about how we could organize our presentation, and made an instant decision.

COLLUSION

"Bart, that's going to be your report," I told him. Then, I looked at Jack and Caitlin. "What else do we have?"

The other two gave me a ten-minute summary of what they believed to be the most important documents we now had on file. I negotiated with them, and together we selected representative examples of corporate misconduct, of poor TEI investments now gone south, and of possible answers to the major question—what caused the collapse of this giant corporation? They returned to their desks and went to work.

I felt good about our plans for the meeting for a couple of seconds, then started thinking about the material that I would present personally. As a basis for my report, I found a spreadsheet that listed the sale of stock, the profit taking that would qualify as "obvious" insider trading.

On my desktop computer I opened a new file and titled it: "The Recovery of Illegal Profits." At the top, I listed the sale of 75,000 shares of TEI preferred stock by Bryan Banks at $41.26, for a total of $3,094, 500.

Then I spent the next five hours pulling data from spreadsheets and transferring the information to my report. As with my son-in-law, I listed names, dates, transactions, and, most importantly, amounts. The total was staggering—over a billion dollars. All three of the names of the investigating committee were there. Billy Ray Powell had sold 50,000 shares at $27.52 for a total of $1,376,000. I wondered what his reaction would be when I asked him to give it all back.

In the summary and conclusions, I listed four recommendations:

That the investigation committee set up an account to receive money.

That the individuals named in my report be contacted and asked to repay their illegal profits.

That an advisory committee of TEI investors and employees be established to disburse the funds to those who had lost their life's savings, their IRAs, and/or their retirement accounts.

That procedures be devised to publicize the plan, to be certain the media and law enforcement agencies would have full access to names, amounts, and progress on the return of the money and its redistribution to the injured parties.

I worked furiously on the report and barely had it finished, copied, and ready to present in time for the four o'clock meeting.

Caitlin, Jack, Bart, and I rode up in the elevator together. The silence during our ascent left no doubt about the apprehensions we felt, individually and collectively, for this meeting. I knew my report, especially, would evoke a negative response.

We walked into the Board Room and as expected, my three young companions reacted. I should have warned them about the grandeur—the intimidation. They rebounded quickly when Billy Ray Powell and his two committee members rose to greet us. I made the introductions, and we took our seats toward one end of the huge table. Powell sat at the end, and I sat on one side with the other two board members. My associates took the first three chairs on the opposite side, facing us.

With no written agenda, I opened the meeting and called on Bart for his report on the Cayman Energy Limited Corporation. He gave an outstanding presentation. His handout was dynamite, and he used it effectively to make his points as he carefully listed the violations of the SEC rules, the unlawful charter provisions, and the billions of dollars lost when the corporation collapsed. He identified no names, made no specific allegations. I watched the three board members—Powell, Wright, and Young—to judge their reactions.

As I expected, they appeared duly impressed.

Next I called on Jack. He reported on another SPE, a Special Purpose Entity, a spin-off corporation that had also been used to illegally hide TEI debt. I thought his material equally well done, documented, and impressive. Again he only reported facts, made no attempt to accuse any persons of wrongdoing, or spell out specific actions that would lead to indictments.

Powell and his committee members reacted with solemnity at the thoroughness of these first two reports. They did not dispute the material or voice any objections.

Then I called on Caitlin.

Her delivery reminded me of a tigress stalking her prey. She spoke in a quiet declamatory style, giving facts that, at first, seemed only informational and completely innocent. Gradually, she tied them together, each one leading to a more intense level of suspicion. As she revealed fact after fact, it soon became evident that the deceptiveness of the illegal actions was the root cause of the problem. TEI, as a corporate whole, had deceived investors, concealed indebtedness, and falsified its financial soundness. Most devastating of all, the insiders who'd perpetrated this fraud had lied to the Board of Directors.

As a result, TEI, the world's largest energy corporation, fell apart like a house whose foundation was eaten away by termites. Caitlin spelled out the generic approach, the deceit, the way it had been done. She omitted the names, who had done what, and the specific numbers. But the method was revealed and, obviously, all that remained to be done was to add the details. She finished her report, and the air hung heavy as the three board members shuffled their papers.

Then it was my turn.

I passed out the listing of ill-gotten gains. And waited.

No one spoke.

Up until then we had talked about the actions of nameless people, of how "they" had made mistakes. Now we looked at names and specific amounts of money. No one spoke and an eerie quietness pervaded the room. Each person squirmed in his or her chair, uneasily, even my three assistants and me.

Finally, Billy Ray Powell broke the silence. "I'm not sure we can do this."

"Whatever support we had expected from the board will be lost as soon as they see their names on this list," James Wright said.

"When you hit them in their pocketbooks," said Dwight Young, the third committeeman, "I think you're going to find less concern for employee retirement accounts."

"So what's the alternative?" Caitlin asked with a boldness that surprised me.

Again the room fell cold and prickled with confrontation.

I was amazed that this young CPA would raise the question so bluntly. Was it naiveté or guts? I only know that I was glad it wasn't me who'd said it. I studied the three men, and watched them fidget. Then, during the silence, I took a moment to mentally total their profits, their sales of TEI stock, the numbers listed on my sheet. For these three board members it totaled roughly eight million dollars.

"I think we'd better sit on this for the time being," Powell said.

"I agree," Wright said.

Young just nodded. Then, he closed up his papers in crisp, rapid jerks. "We through?" he asked.

COLLUSION

"I think that's enough for today," Powell said. "Chris, you have anything else?"

"No, sir," I answered.

"I suggest you and your associates leave us now," he said. "The committee will stay and discuss your report." He stood.

We shook hands and left.

In the elevator on the way down, Bart asked: "Dr. Hartman, what'd you think?"

"I think you wowed them," I said. "And I gave them a bitter pill."

"Yes, but they had to know this was coming eventually," Caitlin said.

"Just not so soon," Jack said, with a nervous chuckle.

You know, Caitlin," Bart added. "I have to admit you were pretty good in there." Then the zinger. "For a girl."

Smiling innocently, she responded, "Gee, Bart, thanks. That's very astute of you." She paused for a moment, then added, "For a guy."

We all chuckled, even the red-faced Bart. I was glad for this moment of levity that helped relieve the tension we were all feeling. I made a mental note that anyone daring to engage Caitlin in a battle of wits was treading on dangerous ground.

Jack's nervous chuckle lingered with me. It was his attempt to characterize the loss of billions of dollars as a surprise. And I could see where he was coming from. Sometimes a sudden personal loss can bring a smile. I remembered a news program where a freak storm had destroyed a home and the newscaster interviewed the beleaguered family. These people laughed at their plight and, at the time, it seemed good and wholesome. Today, however, as we left the elevator and filed into our office, no one smiled at the reality of TEI's disaster.

We locked the office and went our separate ways.

HARRY HAINES

That Friday evening, I drove home with a sense of relief. NPR Radio gave the news and, wonder of wonders, omitted any reference to TEI. Thoughts of family, of an easier weekend, lifted my spirits. Even the rush-hour traffic seemed less of a burden.

As I walked into the house, the phone rang. I answered on the third ring.

"Hello," I said.

"Dr. Christopher Hartman?" a voice asked. I recognized the voice.

"Who is this?"

"B a c k o f f." The voice said the two words slowly and with an ominous quality. I felt a chill start at the nape of my neck and ripple down my spine.

"Back off what? Who is this?"

"Don't try to play games," the voice replied, and then he laughed, the same derisive laugh I remembered from the first call. "You know what'll happen to your grandson if you don't back off." Then his voice changed. It became angry, insistent. "Don't be a fool."

I heard the click, followed by the dial tone. I stood there, frozen, for several moments, unable to move, the receiver pressed tightly to my ear. Then a loud "beep-beep-beep" jarred me back to reality. I hung up the receiver and made an instant decision.

I went into the kitchen and told Jennifer to pack.

Then I called Continental Airlines and booked tickets to Los Angeles for Jennifer, the kids, and myself.

CHAPTER 22

44 Leisure Cove

As soon as we got the kids to bed, Jennifer and I started packing. And, against my wishes, she did laundry. I'd urged her to just "throw in" the kids' clothes. We could wash them later. Jenny wouldn't do it. Hour after hour she loaded every dirty sock, every T-shirt, every soiled article of clothing into the washing machine, then the dryer, and finally, clean and neatly folded, into a suitcase. Winter clothes, summer clothes, bathing suits—she packed until the luggage would hardly close.

The most heart-wrenching aspect of our preparations came when we had to select a few toys and games. It amazed me how much stuff my ten-year-old grandson and my seven-year-old granddaughter had accumulated in their short lives. While they slept, Jenny and I went through both rooms and tried to choose their most cherished items. We went through a process of elimination three times. The first time resulted in an impossible pile of their belongings. The second time, we agreed to limit the selection to only ten items for each child. I let Jenny make the decisions, and I carried her choices to the suitcases, a process that seemed to take forever.

Finally, when we could see that even this reduced quantity could not be squeezed into our limited suitcase space, Jenny blew up.

"This seems so unfair."

I could see that she was close to tears. "Go to bed, Jenny. You're exhausted. I'll finish the packing."

"No, I want to do it," she insisted.

I looked at my watch, surprised to see that it was almost three a.m. "Only three hours until time to rise and shine," I reminded her.

"I know," she said with resignation. Then she carefully made the final selections, about half of the articles we had laid out.

I helped zip the bags, close the suitcases. Then we carried them to the garage and loaded them into my rented Toyota Camry. We set the alarms for six o'clock.

"Surprise, we're going to Disneyland," I said as I awakened the two sleepy youngsters. Luke and Melissa didn't seem to care. Barely half awake, they dressed and fell into the back seat of the car. We stopped at McDonald's for breakfast and made it to George Bush International Airport in time for our plane, Continental Flight #1495, a huge Boeing 777, non-stop to LAX.

The flight went smoothly. We took a cab from the Los Angeles Airport to the Anaheim Fairfield Inn, a small motel located just four blocks from the world-famous amusement park. As tired as we were, Jenny and I walked the kids to the park and started making the rounds. We had fast food for dinner, and finally, at nine o'clock, made our way back to the motel and collapsed.

The next morning Luke found his Erector Set and other personal items.

"Mom, why'd you pack this stuff for a trip to Disneyland?"

COLLUSION

Jennifer looked at me for support.

"Luke, there's a cab coming in a few minutes, and we're going to catch a bus for San Francisco," I said. "On the bus, your mother and I will explain." I could see by his reaction that he suspected something. "We'd appreciate it if you'd help us by packing and carrying your bags to the motel lobby."

He did it, even with his broken arm. I felt proud of my grandson. He might have argued and acted with resentment about being pushed around with no explanation. Luke sensed our anxiety, our need for his cooperation. He carried his bags and came back for two more.

We made it to the Greyhound Bus Terminal where, under the name of John Williams and family, I purchased four tickets for San Francisco, paying cash, and we boarded a large, lightly loaded bus for the twelve-hour trip. I looked carefully to see if anyone followed. As near as I could determine, no one did.

We started the trip with Luke sitting next to me; Melissa and her mother chose seats across the aisle. I could tell Luke wanted to ask questions, but he waited until the city traffic thinned and we were headed north on Interstate-5.

"Grandpa, what's going on?" Luke asked.

"We're taking a trip," I replied.

"I know that. But where are we going?"

"San Francisco."

"You already told me that. What are we going to do there?"

"We've booked a beautiful hotel," I answered. "You'll like it."

"When are we going back to Houston?"

"Well, we haven't really decided."

"It looks like we're running away," he said.

I didn't answer. Instead I marveled at the insight of this ten-year-old. I looked at the cast on his arm and tried to think how best to explain our circumstances. Above all, I didn't want to frighten him. I reached over and put my arm around him, holding him close.

"You're a pretty smart little guy," I said.

"Not really," he answered. "I just want to know what's going on."

"I know you do."

He looked up into my eyes for a moment and, like the day his father died, I felt a closeness to my grandson that words could not describe. Then he leaned his head against my shoulder and looked out the window. I savored the feeling of protecting him as we traveled down the highway. A minute or so later, after the intensity of the moment eased, he relaxed and pulled away.

"You can tell me more. I really want to know, Grandpa."

"I know you do. Your mother and I just don't know what to expect, so we thought it would be good to leave Houston for a while."

"Are we going to Cape Cod?"

"You little so and so." I reached over and tussled his hair. "Why would you think that?"

"Seems like it would be a good place to hide out." He grinned at me as though he had just won a game of hide and seek. I didn't respond. He didn't push for an answer.

I had brought a gift, and this seemed like a good time to present it. I pulled my briefcase from the overhead rack and got it out.

"Luke, do you know what a Blackberry is?" I asked.

"Sorta," he replied.

"This one belonged to your dad. I thought you should have it."

His eyes lighted up and his face broke into a grin. "Thanks, Grandpa."

"Let me show you a few things."

COLLUSION

Our lesson lasted an hour or so and helped ease the boredom of the journey. The rest of the trip passed without incident.

Finally, we arrived at the San Francisco bus terminal at 9:00 p.m. and caught a cab to the Airport Hilton. Again, I watched carefully to see if we were followed, feeling 99% certain that no one was aware of our transfer to the hotel. The luxurious room warmed our spirits. We took turns with our showers and changing into pajamas. Jennifer called room service and ordered four hamburgers. A long, tiring day closed in a party-like atmosphere.

I went to sleep with a more secure sense of our world.

The next morning we loaded our little family and our eight suitcases into the hotel's airport van and transferred to the American Airlines ticket counter. Jennifer and I used the two fake Texas Driver's Licenses, which I had gotten from Detective Joel Wilson. They had our pictures with the surnames changed to Williams. I paid cash for our tickets, then we had a little heart-to-heart talk with the kids about using the name Williams for our trip. Melissa thought it a game. Luke didn't say a word, but gave me a knowing smile.

After we had our tickets, passed through security, and made our way to wait at the gate, I excused myself, picked up a roll of quarters, and settled in at a phone bank. I called my Alcoholics Anonymous mentor and friend, George McClenagan.

Since I'd joined AA, my friendship with George had grown month after month. We shared the challenges of "one day at a time," his divorce, the death of my wife, the ups and downs of our daily existence. He in investments, I in academia—we called on each other for help professionally and personally. I never turned him down when he asked. He did the same for me.

That morning I hoped he'd come through for me again. I knew

he would if he could.

"Hello," he said.

"George, this is Chris. I'm on the way back from Texas and hope you can do me a big favor."

"Sure," he said with an upbeat expectation. "What'cha need?"

"Two things," I said. "I need a ride from the airport, and I need to borrow a car."

"No problem," he responded. "Let me get a pencil."

I could hear the phone rattle.

"Ready to copy," he said.

"American Airlines, flight number 196, arriving Logan Airport at 3:37 p.m."

"Got it," he said. "You want to use my Corvette?"

"I'd rather borrow your Suburban."

"It's filthy dirty; the Vette's nice and clean."

"George, I have my family with me—Jennifer and the two kids, plus eight suitcases," I said. "We'll wash the car for you."

"Sounds like a deal. I'll drive it to the airport to pick you up."

"Thanks, George. I owe you big time."

He hung up, and I returned to the gate area just as they started boarding. We found our seats on an American 767, non-stop to Boston's Logan Airport. After our meal I took an opportunity to work again with Luke and his Blackberry.

"What's your password?" I asked.

"You know, you helped me pick it," he said.

"Why don't you tell me again, just so I'll remember?"

"Get lost."

"Let me watch you punch it in."

With his stylus, he tapped in the seven letters and the

COLLUSION

Blackberry's menu came up.

"Let's do a memo," I said.

He punched in the command for memos.

"Let's see you write a message to me."

Using the stylus he wrote the following:

Grandpa, I really like my Blackberry and I'm going to use it to keep my school assignments.

Luke amazed me at how fast he tapped in the memo. He did it much faster than I could. I showed him a game and how he could download or upload data. He loved it.

Before I realized it, the flight attendant gave instructions to turn off all electronic devices. We put the Blackberry away and prepared for landing.

George met us with a clean Chevrolet. We dropped him off at his home in Somerville, swearing him to a pledge of secrecy. I criss-crossed the highway three times to be sure no one followed before we picked up Interstate 93 and headed south, then southeast on Highway 6 for the three-hour drive to Hyannisport.

We arrived at the beach house just as dusk fell on the Atlantic. The smell of the ocean, the sound of the surf, and the reassurance of familiar surroundings gave me a feeling of safety, a sense of security for me and my family. With it, came the ability to relax. I felt the best I'd felt in over a month—since the phone call from my son-in-law.

CHAPTER 23

123 Breakwater Shores, Hyannisport, Massachusetts

Our house on "the Cape" paled in comparison to Jennifer's luxurious home at 44 Leisure Cove in The Woodlands. With only 1200 square feet, it was less than a third as big, and its gray clapboard siding gave it a weathered, New England look of humility. Everything about the this vacation residence, except the location, made it a decided comedown.

The location, however, was premium. Situated less than a hundred yards from the Atlantic Ocean, the smell of the sea and the sound of the surf definitely raised the value of the property. In fact, I thought, if we had it evaluated, this modest little home would appraise for more than the big house in Texas.

Which did not matter. What mattered was that Jennifer, Luke, and Melissa thought it better than paradise. They loved it.

I stayed for six days.

The first day, Tuesday, we unpacked, went to the grocery store, loaded in supplies, and walked on the beach. We soaked up the feel of New England and reveled in it.

The second day, Jennifer *Williams* enrolled her two kids at

COLLUSION

Hyannisport's East Elementary School. The principal didn't like it. He wanted letters of transfer from their previous school. Jennifer lied. She told him that she'd get the paperwork right away. I called Detective Joel Wilson at Houston PD and asked for his help. He agreed to call the Barnstable County Sheriff's Office and intercede on our behalf. He thought he could get the local sheriff to contact the East Elementary principal and work out a plan to delay the kids' transfer documents.

The next day, Thanksgiving, we drove to Plymouth. Located less than an hour's drive up Highway 6, we looked at *the* rock, took the tour of a replica of the Mayflower, and visited the Pilgrims' Museum. It wasn't difficult to find a nearby restaurant serving turkey and dressing, complete with waiters and waitresses dressed in seventeenth-century clothes. We enjoyed a unique celebration of the holiday, and the kids loved it.

We had a lot to be thankful for.

Friday and Saturday passed without incident.

On Sunday morning, with Luke and Melissa safely buckled in the back seat, Jennifer drove me to a taxi stand in downtown Boston. We said our goodbyes, and I took a cab home.

I called George and arranged to visit with him after our AA meeting that evening.

I've attended meetings in other towns and in other parts of the country. However, none are as helpful to me, as satisfying and supportive, as the group that meets in the basement of Cambridge's St. Andrews Episcopal Church. In familiar surroundings, and with friendly faces, we went through our time-honored ritual, the reading of the twelve steps and then the selection of one for discussion. That night we chose step one, how alcoholics are powerless to act on our own and need the help of a Higher Being to deal with the forces that had driven us, individually, to drink. I listened intently.

After the meeting closed, George approached me. "You were pretty quiet tonight," he said. George, like me of course, is a recovering alcoholic. He's an investment broker, and while I don't think his profession has anything to do with my relationship with him as my sponsor, I do admire him greatly and seek his advice. As the others left, I lingered behind, emptying the ashtrays, cleaning the coffee urn, setting the chairs in order. Soon, everyone was gone except George and me.

"Problems?" he asked.

"Yeah," I answered. "How about a sandwich at Shay's?"

He nodded, and we walked the block and a half to Shay's Wine Bar and Grill, our favorite little restaurant at 806 John F. Kennedy Street, on the south edge of Harvard Square. We found a corner booth and ordered the special, a Bar-B-Q Beef Sandwich Dinner, the only customers in the wine bar without alcoholic beverages.

"How're you doing?" George asked.

"Holding on by my fingernails," I replied.

"Day at a time, like the rest of us." His words paraphrasing the AA creed communicated his concern for me. I knew he wanted me to get through my problems without turning to alcohol.

"This is a little different."

"Tell me about it."

"I wish I could unload, give you chapter and verse, all the details, but I can't."

"Tell me as much as you can and I'll listen," he said. "Sometimes it helps to share, even if only a part of the burden."

We sat in silence for what seemed like a very long time while I

COLLUSION

tried to figure out how much I could tell him. George eyed me with concern.

"Chris," he cautioned, "this is the kind of thing that's dangerous for all of us alcoholics. You know that."

"Stress?" I asked.

He shook his head. "No. Indecision. I trust you still recall the serenity prayer." He said it with a sense of irony. Each of us knew every word—by heart.

"God," he said quietly, repeating the prayer, "grant me the serenity to accept the things I cannot change, the courage to change the things I can, and the wisdom to know the difference."

"I'm not sure if any of the prayer applies to my circumstances."

"It *always* applies, Chris. Use it. It'll keep you from trying to find your solution at the bottom of some bottle."

The food came. The few seconds of interruption gave me time to decide.

"Okay, here goes. Last week I was in Houston working on an assignment, and I received a threat against my family."

Startled, George gave me a hard look. "Why didn't you call?"

"I thought I could handle it myself."

"You thought?" he asked. "Have you forgotten that rational thinking about alcohol is what got you into this?"

I nodded. "Yeah, I know."

"So, how *did* you handle it?"

"I played "Go Fish" with my seven-year-old granddaughter."

George's serious face transformed in an instant. He looked at me and smiled ear to ear. "The perfect solution. No one wants to look like a lush in front of their grandchildren."

"It's only temporary," I said. "The threat is still there."

151

"And if you had chosen to intellectualize the problem—"

"It'd still be there."

"Looks to me like you're going to have to face the threat."

"I'm trying."

"Anything I can do to help?"

"I think you've already done it." It had helped to share part of the burden.

"Chris, let's enjoy our dinner."

George took a big bite of his sandwich. I took a small bite of mine. It seemed better to eat in silence, which we both did.

George finished his meal. I quit, mine only half-eaten. We sat, each with our own thoughts. After a couple of minutes, George spoke, "I have a suggestion."

"Go ahead," I answered. "That's what I'd hoped for."

"You're a smart guy."

"Flattery is not the answer I was looking for."

"Damn it, Chris, just listen."

"Sorry."

"Assuming I'm right—that in fact, you are intelligent—you'll have to be careful that you don't use your intelligence as a crutch. Intellect could be the worst thing you've got going for you."

"Thanks, but—"

"The answer is, you're going to have to ask your God for help, and you can't solve this threat against your family with booze."

"Of course, I know that."

"Consider your alternative—to get rip-roar'n drunk."

I looked away. The threat sounded attractive in more ways than one. "It would certainly be an escape from the reality."

"Running away is the same thing as capitulating."

"These guys could carry out their threat!"

"It sure sounds like it. I guess I'd be willing to bet on it."

"Are you implying that I'm betting the lives of my family?"

"Yes, against the bottle."

A sobering thought. Again, as he had many times before, George had found a way to compare the attractiveness of an alcoholic stupor to something I held near and dear, in this case the safety of my two grandchildren. Viewed in this frame of reference, a glass of pale gold, twelve-year-old Scotch whiskey lost all its allure.

"George, you son-of-a-bitch," I said, with a smile.

"Your choice. It's all in how you look at it." He glanced at his watch. "You've got my home and work numbers?"

"Yes."

"Call me," he said. "Call me every day. Even if you're in Texas, call me and let me know how you're doing . . . and get to meetings!"

We each paid our tab. Outside, he walked toward the parking garage. I headed for home, a short six blocks away.

The next morning I returned to my old routine, a brisk thirty-minute walk to campus, my favorite breakfast at the Spangler Center, and the few steps to my office in the building next door. My associate, Donna Woolbridge, seemed glad to see me. She followed me into my office.

"Dr. Hartman, people have been looking for you."

"Tell me," I said.

"We usually refer your calls to the Houston numbers. I give them your numbers at the office at the TEI Building and your daughter's home."

"That's exactly what I wanted you to do."

"But that doesn't work." Donna looked and sounded distressed.

"Your office tells people that they don't know where you are, and there's no answer at your daughter's home. No one's seen or heard from you since a week ago last Friday."

"I appreciate your concern," I said, "but as you can see, here I am."

"It's more than concern," she continued. "We called the Houston Police and the Cambridge Police and filed missing person reports. We thought something had happened to you."

"Well, again, as you can see, nothing has." I smiled.

"Dr. Hartman," she scolded. "We were worried. Really worried."

"Yes, Mother."

Her face turned red. And for the first time in our working relationship, she was speechless. She stood there, embarrassed, trying to decide what to do or say.

I helped her out. "Donna, have a seat. I need you to do a few things for me." I handed her a yellow legal pad and a pencil. "Make a list."

"People called," she said, again. "I didn't know what to do."

"I understand," I said. "And I apologize. Next time I'm going to be out of touch for a few days, I'll call and let you know."

"Thank you."

"Ready for the list?"

"Yes, sir."

"Call the police. Tell them I'm okay."

"They'll want to know where you've been. What shall I say?"

"Tell them I've been at home working on the TEI report."

She stopped writing, and looked at me with frown. "I tried to call your home a dozen times. The Cambridge Police went by and checked. They called me and reported no one there."

I took a big breath. I looked at her, trying to think what to say. Our eyes met, uncomfortably, for a second. Then she looked down and I could tell she regretted her insistence for an explanation. Silently, I made a decision to fudge a little.

"Donna, did you know that I'm a recovering alcoholic?" I asked.

"No, sir," she responded, softly.

"Well, I am."

She reacted like most people. She sat there, obviously trying to think of what to say next, to avoid talking about alcoholism.

Then, to protect my family, I lied. "This past weekend I fell off the wagon."

"Dr. Hartman, I'm sorry. I didn't know."

"I'm okay now. I went to an A.A. meeting last night, and I'm getting my life back on track."

"Is there anything I can do?"

"Yes," I said. "You could help cover for my absence. Tell people I was home working on the report."

"Yes, sir. I'll be glad to help you."

"Thanks."

"No problem."

"And, Donna," I looked her in the eye and gave her my best look of reassurance, "I really am okay now."

"Yes, sir. You look fine."

"So, back to the list?"

She nodded, picking up the yellow pad. I dictated a couple of letters and asked her to respond to most of the phone calls using the "working at home" story. She left, and I started through the stack of mail on my desk.

The second envelope had a familiar look to it. A plain, white, number-ten size, no return address, and with a Houston postmark, it looked identical to the mysterious pocket of paper that had carried the "deep throat" message. I ripped it open, anxious to see its contents. The message, neatly typed, read as follows:

Dear Dr. Hartman,

Check the TEI Building Blueprints. They are filed somewhere in the Building Maintenance Office. A small spiral staircase connects the top two floors. It's never used because it was poorly designed, too narrow, too steep, and the elevator is nearby, just down the hall. This staircase could have been used by the person who murdered Bryan Banks.

A Friend

I read and reread it. I found my copy of the first note and compared them. The previous note, which at the time I'd discounted and almost tossed, turned out to be 100% accurate. This note practically confirmed the plausibility of Bryan's murder.

And more importantly—if true and there really was a hidden stairway—it pointed to someone on the fiftieth floor as the killer.

CHAPTER 24

Harvard Business School, Morgan Hall, Office 223

I called Detective Joel Wilson in Houston and waited for him to get to the phone.

"Where are you?" he said, out of breath.

"In my office at Harvard," I answered.

"You okay?"

"Yes, I'm fine."

"Your family?"

"They're safe."

"You get the kids in school?"

"Yes," I said, "Thanks for calling the sheriff in Hyannisport."

"Chris!" he yelled. "You need to be careful. Your phone may be bugged, and if it is, you just gave away their location."

The fear returned. It felt like a bolt of electricity and gripping my muscles. I sat there in a stupor and cursed myself, silently.

"Sorry, I shouldn't have yelled," Joel apologized.

I couldn't respond.

"It's unlikely that they've bugged your phone at Harvard."

More silence.

"Chris, you still there?" he asked.

"I . . . I . . . don't know what to say."

"You thinking about how to be more careful?"

"I . . . I'm trying." I felt my pulse ease. "I went to a lot of effort to move Jenny and the kids."

"We traced you to Los Angeles," he said. "LAPD checked all the hotels and found your reservation at the Disneyland Fairfield Inn."

"You could find us?"

"Chris, if we found you, so will the guys who are after you."

"Go on."

"We lost you at the bus station."

"That's good news, I suppose." It made me feel a little better.

"I have to admit, you've made it hard to find your family."

"And then I make a stupid slip on this phone call."

"Hey, what's done is done," he said. "Maybe you'll be more careful in the future?"

"For sure. And I have something else."

"Is this something where you should use a pay phone?"

Reality hit. My life had changed, and it called for new thinking. "Yes, I'll call you back in ten minutes."

We ended our conversation, and I walked to a bank of pay phones near the post office in the Spangler Building. In a minute, I had Joel on the line again and told him about the note I received in the morning's mail. He reacted with disbelief.

"Joel, shouldn't we check this out?" I asked.

"We already did," he answered. "Right after we suspected a murderer may have been hiding in the closet and would need an escape route, I, personally, went to the building superintendent and looked at his blueprints. There's no stairway."

Joel's answer stunned me. When I read the note I was so sure we had found something, an important clue that pointed to someone on the corporate level, the fiftieth floor. "Damn," I said.

"But let me think about this," he said.

"Sure."

"Were you careful when you opened the note?"

"No, I just ripped it open."

"Next time, if there is a next time, get some gloves. Try not to mess up the fingerprints."

"Sorry, I didn't think."

"I need to get the note and have our CSI people examine it."

"I'm coming to Houston tomorrow."

"Put it in a plastic bag and bring it."

"Yes, sir."

"When you get to your office, give me a call. I'll stop by."

"Got it."

"One more thing."

"Yes?"

"You've got to be more careful."

"Yes, sir."

He hung up. No goodbye. Not a friendly end to our conversation. If he was trying to impress me, to convey the idea that the safety of my family was dependent on me, he'd certainly made his point. I would not make another slip on the phone.

I called Jenny from the same pay phone and cautioned her about the possibility of wiretaps. She agreed to use her cellphone when calling me, and when talking, to avoid any reference to her location.

I returned to my office and spent the rest of the day making preparations for the next day's trip to TEI.

HARRY HAINES

The following morning I caught Continental's flight 683 to Houston. The same stewardess in first class recognized me, and we chatted briefly on my involvement in the TEI investigation. I had the breakfast menu memorized: cheese omelet, large orange juice, fruit compote, and steaming hot coffee. Predictable and reassuring. I wished all my life could have those qualities.

One thing differed on this trip. Rain.

Air traffic at George Bush International backed up, and we circled for an hour. Finally, when our clearance came through, we landed into a cold, damp, dreary, November day.

At airport parking, I retrieved my rented, white Toyota, and made the long drive to the TEI parking garage with windshield wipers thrashing at full speed. The lousy weather helped my attitude; taking my mind off the problems at hand. And when I walked into the office, Caitlin, Jack, and Bart gave me a warm reception. The place felt cozy, more like a refuge than a center of conflict.

By now, I had learned how to deflect the expressions of concern over my absence. We went through the ritual of my disappearance, and then gathered around our conference table, with coffee, to review the status of each person's work.

"We've tracked all the SPEs," Bart said. "We have a list as long as my arm of all their illegalities."

"That's going to be the heart of our information," Jack said, "but the repercussions are the juicy part. We've found hundreds of indictable offenses." He passed out a thick report.

I scanned it for a few minutes to find money laundering, financial statement fraud, and dozens of other illegal acts. Jack had specifics— the details of white-collar crime that amounted to billions of dollars. Impressive work.

COLLUSION

"I've been working on Stephen Svensen," Caitlin said. "There's no doubt, they stepped across the line."

"Collusion?" I asked.

"Big time," she answered. "TEI, as a corporation, could never have gotten away with all this duplicity without help from their auditors." She distributed a list.

For the next few minutes, I scrutinized her documentation of the specific violations. The long list of charges appeared overwhelming. If Caitlin's accusations held up, if we proved even half of the wrong-doing, Stephen Svensen was in big trouble, much worse than anyone suspected. As I read item after item, I thought this would probably mean the end of the accounting firm. Silence came over our little group as the implications sank in.

"And I have some good news," Caitlin added. "The Powell committee has established the fund you requested." She laid out a recent copy of the *Houston Chronicle*. I read the headline, "TEI Investigative Committee Establishes Fund to Receive Returns." The article quoted William R. Powell, listed several hundred names—ones I had given him, of individuals who were suspected of insider trading—and spelled out specific amounts. He used my total, over a billion in ill-gotten gains.

Then came the surprise of the morning. Not only had the article listed the suspects, they reported the first four returns to the fund and made a big deal about it. On the front page, the *Chronicle* featured a little chart. The names and figures were given as follows:

NAME	SHARES	PRICE PER	TOTAL
Bryan Banks	75,000	$41.26	$3,094,500
William R. Powell, Jr.	50,000	$27.52	$1,376,000

HARRY HAINES

| James Wright | 100,000 | $28.86 | $2,886,000 |
| Dwight Young | 95,000 | $39.37 | $3,740,150 |

I hadn't yet given Jennifer's check to Powell, but he went ahead and listed Bryan's name. I felt good about it, but what I found to be even better news was the return of almost eight million dollars by the three members of the investigative committee. To use the time-honored cliché, each of them had put his money where his mouth was.

They led the way by personal example.

And the newspaper article went on to outline the Powell Committee's plan to appoint a blue-ribbon panel to oversee the return of this money to those who had been hit hardest by the TEI debacle. Obviously, the returns from insider trading could never repay all that had been lost, but it would make a sizeable down payment. As I read the details, I thought it *excellent. Everyone should be pleased.*

Everyone except those whose pocketbooks were being deflated, one of whom was probably the mysterious voice on the phone.

"Dr. Hartman?" Caitlin interrupted.

"Yes?" I returned my thoughts to the meeting at hand.

"I think we're ready to write the report," she said.

I felt the same and started to say so, but the door opened, and Detective Joel Wilson interrupted our meeting.

"Sorry to break in," he said. "May I see you for a minute?"

"Sure," I answered. I turned back to address my three assistants. "Go. Start filling in the names, dates, amounts—all the specifics." They rose and went back to their desks.

"My apologies for breaking up your meeting," Wilson said, "but, I have some big news."

"Lay it on me," I answered.

"I remembered the name of the construction firm, the people who built this building, Reid and Strickland."

"Okay."

"I know Gary Strickland. He and I are both members of the Downtown Rotary Club I called him, asked if he still had his copies of the construction blueprints."

"Oh." The light bulb came on.

"He did. So I paid him a visit and guess what we found?"

"The staircase?"

Wilson had been holding a long, round container at his side. Now he held it up. "May I?" Without waiting for an answer, he opened the container and unrolled several large blueprints across my desktop. We looked at the plans for the forty-ninth floor.

"Here, in a closet by the restroom at the back of Bryan's office..

I could see a tiny spiral staircase. "Ominous," I said.

"It's concealed. I went up and looked. It's in a closet behind a stack of boxes. I'd never have found it if it hadn't been for these plans."

Joel removed the first of the two pages and we looked at similar plans for the fiftieth floor.

"There's a small hallway that connects to these two offices."

I could see the spiral stairway ended in a connecting hallway between the corporate suites for the CEO and the CFO. "The hallway between Zimmerman and Upton?"

"Someone went to a lot of trouble to replace these two pages in the building plans—the blueprints that were on file at TEI."

"Who would do that?" I asked.

"Who *could* do it?" he asked.

"Someone with connections."

CHAPTER 25

The TEI Building, Office of the Special Investigation

Joel Wilson and I squirmed in our chairs without speaking.

My mind raced with possibilities, all of them bad—and dangerous. I stared at Joel and sensed that his thoughts paralleled mine.

I remembered our breakfast at the Wyndham Greenspoint when he told me about withholding information from his boss.

"Have you shared this with your captain?" I asked.

"No," he said. "I was waiting until I found hard evidence."

"Damn, how much harder does it get?"

"Chris, I just now went upstairs to confirm it. But, since I was in the building, I wanted to show it to you."

"And?"

"I'm on my way to headquarters to turn it over to the department."

"Good. Does this mean they'll reopen the case?"

"Obviously."

"And change Bryan's death from suicide to murder?"

"If it were up to me, I'd do it immediately," he said.

"How could there be any question?" My voice, suddenly louder, reflected my reaction. The evidence seemed overwhelming,

164

unquestionable.

"Chris, we made a mistake," he answered. "The department, understandably, is going to be more careful the second time around."

"The Blackberry removal, threats against my family, and now the change of blueprints—how could anyone continue to support a suicide theory?" I said, irritated.

"I agree."

"What are you waiting on?" I yelled, letting my wrath erupting full-force.

"Nothing." He said it calmly. "I just told you, I'm on my way to see the captain." He rolled up the blueprints, slipped them into the container, and turned toward the door.

I stood, too, trying to control my anger. "Joel, wait." The last thing I wanted was ill feeling. I waited a moment until I could speak calmly. "You've made a major breakthrough, finding these changes in the blueprints."

"Thanks."

"This will likely be the evidence that seals the case."

"Let's hope."

"I appreciate all you've done." I said. "I really do."

He shook my hand, but the tension was so thick I could feel it as he turned and left.

I tried to get back to work. I couldn't do it.

In the days before alcohol took over my life, I'd use the bottle to defuse my pent-up frustrations. At times like this, a trip to the bar provided an easy way to cope with life's dissatisfactions. But today, I reached into my pocket for my chip, pulled it out, and read the words "One Day at a Time" engraved on one side. I turned it over and, for the zillionth time, calculated the date on the other side, the day of my last drink—one year, three months, two weeks, and six days ago.

It worked one more time.

As I returned to my desk, I glanced at my watch. Almost five o'clock. Quitting time for most employees. As others stirred, making arrangements to close down for the day, a young woman came into the office and stopped at Caitlin's desk. I overheard my name. Caitlin pointed toward me, and the woman walked in my direction.

"Dr. Hartman?" she asked.

"Yes," I said.

Without speaking, she handed me an envelope with my name on it, turned, and left. I ripped it open and read the brief message:

Dear Chris,

I'm going to Frank's Pizza at eight o'clock this evening. I'd like to talk with you about some things that happened late this afternoon. Could you join me? Be sure you are not followed.

Elizabeth

Three hours. I had plenty of work to fill the time, so, with renewed tenacity, I pushed myself to write the report. For the next hour I attempted to compose the executive summary. After starting over several times, it became obvious that my energy for creative writing had reached its threshold of frustration. I shut down my computer, took my unsuccessful attempts to the shredder, and left. Elizabeth's admonition to be careful that no one followed weighed heavily, and I decided to again use the successful routine of our last dinner meeting. I drove to the Galleria, parked outside Macy's

Department Store, and walked in to join the mob of shoppers. After being reasonably sure no one had tailed me, I walked to the Wyndham Hotel and took a cab back downtown to the *Houston Chronicle* Building. I went into the lobby, and sat down to read a newspaper. At a quarter to eight, I slipped out the back door and crossed the street to Frank's Pizza. Taking the same, back-corner booth. I waited.

When Elizabeth came in, I didn't recognize her. She wore jeans, sneakers, baseball cap, and a red T-shirt that said "Ft. Bend Hard Hitters" on the front. She slid into the booth and smiled.

"Isn't this the wrong time of year for softball?" I asked.

"We practice inside," she replied.

"At the Astrodome?"

"No, at a local high school."

A waiter came for our order. We selected a medium-sized supreme, with Diet Cokes

"So, how've you been?" I asked.

"Much better, until this afternoon," she answered. "But I still have a job."

"So what happened this afternoon to tip the scales?"

"A detective from Houston PD came and examined the forty-ninth and fiftieth floors," she said. "Evidently, this created quite a stir upstairs."

"The detective, Joel Wilson, came by to see me."

"So you know?"

"Only what he told me. Tell me what you found out."

"I've been working closely with Jerry Norton's secretary, and she came down to quiz me about the detective's investigation."

"What'd you tell her?"

"Just the facts."

"Elizabeth." I said her name sharply. "This is important. I need to know the specifics of your conversation."

"Okay, okay."

"Sorry, but I would like you to recount, word for word, as best you can remember, what was said."

"Well, the detective came into the office in the middle of the afternoon, showed me his badge, and asked to see Bryan's office."

The waiter brought our drinks and we paused for a minute.

"Go on," I said when we were alone again. "He wanted to see the office."

"Yes. I unlocked the office and watched him look around for a few minutes. Then he asked me to leave and close the door—which I did."

"Then what happened?"

"In about fifteen minutes he came out, thanked me, and left."

"That's all there was to it?"

"Until Norton's secretary came to see me about thirty minutes later."

"This is important, Elizabeth," I said. "Take your time. Try to remember exactly what was said."

"She came in with a casual air. Right away, I sensed something was up."

"How so?"

"She's never casual. It's always business."

"Go on."

"First, she asked me how the week had gone, then she asked about my plans for the weekend."

"What did you say?"

COLLUSION

"I said it had been an easy week—which it had. And I told her about my softball practice this evening."

"Then what?"

"Then it hit the fan. She asked about the detective's visit."

"And?"

"I told her, exactly what I've told you."

"I don't understand."

"As soon as I told her I'd left Detective Wilson alone in the office, she started carrying on like I'd just committed larceny."

"She was upset that you didn't know what the detective wanted?"

"She was furious."

"What did she say, or yell?" I asked.

"I think I can quote her verbatim."

"Please."

"She screamed at me, 'You stupid Mexican Spic, why didn't you call security, call me, call somebody?'"

"Wow."

"I wanted to slap her, to call *her* a few names."

"What did you do? How did you react?"

"I bit my tongue, and tried to calm her down. I told her I checked the room and found nothing disturbed. I don't know if she believed me or not, because the next moment she left in a huff."

"And that was it?"

"I stewed about it. I could see I'd lost favor with the fiftieth floor. And I thought I'd better talk with you, so, I wrote you the note."

The waiter brought the pizza, and I was grateful to have a few moments to think about Elizabeth's news. When he left and I watched as Elizabeth quietly took a small bite.

"They can see things are unraveling," I said.

169

"What things?" she asked.

I took a big bite of pizza. It gave me time to avoid answering..

"Elizabeth, there's some really heavy stuff going on. I mean more than the financial problems."

She reached over and placed her hand on my arm. "Remember. I want to help you."

I had the unmistakable feeling that she sensed the perils beneath the surface.

"Elizabeth, you've got to be careful. You could be in danger." I placed my hand on hers. "Listen to me. You need to convince everyone that you don't know anything or suspect anyone."

"Forget about me, Chris. I can take care of myself. What about you?" she asked.

"I'm already in this up to my eyebrows."

"I can help," she said, again. "I want to."

"The best thing you can do is stay out of it," I pleaded. "Don't do anything to raise suspicion or put yourself in danger. This may be over soon. And if you survive just a little longer, you'll be okay." My words carried a double message. Survive meant more than her job. I hoped I wouldn't have to explain.

She didn't ask.

We ate silently, Elizabeth seemingly avoiding me. I sensed she was wrestling with big decisions.

"Please, do this for me," I urged.

"Stay out of it?"

"It's the best thing you can do to help me."

"I can do more."

"Please, Elizabeth."

She touched her napkin to her lips. Her eyes avoided mine and

COLLUSION

I had the distinct impression she wanted to share more information with me. Instead, she looked at me, gave me a little smile. "I will."

We finished our meal in silence. And, when we walked to her car, it seemed perfectly natural to hold he hand. At her car, though, things became awkward.

"May I give you a ride?" she asked.

"I'd better take a cab." We stood close together, and I thought of kissing her goodnight, but the damned baseball cap hid her face and her mood. Instead, I squeezed her hand.

She slipped behind the wheel and I watched as she drove away.

A cab to the Galleria, a walk to my car, a thirty-minute drive to Jennifer's house, and I was ready to call it a day. Five seconds after my head hit the pillow, I fell asleep.

The next morning I went out to get the paper, anxious to read about the reopening of the new developments in the TEI case, hoping the police would announce that Bryan's death would be categorized as murder, not suicide. I scanned the headlines.

The lead story gave details about an oil spill.

I searched the front page for the TEI case. Nothing.

Below it, I saw a story and a photograph about a car wreck.

LOCAL POLICE DETECTIVE KILLED IN ACCIDENT.

The photograph showed the charred remains of a Houston PD Ford Crown Victoria. The caption stated that Detective Joel Wilson had been killed when his police cruiser had been rear-ended. The second driver, a TEI security guard, driving a white Ford pickup, said the police car had braked suddenly, causing the accident. The article went on to extol the exemplary record of Joel Wilson, and the outstanding service he had given to Houston PD.

CHAPTER 26

44 Leisure Cove, The Woodlands

Reading the details of Joel's death frightened me. Then my fear changed to anger. As I read on, my anger turned to rage, and the fury within built as I struggled to think of ways to respond. I called Houston PD, gave my name, and asked to speak with Joel Wilson's immediate superior.

Captain Michael O'Kelly came on the line.

"Captain O'Kelly, I need to see you immediately," I said. "I have information about Joel Wilson's death."

"What is your information?" he asked.

"His death was not an accident. It was murder."

"Why do you say that?"

"It's a long story, but I have facts which, if you investigate, may prove my accusation."

"Do you know who committed the murder?"

"No, but I have some suspects for you."

"What's your name again?"

"Christopher Hartman. I'm in charge of the TEI investigation."

"And you think Wilson's death is related to the TEI mess."

"I know it's related."

"Tell me why you think it's related."

"Listen, I need to see you. I'm in the Woodlands and can be there in an hour."

Silence.

"I'm coming in. Will you see me?"

"I'm very busy this morning."

"This is the murder of a Houston police detective," I yelled. "What's more important than this?"

"Detective Wilson's unfortunate death was caused by an automobile accident."

"Listen, you idiot. That car wreck was planned. He was murdered."

"So you say."

"So I can prove."

Silence.

"I'll be there in an hour!" I hung up.

Breathing hard, the first thought that came to my mind was that he'd damn well better see me.

Sitting there, thinking about Joel, I wished I hadn't called O'Kelly an idiot.

Houston traffic was worse than usual. The drive took almost an hour and a half causing, I imagined, the reluctant captain to be even less inclined to see me. A uniformed policewoman at the front counter received me with indifference.

"I'm here to see Captain O'Kelly. My name's Chris Hartman. I think he's expecting me."

"Have a seat," she said. "I'll tell him you're here."

After ten minutes, I went to the counter. "How much longer?" I asked.

"He knows you're here," the policewoman replied. "I'm sure he'll be with you as soon as he can."

"This is urgent."

"Yeah, everything is urgent," she replied. Her phone rang, and she turned away.

I stood there.

"That was the captain. He'll see you now." She pointed to a door. "I'll buzz you in. Down the hall, last room on the right, number eleven."

"Thank you."

"Would you like a tip?"

"Sure."

"Don't act so pushy. Captain doesn't like to be pushed."

Without a reply, I turned and started toward the door, realizing too late that I had been rude to a woman who was only trying to help me. I went back to the counter and gave her my best smile.

"Thanks," I said.

"Worth a try." She smiled back.

I went to the door and she buzzed me in. As I walked toward the captain's office, I struggled to collect my thoughts. The door was open so I entered without hesitation.

"Good morning, Captain." I extended my hand.

He rose, and without a smile shook my hand. His resentment bordered on hostility.

"I'm the idiot, not you," I said, "and I hope you'll accept my apology."

The expression on his face softened. "We've lost a good man."

He pulled out a yellow pad, picked up a pencil.

"I have some information that will help explain his death."

"So you said."

I told him everything. The missing Blackberry and its return, the photographs that showed the clear spot amid the blood splatter on Bryan's desk, Luke's broken arm, the two calls threatening my family, and finally the two letters from "A Friend." I showed him a photocopy of the first letter and the original second letter which, following Joel's instructions, I had placed in a clear plastic bag.

"That's quite a story," he said, and the way he said it made me wonder if he was simply patronizing me.

"There's one more incident you need to know about," I told him, "and I think this is what got Joel killed."

His eyebrows narrowed as he glanced at me over his yellow notepad. "An accident killed him," he corrected.

I held up my hand. "Hear me out, please."

He leaned back in his chair. "You have my attention."

I told him about Joel's trip to Reid and Strickland, his finding the original blueprints, and his visit yesterday afternoon to locate the stairway. "Joel came by my office and showed the plans to me."

"I've looked at his case file," the captain said. "There's no mention of this."

"At about four-thirty yesterday afternoon, he told me he was on his way to report all of this to you."

Did I sense a slight shift in his attitude?

"Something you don't understand," he said. His gruff voice suddenly softened. "I work closely with my detectives, especially on big, high-profile cases like TEI."

"Yes, sir."

"Joel never said anything to me about Bryan Banks, about changing the case from suicide to murder."

"I know. He told me yesterday afternoon that he'd held back his suspicions. And he said you'd be pissed when you found out."

O'Kelly's face turned red. He looked away from me for several seconds. Then he turned back and gave me an icy stare. In a voice, barely above a whisper, he said, "Joel Wilson and I worked together for fifteen years. He never, not once, ever held back on me."

"Yes, sir, he told me that, too."

"I don't believe you. I don't believe Joel knew this information. And if he had it, I don't believe he would tell you before he discussed it with me."

"Yes, sir."

"And another thing. If it turns out that you are, or have been, withholding information, I'll see that you are indicted for obstructing justice."

"Yes, sir. I understand."

"Now get out of my office," he said. If it were possible, Captain O'Kelly's face turned even redder.

I stood, walked to the door, hesitated, and turned to face him. "Just one more thing?"

"Get out!" he shouted.

I wanted to caution him about involving Elizabeth. Clearly, he was in no mood to hear more suggestions from me.

Driving to the TEI Building, I wrestled with my situation and wondered what to do next. It seemed untenable. Not only had I lost my closest ally, Joel's death gave immediate and tangible proof of the ruthlessness of the enemy.

And my name was either at, or near, the top of their list.

COLLUSION

And my family was there, too.

Seated at my desk, I tried to think what to do. Caitlin stared at me for a few minutes, then came over and took a chair.

"You look drained," she said. "Are you all right?"

"Yes, I'm fine." As I said it, I shook my head, grabbed a yellow pad, and wrote the following message.

This place is probably bugged. Be careful what you say. Warn the others.

She nodded. "Don't hesitate to call on me if I can help." She went back to her desk and I watched as she wrote a note, showing it to both Jack and Bart.

Joel Wilson's death was a tragic loss, and I wondered what I could have done to prevent it. Self-recrimination washed over me. I broke into a cold sweat. Yesterday, Joel had talked with me. Today he was dead.

I had an overpowering urge to buy a bottle of Scotch. One thing for sure, I had to get out of my office. I left.

My mind in turmoil, I drove north on I-45. My rational thinking went into a tailspin, and the car continued as though on autopilot. I wasn't aware how long or how far the drive north lasted, but, for sure, I was well past The Woodlands when I pulled off and found a retail liquor store.

After purchasing a one-liter bottle of Chivas Regal, I decided to drive back to 44 Leisure Cove and find solace in an alcohol escape. The decision felt good, the best possible answer to my frustration.

At home, I went into the kitchen, emptied a tray of ice cubes into a large bowl, and found a gold-rimmed highball glass that seemed just right. I carried the glass, ice, and bottle through the house, searching for a suitable place to drown my sorrows. For some unknown reason, Bryan's desk reached out with special appeal. I settled into his high-back, leather desk chair and flipped on his computer.

While the computer booted its opening routine, I filled the glass with ice, broke open the Scotch, and poured the golden liquid to within a half-inch of the rim. It smelled wonderful.

As the computer's desktop appeared, I searched through Bryan's files to find something interesting, something good to go with my drink, something intriguing that would provide good reading as I slipped away into a drunken stupor. While jiggling the highball glass in my left hand, I held the mouse in my right, and scrolled an alphabetical listing of his files. In the "B's," I discovered a folder titled "Blackberry backups." I double-clicked to open and found several dozen dated documents.

I set my drink down for a minute to scan the dates.

They started in mid-summer and appeared at regular weekly intervals. Then, in September, the dates became more frequent. In October, the dates shifted to a daily basis. The last date, October 1, I remembered, was the day before Bryan's death. I double-clicked the icon to open the file. In the notation, he identified the backup with a short description that included my name.

DATE: Monday, October 1
NOTE: Data for meeting with Chris Hartman

Suddenly, it dawned on me. I realized that each time Bryan connected his Blackberry to this desktop computer, the software automatically created a backup file. At work, he had carefully erased all copies. And his Blackberry, when it reappeared, had come back with the data wiped clean. But no one had thought to check this machine, his home computer, for backup files.

Excitement surged through me at the magnitude of this discovery. Having never used drugs, I don't know what a high from cocaine feels like, but I'd wager a case of Chivas that the elation would not compare to the rush I felt at that moment.

I had found TEI's top-secret corporate data, and the material my son-in-law prepared for the meeting we never had.

CHAPTER 27

44 Leisure Cove, The Woodlands

I couldn't sit still.

Adrenaline raced through my body and elevated my heartbeat. Excitement oozed from every pore as I thought about the implications. My brain jumped ahead to the possibilities of how I could best use Bryan's information.

I roamed around the room, hoping physical movement would help me control my emotions. As I paced back and forth, thinking furiously, my eyes fell on the bottle of Scotch and the highball glass. I picked them up, carried them to the kitchen, and dumped both into the sink.

The smell of expensive Scotch no longer held any enticement.

Hurrying back to Bryan's desk, I turned on the printer and printed out the file. It was quite long, over a hundred pages. Much of it paralleled data we'd found in the Svensen shredding list. However, what was new, what pleased me most, was Bryan's summary. He took the raw data, the facts, and wrote his interpretation of the consequences for the corporation.

He named names.

COLLUSION

I read with fascination his characterization of who had done what. He believed the Stephen Svensen auditors were the key players. They knew TEI's corporate officers were cutting corners. If Dennis Johnston and other top Svensen accountants had met their responsibilities that would have stopped the financial statement fraud.

This fraud, alone, was enough to cause the downfall of the world's largest energy corporation.

With pinpoint accuracy, Bryan had predicted that eventually TEI's hidden debt would be found, and when the truth came out it would cause an unstoppable freefall in the stock price. And he had the foresight to see that the SPEs, the special purpose entities—TEI's partnership corporations like Cayman Energy Limited, would lead the way. The SPEs would go belly-up and, like falling dominoes, take TEI with them.

Bryan had seen it coming.

He couldn't stop it.

He'd wanted me to review his options and advise him what to do. He'd made a list. I read it with fascination. At the top of the list was his realization that he'd broken the law when he sold 75,000 shares of stock at $41.26. He could see, correctly, that he would be cited for insider trading because he knew, in a very short time, the stock would fall. He'd planned to ask me the next morning whether, if he repurchased the stock, this action would protect him from the charge.

His list contained nineteen other questions, most of which would have been difficult, if not impossible, to answer at that time. Now, however, the answers were much more apparent. His first and most important question, in my opinion, was what to do about the auditors.

Dennis Johnston and his Stephen Svensen colleagues had placed themselves between the proverbial "rock and hard place."

They wanted to keep their largest client—TEI—and the lucrative contracts which Bryan estimated at $5.5 million per year. To do this, Svensen would have to go along with Upton, Norton, and others.

No collusion. No contract.

Obviously, Johnston had "gone along," hoping he could ride it out. Unfortunately, things came unraveled. The rules about financial statement fraud, which had been put there for good reason, had caught up with him. With everyone.

Now it was my turn.

I had to blow the whistle.

This was not the same as attacking TEI corporate officers—people like Richard Zimmerman, Reed Upton, and Jerry Norton. But it was close.

I needed to find a way to do it without getting myself killed. Or worse yet, without endangering others, as I had done with Joel Wilson. It would require careful, thoughtful planning.

Tired, but relaxed and more confident, it was obvious what I had to do. Still, I decided to sleep on it.

The next morning I showered, shaved, dressed, and picked up a Danish to eat in the car on my drive downtown. After breakfast, I called Dennis Johnston on my cell phone and arranged to meet him in his office.

When I arrived, his secretary showed me in without waiting.

Dennis stood behind his desk, his dark blue sports jacket parted to allow him to stick nervous hands into light khaki pant pockets. He looked at me with a somber face. I could tell immediately that he suspected bad news.

"Coffee," he said.

COLLUSION

It was more of a command than a question. "No," I answered.

He poured a cup for himself, sat and looked at me with apprehensive eyes. "What's up?"

"Denny, I haven't written my report yet, but it's obvious I'll have to include some things that are unfavorable to Stephen Svensen."

"So, what else is new?"

"Let me read you an outline."

"Go ahead, take your best shot."

I pulled out Bryan's summary. Johnston sipped his coffee. He carried his self-assurance well. If I hadn't had the list before me, I probably would have been intimidated. In the world of forensic accounting, a bluff often carried the day.

I read Bryan's listing, starting with the SPEs. Six of them, all illegal, all approved by Stephen Svensen, all now bankrupt, a loss that totaled over three billion. Then I read thirteen other specific financial acts where the auditors had signed off on TEI's illegal transfers, money laundering, kickbacks, and financial statement fraud.

Dennis Johnston's look of self-assurance crumbled into panic.

"God, Chris, you can't print that," he said.

"Sorry, Denny, I have no choice."

"We'll sue you for defamation," he exploded. "That stuff would destroy our company."

"It's all a matter of public record," I answered. "Either you did it, or you didn't. And if you did, you deserve the consequences."

"Wait, let me contact our corporate headquarters," he pleaded. "I'll bet they'll find a way to oblige you."

"A bribe?"

"Of course not."

"A consultant's fee for accommodation?"

"Chris, you know complex accounting procedures, like most of those on your list, are subject to various interpretations."

"Fine. I'll just report them and let you and your corporate headquarters make the interpretations with federal officials."

"There's no need to do this." Beads of perspiration glistened on his forehead.

"Just my conscience."

"Damn it, Chris, I'll have to report this to Billy Ray Powell and the TEI Board."

"Go ahead. Do what you have to do."

"And to Zimmerman, Upton, and Norton." He stood, spitting out their names like a threat.

I didn't care, and I suppose my face showed it. "Sure."

"They're not going to like your high-handed, hardball approach."

"I know."

"They have their ways of responding." Johnston slammed his fist against his desk.

"Is that a threat?"

"Yes. Well, no. I mean, it's unnecessary," he pleaded. "We can work this out."

"Denny, obviously, we're on different sides," I said. "I like you personally, and I will always appreciate the comments you made about my son-in-law back in October."

"But—" He fell back into his chair, the bluster fading from his voice.

"But I've got a job to do."

He looked down at the floor, the starch now gone from his persona.

"I wanted you to know what's coming down the pike," I said. "I've given you warning so you can make plans. Maybe you should try to distance yourself from TEI before all this becomes public. I remember that you and I talked briefly about the opportunities for accountants in academia."

Silently, he shook his head. "Too late," he whispered.

I left.

Back at my office I had a phone message to call Captain O'Kelly, Houston PD. I dialed the number, and as the number started to ring, the thought hit me that all of my calls were probably being monitored. I hung up before O'Kelly answered.

Walking across the street to a Starbuck's Coffee Shop, I found a pay phone and redialed the number. The Captain came on the line.

"Chris Hartman, returning your call," I said.

"Thank you, Dr. Hartman," he answered. "I'd like to meet with you."

After the way we'd parted, his words surprised me. "Sure," I said after a brief hesitation.

"Bryan Banks's office in thirty minutes?"

"Okay."

"Thank you. I'll see you there."

I sensed he was about to hang up. "Captain, I have a suggestion." I heard him take a deep breath, a breath of annoyance.

"What is it?" He said it curtly, his resentment unmistakable.

"The last time a policeman went into that office to look around, TEI's corporate people didn't like it."

O'Kelly's response surprised me. He chuckled. "People usually don't like it when police come nosing around."

"I think this situation is more serious. The last time a policeman 'nosed around' that office he was killed in an automobile accident, less than an hour later."

"Joel?"

"Yes."

Silence. I could almost hear his brain working, thinking through my words of caution. Finally he asked my advice. "What do you suggest?"

"Be careful not to make a big splash. Don't go to the fiftieth floor."

I could hear the rustle of paper. "Room 4901?" he asked.

"Yes," I answered. "I'll go up a few minutes early, make arrangements with the secretary."

More sounds of paper shuffling. "Elizabeth Garcia?" he asked.

"She's on our side."

"Okay. Meet you there in forty-five minutes." He hung up.

I picked up a cup of coffee to go and headed back to my office to write two short notes.

> *Caitlin, please take this note to Elizabeth Garcia. She's the secretary in Bryan Banks's old office, room 4901.*

Elizabeth,

Captain Mike O'Kelly, Houston PD, is coming to look at the closet this morning. I'll meet him there within the hour. Do what you can to get us in and out without anyone from the fiftieth floor knowing about it.

Chris

COLLUSION

I put Elizabeth's note in a small envelope and gave them both to Caitlin. She read her note, took the envelope with Elizabeth's name on it, and left. I waited. Ten minutes later she returned and gave me a thumbs up. The minutes ticked by slowly. At the appropriate time I took the elevator to the forty-ninth floor and walked to the infamous office. Alone, Elizabeth sat at her desk.

"Is the door unlocked?"

"Yes." She rose and opened it.

I walked over, and we stood close. Her perfume swept over me. It was an awkward moment—the feeling of closeness, yet the formality of our separate space. The sound of the door caused us both to look. Captain O'Kelly came into the room and we stepped apart. I made the introductions.

"Elizabeth, I think it better for you to stay out of this," I said.

O'Kelly nodded.

We went into Bryan's office and closed the door. I led him to the closet and turned on the light. The small room was narrow but long—about six feet wide and probably fifteen feet from the doorway to back wall. With shelving on both sides, the space between was probably less than four feet. In the narrow aisle, we walked to the back where cardboard boxes were stacked, floor to ceiling.

"Joel said the spiral staircase was behind these boxes," I said.

"Let's have a look," O'Kelly replied. He reached up and worked the top box down. He handed it to me and went after the next one. For the next few minutes we unstacked the boxes, one by one. Gradually, the space behind the boxes revealed itself.

It was a blank wall.

CHAPTER 28

Express elevator, the TEI Building

In the elevator going down, I told O'Kelly about Joel's visit to the construction company and their blueprints. When we reached the ground floor, I walked him to the door where we stopped to talk.

"I think we should go look at those blueprints," I said.

"You go, if you want," O'Kelly said. "I've already wasted too much time on your mistakes."

He stomped off, leaving no doubt about his evaluation of me and my suggestions. The security guards watched with interest. I felt like a fool as I returned to the elevators.

Back in the office I decided to forego the dispute with Captain O'Kelly and deal with it later. Instead, I called a meeting of my three assistants. Since we now believed the office was bugged, we took frequent "coffee breaks" or met for lunch at nearby restaurants. That day we took a cab to Frank's Pizza. I passed out copies of Bryan's data. For the next hour, Caitlin, Jack, and Bart read while I sketched out a plan on how to use the information. The facts spoke for themselves. Our job was to present them in an organized and succinct way. The lunch hour passed swiftly, with occasional comments or questions passing among us.

Finally, Caitlin shuffled her stack—indicating she had finished—and looked at me with a shake of her head. "Dr. Hartman, this is incredible. I thought the Svensen shredding lists were the ultimate gold mine, but this is even better."

She got up and secured coffee refills for each of us. Jack and Bart finished. With fresh caffeine, I started down the list of writing assignments.

"This will be chapter and verse about Stephen Svensen."

"What about TEI?" Jack asked.

"That comes later," I answered.

"Seems to me the information is inseparable," Bart said.

"Facts are facts," I said. "But we're writing a report about auditors, about Stephen Svensen's failure to report illegal actions."

"Wait a minute," Caitlin said. "Surely we're not gonna let these TEI guys get away with this?"

"No, of course not," I replied.

"Why not nail them now?"

"Trust me," I said. "It's better to go after the accountants first."

The three sat there, sipping hot coffee.

"Lay the groundwork?" Jack asked.

"Build the case, layer by layer," Bart said.

I sipped my coffee silently.

Caitlin squirmed in her chair. "Dr. Hartman, is there something you're not telling us?"

"Yes." I thought about the deaths of Bryan and Joel, and the threats against my grandchildren. Without speaking, I mulled over my plans to keep these three away from the danger.

The silence among us weighed heavily. Caitlin, especially, made it obvious that she didn't like to be kept in the dark. She rolled her eyes, exchanged glances with Jack and Bart. I looked away and waited.

Finally, Jack broke the tension. "Caitlin, time to move on," he said.

"Tell me my assignment," Bart said.

She shrugged, "Me too."

I ran down the list. They had their copies of Bryan's executive summary, and we checked off the topics. Bart would work the SPEs. Jack took the next six topics, which included financial statement fraud and money laundering. Caitlin agreed to cover the remainder. I assigned myself the finger pointing—the job of naming names and spelling out the specific acts which should be subject to government indictments.

Back on the street, Jack, Bart, and Caitlin caught a cab back to the TEI building. I waived them off and then took a minute with my cell phone to call the cabin on Cape Cod. Jennifer answered on the first ring.

"Greetings from Houston," I said, the sound of street traffic almost as loud as my conversation.

"Dad. It's so good to hear your voice," she answered, her words bubbly, the emotion unmistakable.

"You and the family okay?"

"Any move has its problems."

"Tell me," I said. "Maybe I can help."

"We both know you need to give all your attention to finishing your report." She paused as though deciding what else to say.

I waited, trying to give her space.

"Last night the kids asked when we could go back to Houston.

COLLUSION

What should I tell them?"

"Tell them, when it's safe, that grandpa is working on it, and it won't be long."

"You know how it is with a ten-year-old or a seven-year-old," Jenny said. "They want a concrete date."

"Wish I could give you one."

"How about a guess?"

Her words pulled at my heartstrings as I rued the day my family ever became associated with TEI. "Jenny, I'm trying as hard as I can."

"Dad, that's okay," she said and I felt her voice soften—a shift in her concern from the kids to me. "Don't worry about us."

A big eighteen-wheeler on Travis Street roared by and the noise made it increasingly difficult to communicate. Standing on the sidewalk, only a few feet away, I could see this was not the place to get into a serious discussion about life-threatening issues.

"I love you," I said. "Give the kids a hug for me."

"I love you, too, Dad, and the kids think their grandpa's number one."

We punched off. I found a taxi back to the TEI Building. A renewed pressure coursed though my brain—a resolve to work faster on the damn TEI report and get my family back to their normal life.

In my office, I called Reid and Strickland Construction Company, asked to speak with Gary Strickland. He agreed to meet me at his office at four o'clock. I spent the next several hours writing and watching the clock. At three-thirty, I said my goodbyes and drove to the construction company's offices in South Houston.

Gary Strickland wore work clothes. In khaki shirt and trousers, steel-toed boots, and hard hat, he looked like more like a job foreman than the millionaire owner of Houston's largest construction company. He took off the hat and offered coffee.

"No thanks," I said, "I'm coffeed out."

"What's up?" he asked.

"I'm a friend of Joel Wilson."

"Me, too," he said, "Joel was an honest, dedicated cop."

"And a great person," I added.

"Houston PD needs to fix those damn gas tanks," he grumbled.

I thought about discussing the details, but decided against it. "I'm doing a follow-up on his last two days," I said. "We suspect he may have found information related to the TEI investigation."

"What does that have to do with me?"

"You built the building?"

"Yes."

"The day before Joel was killed, did he come here to look at your blueprints?"

"We talked about it at Rotary," he said. "I don't know that he actually came and looked at the construction plans."

"He did," I said, "and he showed me his copies of the forty-ninth and fiftieth floors."

"So?"

"I think something he found out about the building may have gotten him killed."

Strickland's breath caught. "Damn. How could that be?"

"Could we go look at your plans?"

"You bet," he said. "Let me call to be sure someone's there to help us find them."

He called, made arrangements. We walked to the Engineering Department where a file clerk pulled the blueprints. They were huge.

"All we want are the floor plans for the forty-ninth and fiftieth floors," I said.

Strickland turned to the file clerk, a gray-haired woman named Mary Jo. "Would you help us?"

Mary Jo plowed through hundreds of pages and, in seconds, found the plans.

Strickland complimented her. "Mary Jo, that's the fastest I've ever seen you work a set of blueprints."

She blushed. "It's the third time in three days I've done it. I'm getting familiar with these plans."

"The third time?" I asked. "Tell us about the others?"

"A police detective a couple of days ago."

"Joel Wilson?"

"I don't remember his name, but he showed me his shield."

"Who was the other?" I asked.

"A guy from TEI Security. He showed me his I.D."

"Name?"

"Again, I don't remember."

"Mary Jo," I asked, "did you stay with him while he looked at the plans?"

"For a minute," she answered. "He wanted to study them so I went back to my desk."

I looked at the plans and realized they had been replaced. There was no spiral staircase shown on either the forty-ninth or the fiftieth floor.

"Damn!" I shook my head.

"What's wrong?" Strickland asked.

"The S.O.B. replaced these two sheets," I said.

"Show me," Strickland said. He didn't say it, but I could tell by his reaction that he didn't believe me.

I pointed to the closet in room 4901. "On the copies that Joel Wilson showed me, there's a small spiral staircase right there."

Again, in disbelief, Strickland looked. He turned to the file clerk. "Mary Jo, how could this be?"

She looked. "This is the floor plan. Let's check it against the steel drawings." She rustled through the huge stack of blueprints.

While she searched, Strickland explained. "There are different drawings for each of the subcontractors. These multiple copies vary for steel, for heating and air conditioning, for electrical, etc. But all will show the basic walls and staircases."

"Here it is," Mary Jo said. She rolled out a blueprint for the steelworkers for the forty-ninth floor.

It showed a small, steel, spiral staircase at the back of the closet.

"I'll be damned," Strickland said, shaking his head. "Someone is going to a hell of a lot of trouble to try to hide that stairway."

CHAPTER 19

Houston PD Headquarters

The next morning I again approached the policewoman at the counter. "Hi. I'm Chris Hartman. Remember me?"

"And you want to see Captain O'Kelly?"

"Yes, please."

She glanced at her computer screen, clicked her mouse. "I don't have your name on his appointment schedule."

"He's not expecting me." I gave her my best and most ingratiating smile. "Could you work me in?"

She turned away and picked up the phone. I couldn't hear what she said. In a moment, she turned to face me. "He's very busy. How much time do you need?"

"Less than five minutes."

"He says less than five minutes," she repeated into her phone. After a brief pause, she said, "You know the drill," and pointed to the door. "I'll buzz you in."

I walked through the steel door with its bulletproof glass and continued back to the room at the end of the hall where I found O'Kelly on the phone. He gestured to an empty chair.

I sat, unrolled the blueprints on his desk, and placed books on the ends to hold them flat. I waited while he finished his conversation.

"What is it?" he asked before the receiver hit the cradle. "I don't have much time."

With a red pen, I circled the spiral staircase at the end of the closet.

He recognized it immediately.

"Well, I'll be damned. Where'd you get this?"

"Reid and Strickland Construction Company." I moved the book on one end, allowing the top drawing to roll back. "Here's the fiftieth floor." Again, I circled the stairway with my red, felt-tip pen.

He slouched back in his chair, rubbed his face with both hands. "All right, how do you explain this?"

I told him about the exchange of blueprints. When I finished, he said almost the same thing as Gary Strickland.

"Someone's going to a hell of a lot of trouble to try to hide this damn stairway."

I grinned, an impish impulse I couldn't help.

"Guess you and I better go check it out?"

This was not the reaction I'd expected, and sensing genuine contrition on O'Kelly's part, I immediately sobered. "I've thought of a plan," I said.

He nodded. "I figured you had. Lay it on me."

"Let's take a keyhole saw and cut an opening in the sheetrock. I think the best time to do it would be at five-thirty this evening."

He thought about it for a moment. "Okay."

"I'll make arrangements with the secretary, Elizabeth Garcia. Can you bring the tools?"

"Sure."

COLLUSION

"Meet you there, 5:30 p.m." I stood.

He rose and smiled. Not a big smile, just enough to convey approval. He held out his hand. "I'm impressed."

I shook it and left.

Arriving back at the office where everyone seemed hard at work, I went to my desk and wrote another note to Elizabeth.

Elizabeth,

> *Captain O'Kelly and I are going to take another look at Bryan's office. We'll be there this evening at five-thirty and stay about fifteen or twenty minutes. Could you find an excuse to work late and cover for us?*

Chris

I placed the note in an envelope and wrote Elizabeth's name on it. Then I took it to Caitlin.

"Would you take another message for me?" I asked. "Same person, same place."

"Sure."

I handed her the envelope. "I'd like you to wait while she reads the note, then bring me her answer."

"May I ask a question?" Caitlin suddenly had a big, goofy, ear-to-ear smile that implied a hidden meaning.

"Sure, what'd you want to know?"

"Uh . . . are you two dating?"

I smiled back, but kept my mouth shut, neither admitting nor denying a thing.

"Sorry," she said. "I know it's none of my business."

She took the note and left, leaving me feeling more than a little flattered.

Ten minutes later Caitlin returned. "She said yes."

"Thanks," I replied.

"An attractive lady. You could do a lot worse." Caitlin winked at me and walked back to her desk.

I spent the rest of the day writing the Stephen Svensen report. By five o'clock, I had the first draft finished.

One by one the others completed their workday and left the office. At five-fifteen, I shut down, packed my briefcase, and took the elevator to the forty-ninth floor. On the short walk to number 4901, I looked around. The area seemed deserted. I walked into Bryan's old office to find Elizabeth, alone, sitting at her desk. She gave me a warm smile.

"How're you doing?" I asked.

"You want an honest answer?" she responded.

"What other kind is there?"

"The Hartman rule." Her face lit up, and I had the feeling she was making fun of me. "I'll never get into trouble telling the truth."

"It works."

"Yeah, but will the truth let me keep my job?"

"Maybe not," I said, "but, in that case, perhaps the job's not worth it?"

Elizabeth smiled and gave me a big nod. It came across as an elegant gesture, one of consummate assurance.

"So, how're you doing?" I asked, again.

"Worried about what you're doing," she replied.

"If we're lucky, we'll be out of here before anyone catches on."

The door opened, and we both jumped. Two maintenance men

walked in wearing blue coveralls. At first I didn't recognize either, until a familiar voice said my name.

"Chris, it's me," said Captain Michael O'Kelly.

"Wow," I said. I couldn't believe it. He looked completely different in his coveralls and cap emblazoned with the TEI logo.

"This is Sergeant Tony Rodriquez, homicide division," O'Kelly said, nodding to the man in blue work clothes. "Let's get going."

We immediately went back to the closet and started to work. First, we moved the boxes away from the wall. Then Rodriquez unpacked a saw, and cut a large hole in the wall. He removed a piece of sheetrock, about three feet high by a foot and a half wide. Using a flashlight, the three of us looked in.

O'Kelly climbed through the small opening and stood by the spiral staircase.

"Let's go upstairs," O'Kelly said.

"Lead on."

He did and I followed. Rodriquez stayed.

O'Kelly led the way with his flashlight. At the top, the fiftieth floor, we found another blank wall.

"Looks like new construction," he said. He used his flashlight to examine the corners.

In the tiny, cramped quarters I smelled fresh paint. "Seen enough?" I asked, nervously.

"Yeah, let's get out of here."

In less than a minute we were down the stairs, out through the hole, and into the closet. The three of us restacked the boxes, turned off the light, and went back to Elizabeth's desk in the outside office.

"This changes everything," O'Kelly said. "I'll call you."

I nodded. And my brain started counting how many things

would change. The repercussions seemed enormous.

"We're going to need a day or two to figure out how to handle it."

"I understand."

After he and Rodriquez left. I stayed behind to talk with Elizabeth.

"Sounds like the news is good," she said.

"The best possible," I answered.

"Am I to be a part of this?"

"Better if you're not."

"How many times do I have to tell you—I want to help."

"And you are," I said. "We couldn't have done this without you."

She walked over and stood close to me. "I want to do more."

Her large dark eyes said more. I leaned over and kissed her. I didn't expect it, didn't plan it, but it seemed right. I pulled her closer and could feel her heart pounding.

"When this is over, I hope we can see more of each other."

"We will," she answered.

"We need to get out of here. This could be dangerous for you."

"Chris—"

"Later."

She nodded and turned back to her desk.

"We shouldn't be seen leaving together."

Again she nodded. She sat at her desk, and pulled her purse from a drawer.

"Elizabeth—

She put her finger to her lips. "Shhh," she whispered.

Driving north on I-45, I cursed the damn TEI Corporation and the corruption that had so disrupted our lives.

CHAPTER 30

Driving North on I-45

I wanted a drink.

Instead, I pulled out my chip and looked at it. It helped. But not enough. So, when I saw the neon sign, "Chili's Bar and Grill," I pulled over and parked.

Inside, George's admonition, "attend a meeting," weighed heavily on my mind. Waiting to be seated, the aroma of TexMex cuisine added further confusion to my thoughts.

Chili's was crowded, and the young woman taking names asked her standard question:

"Smoking or non-smoking?"

"First available," I answered.

"I could seat you at the bar," she said.

"Sure." *Why fight it*, I thought.

The bartender was busy. I sat for several minutes and looked around, taking an inventory of the beverages of other patrons—margaritas and Mexican beer—one hundred percent.

The harried bartender laid a napkin in front of me. "Happy Hour," he said, "Margaritas are half price."

I almost ordered one, but from somewhere out of the blue, my conscience took hold and instead I said, "Would you save my place while I make a phone call?"

He didn't like my answer. "I can hold it for five minutes." With a frown of impatience, he hurried off.

I walked around to the telephone bank, found a phone book, looked up the numbers for Alcoholics Anonymous, and dialed the first one I saw. The woman who answered told me about a meeting that evening at the Woodlands Presbyterian Church.

"What time?" I asked.

"Seven-thirty," she answered.

I looked at my watch. "Thanks."

"You want to write down the address?"

"No, I know the location."

I went back to my stool at the bar and ordered a Diet Coke.

"You can get a margarita for the same price until seven," the bartender said. He nodded toward the clock.

"Thanks, but a Diet Coke will be fine."

He shrugged. A moment later he brought the soft drink. "You want to order?"

"How about a hamburger to go?"

He handed me a menu. "We have seven different burgers." His tone of voice and his frown left no doubt about his opinion of my status. I was a PITA—a pain in the ass. He waited, pen in hand, his order pad on the bar.

"Number one, the old fashioned," I said.

For the next few minutes I waited, sipped my soda, and thought about my situation. In fifty-five years on this planet, my personal circumstances had seen a good many ups and downs. Recently, with the death of my wife, her battle with cancer, and mine with alcohol, they had been down. Really down. And just when I thought things were beginning to take an upswing, Bryan's death created a disastrous downturn.

The discovery of the staircase, and the fact that someone was going to great lengths to hide it, virtually proved the case for murder. I shook my head in dismay at the implication. When "murder" was considered good news, it made a strong impression about the overall downward spiral of my state of affairs.

I felt certain Joel's death, too, had been murder. Assuming the TEI case now included two possible murders, it didn't take an Einstein to see the implications. With the passing of each day, the threat against my family grew more ominous. I needed to bring the TEI crisis to a conclusion. Quickly.

My hamburger arrived. I paid, added a small tip for the surly bartender, and left. The short drive to Woodlands Presbyterian got me there five minutes early. The next two hours, recharging my resolve against the temptations of alcohol, proved George's advice to be right on target. Happily, I went to Jennifer's house to eat a cold hamburger, and thirty seconds after my head hit the pillow, I fell asleep.

The next morning, with renewed confidence, I showered, shaved, dressed, and headed south on I-45. Another good omen—the morning traffic flowed, and the drive to downtown was as good as it gets in Houston—no fender-benders or lane closings, an occasional slowing but never a complete stop. The result was that I arrived at the TEI garage in less than an hour, a record for the morning drive from Jennifer's house. I walked across the street to Starbuck's for coffee and a blueberry scone. Carrying my briefcase and breakfast, I arrived at the office to find my three CPAs sitting at their desks—all idle. It bothered me that they weren't working.

I went to my desk and found the reason why.

Three stacks of paper lay neatly arranged on my desk. Each had a cover sheet, which I read with interest.

A Review of Stephen Svensen Accounting's Audits of Texas Energy, Incorporated
Part I: The Failure of the Special Purpose Entity Corporations By Bartholomew Nichols

A Review of Stephen Svensen Accounting's Audits of Texas Energy, Incorporated
Part II: Examples of Financial Statement Fraud and Money Laundering By Jack Ward

A Review of Stephen Svensen Accounting's Audits of Texas Energy, Incorporated
Part III: Twenty-Eight Cases of Wire Fraud and Obstruction of Justice By Caitlin Cunningham

Each report ran a hundred or more pages. I marveled at the thoroughness of the work of these young professionals. Their reports documented a total of seventy-four failures of the Svensen audits to report illegal acts. I shook my head as I read the specific examples, each one carefully documented and quoted from published, public documents.

Stephen Svensen now had only two choices.

The accounting firm—one of the so-called "big six" of America's

COLLUSION

largest and most prestigious professional accountants—could admit to gross negligence, or much worse, to criminal intent. Either way, Stephen Svensen was finished.

The only thing lacking was an executive summary. The total of over three hundred pages was too long, too ponderous. The massive detail, while needed for legal justification and future court cases, would overwhelm lay readers.

Writing the summary was my job.

But first we needed a meeting. I arranged with Bart, Jack, and Caitlin to meet for coffee at Starbucks. At ten o'clock we gathered at a booth with our cups of gourmet black liquid.

"Great job," I said.

They smiled, sitting quietly.

"I'll take it from here," I said.

I sipped my coffee, waiting for someone else to speak. No one did.

"I want each of you to take a month off—with pay. Pack your stuff this afternoon, and, when you leave the office, don't come back until I give the word."

"Wait a minute," Caitlin said, "we haven't started on the TEI report."

"That's why you hired us," Jack said.

"We've done the research," Bart added. "We can't quit now."

"Dr. Hartman," Caitlin said, "you're holding out on us."

"Yes, and I'm worried about what's in line for you three when the people about whom you are writing find out that we're about to blow the whistle.

The quiet returned.

"Don't you want us to continue with our writing?" Caitlin asked.

"Only if you can do it surreptitiously," I answered. "If you can go someplace where no one will know what you're writing—yes. I'd appreciate anything you can get done."

"But our data . . . I can't write my stuff without it," Bart complained.

"Take what you can in one small briefcase, no more," I said.

"I could send my stuff in e-mail attachments to friends in Boston," Jack said.

"*Absolutely not.* These guys are going to monitor all your e-mails," I cautioned.

"You could encode it," Caitlin said.

I held up my hand. "Hey. These guys are smart. And they're already suspicious of what you're doing. Tomorrow, when they find out you're gone, they'll start looking for you."

Finally, it began to soak in. They sat there, deep in thought.

"I've worked out a code so that you can call my Harvard office once a week." I passed out three-by-five cards with code words that they could use. "Be sure you always call from a pay phone."

"Wow," Bart said. "This is getting way too Robert Ludlum."

"Ominous," Jack said.

"What about you?" Caitlin asked.

"I'll be careful, just like you," I assured her.

"And your family?" Bart asked.

"I've moved them to a safe place," I replied.

"Are we getting combat pay for this?" Jack asked with a smile. The others chuckled.

"I don't think we should be laughing," I said. "They've already killed two people."

Immediately, the laughing stopped, and their smiles vanished.

"What do you mean?" Caitlin asked, appalled.

COLLUSION

"You remember Detective Joel Wilson. He intended to change the cause of Bryan's death from suicide to murder."

"Really? "Caitlin's eyes grew wide.

"When he left my office last Tuesday afternoon, he was on his way to police headquarters to reopen the case."

"And?" Bart asked.

"Killed in an auto accident," Jack answered.

"That was no accident," I said. "I'm betting my life on it."

"You mean that literally, don't you?" Caitlin asked.

I didn't answer. And I knew we needed to get back to the office. "Remember what I've told you about being careful," I cautioned. As I left them, without thinking, I said, "Take care." The two words suddenly took on new meaning.

Returning to my desk, I started working on my summary of the reports completed by Bart, Caitlin, and Jack. Reducing their three hundred pages to a meaningful synopsis challenged me—a real test of my skills to convert their technical accounting jargon into common, everyday English that could be easily understood by lay readers. By late afternoon I had completed a rough draft and decided to take a break.

The day's mail lay heaped in a pile on the corner of my desk. I poured a cup of coffee and sat down with a letter opener. The first two items were junk mail, which I discarded quickly. The third envelope looked familiar—it appeared identical to the two previous mystery messages. I ripped it open, anxious to see its contents. The note, again neatly typed, read:

Dr. Hartman,

The new man in security named John Smith should be checked out. He came to work at TEI on October 1st. In case you don't remember, that was the day before the death of Bryan Banks. Also, Smith carries a gun.

A Friend

I thought about the note, reading and rereading it. I felt I was aware of a subtle scent. I smelled something. Or was I imagining it?

I instinctively held the note closer to examine the texture of the paper, and in holding it closer to my eyes, the scent was a bit stronger. I held the paper close to my nose and sniffed. It was a delicate perfume, the aroma faint but unmistakable. And I recognized it.

The implication stunned me.

I slouched back in my chair and tried to gather my thoughts.

After a few moments, I left the office, walked across the street and called Elizabeth. When she answered I spoke four words: "Pizza tonight, eight o'clock?"

She answered with one word, "Sure."

I went back to my office and worked on revising my executive summary of the Stephen Svensen report. By seven-thirty I had finished. I packed and left.

Careful to be sure no one followed, I drove to the *Houston Chronicle* building and parked on the street, following my usual procedure, then I walked out the back door, and across the street to Frank's Pizza, I found Elizabeth in the familiar corner booth and slid into the seat facing her.

"I'm looking for . . ." I said, letting the sentence dangle.

She looked at me expectantly, waiting for me to finish.

" . . . A Friend."

CHAPTER 31

Frank's Pizza, Houston

"I was going to tell you," Elizabeth said.

"Why didn't you?" I asked.

"Too intimidated, I guess."

Her answer surprised me. "You? That's ridiculous."

"Oh, really? Dr. Christopher Hartman, the most famous forensic accountant in the country."

"Elizabeth—"

"Why would you be interested in what a secretary has to say?"

"Elizabeth. That's a cheap shot. And unfair."

"No. Especially back in October, before I got to know you."

"But now that you know me, why continue the letters?"

"Hey, I tried," she said.

"You did? When?"

"Yesterday, after the captain left, and countless times before that. I told you I wanted to do more to help you."

"I know. but I've been concerned for your safety.

She cast me a small smile and looked at her menu.

The waiter came to take our order. I welcomed the interruption.

"I propose a truce," I said after the waiter had left.

"Me, too," she answered. "I'm really getting tired of all this cloak and dagger stuff."

"We're on the same side, you know."

"Obviously."

"Total, open, honest communication?"

"I agree."

"No more letters?" I asked.

"Okay, and no more of your bullshit about protecting me."

"Elizabeth."

She shrugged. "Let's call it what it is."

"I had honest concerns. Still do."

"And I'm trying to tell you that, if we're in this together, any attempt we make to protect each other will only help the guys on the other side."

I saw her point. The waiter brought our drinks.

She smiled at me. I smiled back. We continued the standoff, and stared at each other. Then she looked away.

"These guys on the other side play for keeps," I said. "They murdered Bryan and Joel."

"Yes," she said.

"They've made threats against my family."

"I know."

"There's no need for you to endanger your life."

"Wrong." She said it simply, but firmly.

She was a beautiful woman. From our first meeting, I admired the way she carried herself as a person, comfortable with her beauty. However, until that moment, I hadn't taken full measure of her inner strength.

"I care about you," I said.

"I'm flattered."

"I hope it can be a two-way thing."

"Chris, it already is."

"Then why are we arguing?"

"Because you're trying to shut me out," she said, her voice insistent, almost angry.

"I was trying to protect you," I answered.

"Let me use your words—total, open, honest communication."

"But in matters of the heart—"

She shook her head. "In life." She reached over, took my hand.

"I give up." I nodded. "We're in this together."

"All the way?"

"I feel responsible for Joel Wilson."

"You can't allow yourself to feel that way," she said, her voice full of passion. "He was a policeman, doing his job. It would have been wrong for you to hold back any information."

When you put it that way, I guess I can see your point."

"Back to our agreement," she pressed, "we're together."

"You win. I won't shut you out again."

"Good. Let's talk about John Smith," she said.

"Okay," I marveled at her steadfast gaze. Her eyes were black and radiated a feminine beauty that, while tantalizing, I had never considered in a committed, romantic sense.

"He acts suspicious."

"How?" I asked.

"He hangs out on the fiftieth floor."

"What's suspicious about that?"

"He's the only security person who does."

"Elizabeth, that's not suspicious."

"He swaggers."

"Swaggers?" I almost laughed, but caught myself just in time. Elizabeth was dead serious.

"He walks around in an arrogant and boastful way, like he owns the place."

I thought about her suspicions. She probably had a point, but we'd need more to go to the police with. A lot more. "All right. He's arrogant, he swaggers. Anything else you can tell me?"

"One day I took a report up to Norton's office," she said. "I could see and hear them as I approached. Smith was talking with Norton and Upton, but Smith was leading the conversation. *He* was telling *them* what to do. Clearly, his relationship to these two corporate officers suggests more than expected from a security person."

"That's interesting."

"And one more thing. When I walked in, Smith stopped in mid-sentence."

"He didn't want you to hear?"

"Exactly," she said. "And he looked annoyed."

"Describe an annoyed look."

"You know. You can tell when someone is caught doing or saying something they know is wrong."

"The guilty look?"

"Absolutely," she said. "And Smith is not good at hiding his emotions. He looked guilty."

"You think he's a hired gun?"

"He came to work one day before Bryan was shot."

"Hmm." I thought about it for a moment. "Interesting coincidence."

COLLUSION

The waiter brought our pizza, interrupting our conversation. Elizabeth removed her hand and I served us each a piece.

We both tried to eat, but most of the pizza remained untouched.

"Guess I've lost my appetite," I said.

"Me too," she answered.

"We need to be careful."

"Yes."

"My young associates left yesterday."

"Good."

"My daughter and my two grandchildren are in a safe place."

"A Relief."

"That leaves you and me."

"What do you suggest?"

"Same as before. Don't do or say anything that makes you look like a threat," I said.

"I can do that," she said, "but what about you?"

"I'm going to release the report about the auditors."

"Chris, I hope you know what you're doing."

"My report places all the blame on the accounting," I said. "It says the auditors should have warned corporate officers."

"How can you separate the wrongdoing?"

"Easy. That's a standard, ongoing aspect of the vagaries of white-collar crime."

"I really don't understand," she said. "Looks to me like the corporate officers would be more guilty than the accountants."

"They could be," I answered. "It depends on how it's reported."

"Could you give me an example—in layman's terms? Something I can easily understand?"

"Sure. Take financial statement fraud. If the corporate officers

213

intended to hide debt, if their intention was to defraud investors, then their action becomes illegal, and they are subject to indictment."

"Or . . ."

"Or, if they were just conducting complex business transactions—and their auditors failed to catch the technical slips, the financial statements that violated the law—then the corporate officers can blame the accountants."

"Which way are you reporting it?" she asked.

"I'm blaming the auditors," I answered.

"Will it fly?"

"I'm the expert, and—"

"And what?"

"Later, there can be another report providing more information."

"Chris, I don't like this."

"The corporate officers won't either. What they need is a document, signed by me, that exonerates them. This report doesn't do that. It only points the finger at the auditors."

"And leaves unanswered any questions about TEI's corporate officers?"

"Exactly."

"And you think they'll keep you safe until you whitewash their involvement."

"They need someone to give expert testimony on their behalf. I'm counting on that."

"But won't the government see through this?"

"Elizabeth, this is a quagmire of extremely technical, corporate data. The TEI corporate officers are some of the slickest operators in financial history."

"But the bottom line is that they could get away with billions."

COLLUSION

"I know."

"You're not going to let them do it? Are you?"

"I'm going to try. But they don't know that," I said.

For the next few moments, she sat quietly. I could almost see the thoughts churning inside her head. Then her expression changed, to a worried look.

"Chris, I think they do."

She looked away, lifting her hand from my arm, I could feel her backing away.

"This whole thing really scares me," she said.

CHAPTER 32

Driving North on I-45

Driving home gave me a chance to think. I set the cruise control and let my mind scroll. Elizabeth was right. We needed to find a way to wrap this up. The quicker the better. I could start by meeting with Billy Ray Powell and his investigative committee to release our report on the auditors. I mentally placed Powell at the top of my list.

Then there was the stairway. I'd give Captain O'Kelly a call.

John Smith loomed in my thoughts as number three. I wished Elizabeth and I had talked more about the mysterious security guard. Maybe O'Kelly would have some ideas.

I thought about calling Jennifer, but every contact increased the danger, and it was now an hour later in her time zone. A call tomorrow morning from a pay phone would be safer.

I pulled into the driveway on Leisure Cove—tired, knowing there was progress in the case and a full agenda. With thoughts roiling through my head, I fell into a shallow, fitful sleep.

The next morning I called Powell and asked to meet with the board's investigative committee. As usual, he reacted aggressively.

COLLUSION

He set the meeting for four o'clock that afternoon in the TEI board-room.

Next, I called Houston PD and set up an appointment with the captain. An hour later, the familiar policewoman buzzed me right into O'Kelly's office. Instead of the resentment I'd received on previous visits, he greeted me with a smile, a handshake, and an offer of coffee. I returned the gestures and accepted his cup. As we sipped HPD's bitter version of hot coffee, I handed him the third note from "A Friend."

He read it with interest.

"I now know who 'Friend' is, and I'll buy you a steak dinner if you can guess the name."

He shook his head. "I don't have a clue."

"Elizabeth Garcia."

"Really? She's the last person I would've suspected."

"All the better for us," I added. "Makes it less likely the enemy will become suspicious."

"Yes." He sipped his coffee, thinking. His appearance indicating continued skepticism. "Do you know this for sure?"

"We had a heart-to-heart talk last night."

"I'd like to have heard that." He looked at the note again. "Tell me what she said about John Smith."

I related her observations about his shifty behavior.

He returned to his coffee-sipping, meditative mode.

I waited.

"We'll look into this, run a background check, try to do it without arousing his suspicions."

I nodded.

"This could be a big break," he said.

I nodded again.

"Caution your *friend* to be careful."

"I already have."

"Two murders are two too many. The last thing we need is a third."

"I pleaded with her to quit."

"I'd vote for that."

"She refused."

He looked away. Another minute passed.

Finally, I broke the silence. "Earth to O'Kelly."

"Yeah, I'm trying to think through the ramifications."

I told him about my meeting at four with Powell and the board's investigative committee. "My report will place the blame on the auditors," I said.

"Another situation to make everyone nervous," he answered.

"They're already nervous."

"My point is, we have two deaths that have been reported, one as a suicide and the other an accident. As soon as we show our hand—that we're investigating them as possible murders—the shit is going to hit the fan."

"It'll put them on the defensive."

"I think we're better off if we keep our information under wraps while we build the case."

"Agreed," I said. "Especially, the staircase."

"Joel Wilson's rear-ender has raised suspicions, too," O'Kelly said.

"Anything you can share with me?"

"A couple of things. We've been over the car with a CSI team. They think a bomb may have been attached."

COLLUSION

"Wow," I said.

"If it had a trigger hooked to the back bumper, just a light bump from the rear and *boom*, you'd have an explosion. It's what we call 'a bump and run.'"

"So what are your thoughts?"

O'Kelly shook his head, "Unfortunately, the Ford Crown Victoria—the police edition—has a reputation for gas tank explosions in rear-end accidents. But we have almost a hundred Crown Vics in our fleet. This has been the only detonation."

"One in a hundred," I said. "Anything else?"

"Another interesting coincidence," he said. "But they keep coming, one after another, until finally, you have to make an arrest—a case built on circumstantial evidence."

"How long do you expect to keep this quiet?"

"Hard to say," he answered. "I hope not long."

"I feel like I'm sitting on a keg of dynamite."

"Me, too," O'Kelly said, getting up from his seat and extending his hand. "Thanks."

We pledged to keep each other informed. Houston PD would give highest priority to investigating the two deaths and to following up on Elizabeth's suspicions about John Smith. I would go ahead with my report to the board. I left O'Kelly, wondering and hoping.

I wondered what would happen next.

I hoped we could quickly end my part in it.

I thought again about calling Jennifer. The thought that every contact might endanger her caused me to decide against it. I drove on.

Arriving at my empty office in the TEI Building, I spent the rest of the day preparing my report for Powell, Wright, and Young. I revised my executive summary, paring it down to five pages. I added a cover sheet, a table of contents, and took it to the Xerox machine. The finished document totaled 326 pages.

The four o'clock meeting started badly. I passed out the huge report and waited while Powell, Wright, and Young studied it. First they scanned my executive summary. The next thirty minutes was like watching grass grow. I sat at the table wondering how far they would get into the remaining 321 pages, realizing the report was too much to digest in a meeting like this. I should have sent it to them first, and then asked for a conference to discuss it.

Finally, James Wright gathered up his copy and straightened the stack, noisily banging the paper against the table as he rotated the pile four times to align it. "All this seems to say is that the goddamned auditors were asleep at the switch." He slumped back into his seat with a scowl on his face.

"Dr. Hartman," Dwight Young said, "I'm disappointed. You hardly mention any involvement of our corporate officers." Then he, too, shuffled his papers. He had read a fraction of the report.

Powell kept reading. The minutes ticked away as he read carefully, turning pages one by one.

Young stood, walked to the coffee bar. "Anyone want a cup?"

I shook my head. Powell kept reading. Wright ignored the question, and simply stared at his copy of the report with a look of anger and fear. Young returned to his seat.

The minutes ticked by in a fog of inertia.

Finally Powell stopped. "Chris, you've documented the losses." He shuffled his pages. "When we were getting those reports on CEL and the other partnership corporations, I thought something looked too rosy."

"Billy Ray," Young blustered, "he doesn't assign any blame to management. It's as though he's oblivious to any wrongdoing by corporate officials."

"On the other hand," Wright countered, "he doesn't absolve them, either. This pile of shit leaves everyone open for indictment. It's as though his report, for which we are paying through the nose, doesn't know whether or not to involve Zimmerman, Upton, Norton, or any of the other employees."

"I agree," Young said. "Either our corporate officers are involved or they're not. Hartman must answer the question. That's what we're paying him for."

"What good is a report that points the finger at the accountants and leaves everything else up in the air?" Wright asked.

"Billy Ray, I move we not accept this report," Young said.

"I second the motion," Wright added.

The room became quiet. After their explosive rhetoric, the contrast seemed eerie. Neither Wright nor Young had stated their position openly, yet anyone could easily read the inference in their remarks.

Young thought TEI's corporate officers were to blame. He was angry with me because I failed to accuse them.

Wright wanted Upton and the others exonerated. He was disgusted with me for exactly the opposite reasons.

No one at the table wanted a fence straddler.

"Chris, surely this is not your final report?" asked Powell.

"No. These are just the facts. It tells you where the money went and how the auditors failed in their responsibility to report it."

"So, what are your plans?" Powell asked. "When can we expect your *final* report?"

Before I could answer, the door opened and a man walked into the room. He was tall, muscular, fortyish, and moved with a military bearing. His unbuttoned coat fell open slightly as he neared our table, just enough that I could see a handgun in a leather holster underneath his left arm. He spoke with a commanding presence.

"I'm John Smith." he said.

CHAPTER 33

The Board Room, TEI Building

"Identification, please," Smith said.

Two simple words, but the way he said them seemed chilling. His voice reminded me of a Nazi Gestapo officer, and I quickly pulled out my TEI photo ID. My hand shook as I handed over the badge.

Smith scrutinized it, glancing back and forth between my face and the photograph. After what seemed an exceptionally long time, he tossed it on the table in front of me. "Thank you, Dr. Hartman," he said, dismissively. His words implied anything but thanks.

He turned to the others. Wright and Young had their IDs readily available. Powell did not.

Smith grabbed the two identification badges, and as he had with me, took great pains to match their faces with their photographs. His his posture, his tone of voice, both created a milieu of fear and apprehension. Several minutes passed before he returned their IDs.

"Thank you, Mr. Wright and Mr. Young."

He turned to Powell.

"I'm sorry, I seem to have misplaced my badge," Powell said. a bit nervously. I watched in fascination as the chairman of the board of directors reacted with some anxiety to the actions of one of his employees.

The room grew quiet. I half expected Smith to pull his gun. Thankfully, he didn't.

"Please state your name and your reason for being in this room," Smith ordered.

"William R. Powell, Jr.," he answered. "I'm here for this meeting of the board's investigation committee. These gentlemen can vouch for my identity."

"Mr. Powell is chairman of the board of directors of the TEI Corporation." I said it slowly and with as much flourish as I could muster, trying to impress Smith with Powell's position.

Wright and Young nodded.

Smith didn't flinch or back off. Instead he glared. His eyes searched each of us, as though looking for the slightest hint of suspicious reaction. Finally, he returned to Powell.

"Mr. Powell, our security force is charged with the protection of the corporation and its employees. In the future, we'd appreciate your cooperation."

Here was a security officer "dressing down" the chairman of the board. And even more unbelievable, the chairman's reaction was one of intimidation. Watching Smith was like observing an academy award performance. He didn't pull his gun. He didn't have to. His physical stature, his assertive voice, and his commanding presence carried the effect of bullying terror.

And Smith was smart.

He conducted his coercion under the guise of legitimacy. In a semantic paradox, he turned the tables, making it appear that he was upholding his corporate assignment, while Powell, because he didn't have his ID badge, was now cast in the role of an offender. The chairman of the board was visibly shaken.

I had to admit, Smith scared me, too. At first.

But the more I backed off and analyzed his tactics, the more it became obvious to me that Smith was nothing more than a smart, highly paid thug. Nevertheless, I breathed a sigh of relief when he left the room.

"Damn. Who the hell was that?" Young asked.

"I think he's the new head of security," Wright answered. "He's the point man in Upton's new initiative to tighten building safety."

"I don't like the way he came in here and read us the riot act," Young said. "That was uncalled for."

"He's just doing his job," Wright said.

"Seems to me that was over the top," Powell said.

"I agree," Young said.

The four of us sat at the table for a few moments, pondering the interruption. I sensed that Powell wanted to respond in some way, but didn't know how. After a brief silence, he changed the subject.

"Chris, we were talking about your final report," he said. "What can we expect?"

"I'm working on it," I answered, "and should have it ready soon."

"That's good enough for me," Powell said. He turned to the other two. "Any questions?"

Both shook their heads.

"Chris, we need to wind this up," Powell said.

"I understand."

"Sooner is better."

"Yes, sir."

Powell stood, shook my hand in a gesture of dismissal, and then said, "The three of us are going to stay for a few minutes."

I nodded and left.

The long ride down in the elevator gave me a chance to rethink the remaining tasks on the day's agenda. I mentally scrolled through my options, writing my final report, calling O'Kelly, and calling Jennifer. I decided to walk to Starbuck's and make the two phone calls.

O'Kelly was out of the office. I left my name and cell phone number, and immediately called the cabin on Cape Cod.

"Hello," Jennifer answered.

"How're you and the kids doing?" I asked.

"Fine."

Her one-word answer didn't sound "fine."

"How's the weather," I asked.

"Typical."

Over the years I've learned to read my daughter's reactions. Her brief responses told me something was wrong. I made a guess.

"Cabin fever?" I asked.

"Dad—"

"Tell me about it."

"It's nothing, really."

"If it's nothing, then why try to hide it?"

"I'm not hiding anything."

"This is your father speaking, and I'm an expert on Jennifer Ann Hartman Banks. My sensors report you're holding something back."

"I'm just tired," she said.

"Sometimes it helps to tell your ole dad why you're tired."

"You've got enough to worry about. I don't want you to worry about us."

COLLUSION

"The kids having trouble at school?" I asked.

"Dad."

"Tell me about it."

Even though I couldn't hear any audible cues, I suspected she was crying.

"You might feel better if you just open up and get it off your chest," I said. "And what about me? You know I'll worry less if you tell me what's going on."

"Melissa forgot and signed one of her papers with her real name."

"Melissa Banks instead of Melissa Williams?"

"Yes, and the teacher made a big scene in front of the other students."

"So, what happened?"

"Melissa didn't know how to handle it, so, she made up a story."

"And?"

"And the teacher accused her of lying and—" Jennifer started sobbing.

I could hear her put the receiver down. I waited.

After a few minutes she returned. "Dad, you still there?"

"I'm here, Jenny."

"Sorry. It's just that we're trying so hard. And Melissa's only a second grader. It's asking a lot for a seven-year-old to—"

"I know." I tried to think of supportive words.

"And the kids at school talk."

"So you think your cover's blown?"

"I'm afraid so."

I could hear a quiver in her voice.

"Don't worry about it," I said. "What's done is done."

"Does this mean we should move again, go somewhere else?"

I hesitated. Another move would be awfully stressful. "No, I don't think so."

"But, I'm so worried. What if someone comes looking?"

"It won't be much longer."

"Oh, Dad. That would be such a relief."

"Maybe just a few more days."

"And then we can use our real names?"

"You bet."

"And quit looking over our shoulder?"

"Yes."

"Just a minute."

I could hear her blowing her nose.

"Oh, that would be like liberation," she said. Her voice, for the first time, sounded upbeat, confident—the sound of the daughter I knew before the TEI mess.

"We'll plan a big Christmas celebration," I said.

"Yeah, huge."

"Skiing?" I asked.

"We'd love it."

"And you'll use your own names."

"Where?" she asked.

"You pick," I answered.

"I'll start looking," she said. "Okay if I tell the kids?"

"You bet."

"Dad—"

"Yes?"

"Thanks for calling."

My emotions gripped me, I felt tears coming, and I didn't want her to hear it in my voice. "Gotta go. I love you."

COLLUSION

"We love you."

The conversation ended just in time. I stood there at the phone for a couple of minutes trying to regain my composure. Then I took a Kleenex and wiped my eyes. The reality of my family's dangerous situation bolstered my resolve.

I needed to finish the final report and proclaim every incident of white-collar crime for what it was. With clenched teeth, I walked to the TEI parking garage to get my car for the drive to 44 Leisure Cove. Frustrated, fuming, trying to get control of my life, I was more determined than ever to get my family out of danger.

CHAPTER 34

Office of the Forensic Accountant, TEI Building

The next morning I got to the office early and, with renewed vigor and determination, started on the report.

The phone rang.

"Chris, Mike O'Kelly," the Houston PD Captain said.

"Thanks for returning my call," I answered.

"I didn't get your message until this morning. You want to call me back on another line?"

I paused to consider my options. Walking back across the street was a drag. It consumed time I wanted to spend on writing. "Mike, I don't have time. Let's just assume the guys on the other side are listening to everything we say."

My response must have jarred O'Kelly. For the next few moments he was didn't say anything.

"Let me ask the questions," I said.

"Fire away," he answered, "I'm returning your call."

"Have you found anything on the person you were investigating?"

"Yes."

"Enough to arrest him?"

COLLUSION

"No."

"The discovery you and I made yesterday—"

"Go ahead."

"Are you ready to release that information?"

"I think it better to wait."

"And the accident?"

"Same."

"So, we're at the same point we were yesterday morning when I left your office?"

"No."

I thought about his answer and tried to read between the lines. He wanted to hold off on releasing information about the hidden stairway, about the bomb on Wilson's car, and about changing the cause of both deaths to murder. I surmised that he had more on Smith, but not enough to arrest him for anything connected with the deaths of Bryan Banks or Joel Wilson. I made a decision.

"Mike, I need to release my final report," I said.

"I understand, and I agree," he said. "The sooner the better,"

"If I work all day today, perhaps into the night, I think I can have it ready by tomorrow morning."

"Wow. That soon?"

"Could Houston PD post a couple of officers here at my office for twenty-four hours?"

"Chris, you shouldn't have to work through the night," he said.

"It's the way I want to do it. Could you send some troops?"

"Sure."

"Assuming someone is listening, how long before the cavalry arrives?"

"I can have an officer there in minutes."

"Probably a good idea."

"Yeah. And it'll give us time to get organized. I'll assign a three-shift team to you for twenty-four hours, or until you release your final report."

"Thanks, Mike."

"Good luck with your writing." He rang off.

I started typing. Before I finished the first page, a uniformed policeman arrived. Within the hour, a second officer appeared.

A sense of urgency motivated me to work. By mid-afternoon I had the report sketched out and well underway. Using data from my previous report on Stephen Svensen, I could "cut and paste" much of the factual material. The words flowed from my fingertips, energized by the thought that the end was in sight.

Late that afternoon, a second shift replaced the two officers. The new policemen introduced themselves, and we made plans to order pizza for dinner. I learned a third shift would come eight hours later.

Coffee kept me going. And at midnight I had a visitor.

"I won't stay long," Captain Michael O'Kelly said.

"Thanks for stopping by. It helps to have a break."

"How's it going?

"On schedule. I'll have it finished by morning."

"What's next?"

"Xeroxing about ten copies.

"And then—"

"First, I'll call Billy Ray Powell and arrange to give him the official copy. Then I'll notify media and schedule a news conference."

"What's your report gonna say?"

"That the bad guys made themselves rich and brought about the downfall of the world's largest energy corporation."

COLLUSION

"Hell, everybody knows that."

"Correction, everybody *thinks* that's what happened."

"You got proof?"

"I'll have more than 350 pages of facts. The government will have to draw up the indictments."

"Who do you name?"

"Lots of names. You'll have to read the report to get them all."

"Give me the top name," he said. "Is it Zimmerman?"

"No."

"No?"

"I can't find any specific instance where he committed an indictable offense. In my opinion, Richard Zimmerman was an honest, but bumbling, CEO who allowed the corporate officers under him to do sleight-of-hand accounting and hide massive debt."

"He was asleep at the switch while others robbed the cookie jar?"

"Well, yes, to use a couple of clichés."

"So, who should be indicted?"

"Lots of people."

"Upton, Norton, all the financial people?"

I smiled. "Read the report."

"What about the deaths of Banks and Wilson?"

"That's police work," I answered. "Those are up to you."

"You gonna mention it?"

"Don't see how I can. I'm an accountant."

"Yeah, I understand."

"But I'm interested. What've you found about Smith?"

He pointed to the ceiling, to the imaginary microphone.

"Sorry," I said, "I forgot."

"Want to go somewhere where we can talk?"

I looked at my watch and saw that it was after midnight. "Mike, I'll take a rain check. I'd better get back to my writing."

"You're probably right," he said.

"You coming in the morning?"

"Wouldn't miss it," he answered. "What's the timeline?"

Up until his question, I hadn't really thought about it. I grabbed a pen and yellow pad, and sketched out the remaining work. "Assuming I finish the writing in four or five hours, take a couple of hours for Xeroxing, I should be ready to make calls about eight a.m. I'll set the news conference for ten. That'll give me a couple of hours to go home, shower, shave, and change clothes.

"Ten o'clock?"

"Yeah."

"See you then."

He left. Two new policemen came on duty. They introduced themselves as Paul and Cliff.

I went back to writing. Amazingly, my mind and body felt strong, full of energy, a little tired but not the least bit sleepy. Four hours later I typed the last sentence.

It took thirty minutes to print out the finished report on my laser printer. Paul and Cliff helped me photocopy and collate. By seven-thirty we had ten neat stacks, all ready to hand out.

I called Billy Ray Powell.

"Hello," he said.

"This is Chris. I have the report finished."

"Hey, you've put in some overtime."

"Yes, some."

He chuckled. "You sound a little bushed."

"I want to release this to the media."

"Fine with me," he said. "When?"

"I'd like to set up a news conference for ten o'clock."

"What can I do to help?"

"I think it would be good for you to be leading the charge. To be the spokesman."

"Nothing I'd like better."

"Would you call and arrange to do this in the boardroom?"

"You bet," he said. "We gonna name names?"

"Complete, total, open disclosure."

"Hot damn. I can hardly wait."

"You set it up," I said. "I'll contact the media."

"See you at ten o'clock." He hung up.

For the news conference, I decided to contact *The Houston Chronicle* and all the local TV stations. I pulled out the phone book and looked up numbers. Just as I had completed my list and reached for the phone to begin dialing, it rang.

"Hello," I said

"Dad." My daughter's voice trembled, shaking as it had twenty-five years ago when, as a little girl, she called for me in the night. "They're here."

"Who's there?" I asked.

"Three men, with guns."

CHAPTER 35

Office of the Forensic Accountant, TEI Building

"Jenny." That's all I could say.

One word, and then a recognizable voice came on the line. Hearing that same Gestapo-like ring of authority and intimidation, my initial reaction was much the same as two days earlier, in the meeting with the Powell committee.

Fear.

The only difference was the degree. In the boardroom, I had felt an ominous chill. This was worse. Much worse. A cold, debilitating numbness surged through my entire body and, in a sudden paralysis, I couldn't breathe. I clutched the phone as the voice of John Smith seized control of my life.

"Listen carefully," he said. He spoke distinctly, malevolence cutting into my ear like a knife. After the two words, he paused. His silence caused me to grip the phone even tighter. I felt faint.

"We want your report to absolve TEI corporate officers of any indictable offenses." He waited.

I could hear his breathing. I opened my mouth to respond. Disoriented and overwhelmed, I couldn't think of anything to say.

COLLUSION

"What happens now is up to you," Smith said.

More silence. I felt the pounding of my heart. It raced out of control with nothing I could do to stop it.

"We've read and studied your preliminary report," he continued. "You've done an excellent job of naming the Stephen Svensen accountants. It will be easy for you to make them entirely responsible for TEI's problems."

The realization that Smith was familiar with my report increased my anxiety. Beads of perspiration broke out on my forehead and ran down the sides of my face.

Smith went on. "You know, and we know, that you've left many unanswered questions about TEI's corporate officers."

I tried to speak, unsure if my voice would work. "Yes," It was a whisper-like rasp, but he heard and understood.

He continued. "All that's needed is a brief, expert summary on behalf of our corporate officers. If you vindicate their actions, this will all go away and everyone *lives* happily ever after."

I fought for control.

All I could think about was my family, Jenny, Luke, Melissa, and the word "lives."

The line went dead.

I'm not sure how long I sat there holding the phone.

"Dr. Hartman," Cliff, the older policeman, said.

"You okay?" the other one, Paul, asked.

"You look gray, like you're about to collapse," Cliff said.

Paul, poured a cup of hot coffee and brought it to my desk. "Drink this."

"You've been at this all night, pushing yourself too hard," Cliff said.

They looked at me with concern.

I tried to think what to do.

"You're perspiring." Paul handed me his handkerchief. "Are you in pain?"

A simple question, one that I could answer. "No." I wiped my brow.

"What can we do to help?" Paul asked. "Do you want to lie down?"

"No," I said. I sipped the hot coffee. It burned my tongue.

"Should we call for medical help?"

"No," I said. "I'll be all right. Just give me a few minutes." I took a deep breath, exhaling slowly.

"The report—" I gestured to the ten stacks of paper on the table.

"Yes," Cliff answered. "What about it?"

"Could you help me find a safe place?" I asked. "We need to hide it for a few days."

The two policemen looked at each other. "The property room?" Paul asked.

"That would be safe," Cliff answered.

"Explain," I said.

"We can stack all ten copies in a box and take it to the evidence room at police headquarters."

"You're sure—very sure—the reports would be safe there?"

"They'd treat it like evidence in a police investigation," Cliff replied.

"I can't think of a safer place," Paul added.

"Okay," I said, "let's do it."

"Can you go with us?"

"I wouldn't have it any other way."

COLLUSION

Doing something physical helped. Together, the three of us stacked the reports in a box. Gradually, my rational thinking returned, and my emotions eased to a level less than frantic. As the two policemen made preparations to leave, I downloaded the report from my computer to a small flash drive. After erasing the data on my hard drive, I shut down the computer, and the three of us walked from the house. We loaded the box into their police cruiser and drove to Houston PD Headquarters.

During the drive, I had another thought.

"Can you contact Captain Michael O'Kelly?" I asked.

"Sure," Cliff answered. "You want to speak with him?"

"Yes, please."

In a few minutes, I heard O'Kelly's voice on the police radio. They handed me the microphone. Without telling him the details, I arranged to meet him in his office.

Arriving at the police headquarters building, we checked the box for safekeeping. I made my way to O'Kelly's office. He greeted me with a question about my appearance.

"Damn, you look like the last rose of summer," he said.

"I know," I answered. "It's been a rough night." I told him about finishing the report, and receiving the phone call from Jennifer and then Smith.

He answered with silence.

From my previous association with Mike, I guessed he was thinking how we could respond.

"I want to cancel the ten o'clock meeting and, instead, go to my cabin on Cape Cod. That's where—"

"Let's do it," he answered. "Sooner the better."

"I can probably get Billy Ray Powell to cancel the meeting and

239

loan me his Lear Jet."

He nodded. "Set it up. I'll go with you to check on your family."

I called Powell. Thirty minutes later we were at Hobby Airport boarding the plane. Once airborne, we analyzed our situation and made plans. The Lear had excellent communication systems. O'Kelly called the Barnstable County sheriff, alerted him to the kidnapping, and arranged for him to meet us at the Hyannisport Regional Airport. The sheriff would bring as many deputies as he had available, probably four cars and eight men.

Then O'Kelly called the Boston Office of the FBI. Again, the response was immediate support. The field office head would meet us at the airport with six agents and three unmarked cars.

The flight took just under three hours. I checked my watch, adding the hour for the Eastern Time Zone, and computed the time at twelve-thirty. We taxied to parking and opened the door to find two men waiting. One wore a tan uniform with an insignia of the Barnstable County Sheriff's Office. The other was dressed in a dark suit with a nondescript striped tie. He looked like a lawyer or a banker, but he introduced himself as Agent Leonard Parsons, head of the FBI's Boston Office. The four of us walked quickly to the small terminal building.

"We've arranged to use the airport's conference room as a temporary headquarters," the sheriff said.

I counted six more men. Two wore suits, the others uniforms.

"We have surveillance of the house at 123 Breakwater Shores in Hyannisport," Agent Parsons said. "It appears to be empty."

"Apparently the kidnappers have taken the hostages elsewhere," the sheriff said.

"We expected that," O'Kelly responded.

"We have a plan," Parsons said.

COLLUSION

"Let's hear it," O'Kelly said.

"Someone needs to go into the house, confirm that it's empty, see if they left any clues."

"I agree," O'Kelly answered.

The sheriff nodded.

"Okay then, I think the best person to do this would be Dr. Hartman," Parsons said. "It's his house. If anyone is there, his coming to the door would be the least suspicious."

"Yes." O'Kelly said.

Parsons looked at me. "Could be dangerous," he added.

"I want to do it," I answered.

"We have a rental car for you." Parsons handed me a set of keys and a cell phone. "Drive up to the house as though you're alone. Go in, see what you can find. If it's empty, and we're pretty sure it is, call us at 555-1234."

We left.

I drove by myself to the house.

Walking up to the front door, I found it locked. I used my key, went inside, and called out, "Jennifer?"

No answer.

"Anyone home?"

Again no answer. I walked through the house.

It was empty.

CHAPTER 36

Cabin at 123 Breakwater Shores in Hyannisport, Massachusetts

I called Agent Parsons on the cell phone. "Empty."

"Walk through the house slowly. "Tell me what you see."

"I'm in the kitchen," I said.

"Dirty dishes, any sign of a struggle?"

"No sign of struggle. Breakfast dishes are partly loaded into the dishwasher."

"Go to the next room," Parsons said.

"I'm in the living room," I answered. "Same thing—it's just an empty room."

"Any sign of a struggle?" Parsons asked. "Anything unusual?"

"Nothing to indicate a struggle. Some clothing and kid stuff left scattered around. Looks like they may have left in a hurry."

"Go on."

I walked down the hallway. Again, nothing unusual. I looked at the hall bathroom, the master bedroom, and its attached bathroom. Nothing. I reported each room in turn.

The last room was a small bedroom at the end of the hall.

"I'm in Luke's room, now."

COLLUSION

"What do you see?"

"The bed's unmade, but that's about it." I walked around, looked in the closet, and didn't see anything. Walking through the door, back into the hallway, I confirmed, "Nothing unusual."

The minute the words left my mouth, I realized that wasn't true.

"Luke is a neat nick, he always makes his bed," I said.

"This morning was different," Parsons said, "the kidnapping would explain why he didn't make his bed."

"But he ate his breakfast," I said. "Luke was up and around," I reasoned. "Wait a minute." Carefully, I pulled the covers back.

"Find anything?" Parsons asked, again.

"Yes," I said. "His Blackberry."

"Blackberry?"

"I gave Luke his father's Blackberry," I explained. "On the flight from San Francisco to Boston, it was a gift to boost his spirits. To compensate for having to move."

"A ten-year-old who uses a Blackberry?" Parsons asked. He sounded like he didn't think much of the idea. "Check out the rest of the house, Chris. We may not have much more time."

"I'll bring it with me," I said. "Wouldn't hurt to take a look at it."

I pocketed the Blackberry and quickly went though the house a second time, reporting to Parsons on the cell phone. "There's nothing here that I can see. You want to come look for yourself?"

"No, we need to clear the house in case they come back," he said. "Let's meet at the airport conference room."

Parsons assigned two agents to watch the house. The rest of us left. I carried the Blackberry in my coat pocket. We gathered at the makeshift headquarters.

"Let's take a look at your gadget," Parsons said.

"Luke and I, together, decided on the password, 'GETLOST.'"

I punched in the seven letters, and it worked. We scrolled through school assignments, a computer game, and a listing of basketball scores for the Houston Rockets. At the end, we found his file labeled "Memos." I opened it to find four. The last one was named "GRANDPA." I opened it to a four-word message: GRANDPA, RENTED HOUSE, TRURO.

"What do you think?" I asked.

"I think it's a clue," the sheriff said.

"Could be," Agent Parsons agreed.

"Truro's a small village, out at the end of the Cape, near Provincetown," Parsons said.

"Truro is the smallest town on the Cape," the sheriff added. "And this time of year, it's practically deserted."

My heart began to race. "Sounds like an ideal place for kidnappers to hide hostages," I said.

I looked around the suddenly silent room and studied the faces.

Parsons broke the silence with a question to the sheriff. "Tell us what you know about Truro."

"It's a post office, a town hall, a shop or two," the sheriff answered. "You know you're there by a small sign that says 'Downtown Truro' at the plaza entrance. They have a three-person police force and I know the chief—Henrietta Bozeman—everyone calls her Hank."

"What's the driving time to Truro?" Parsons asked.

"Less than an hour," the sheriff replied.

"Call her, brief her on our situation, and ask if she could meet us in an hour. Ask her to suggest someplace secluded."

The sheriff pulled out a small notebook, looked up the number,

COLLUSION

and dialed it on his cell phone. While he was making the call, Parsons organized the group. There would be four cars with ten people—six agents, the sheriff, one deputy, Captain Mike O'Kelly, and me.

The sheriff announced that Chief Bozeman would meet us at the Truro Historical Museum, a small complex north of Truro that was closed for the winter.

I rode in the lead car with Agent Parsons, Captain O'Kelly, and the sheriff.

"I'm really worried about this," I said.

"Yes," Parsons said, "we all are."

"We've heard that Smith is a hired gun," I said. "Captain O'Kelly and I think he has already killed two people on this case." I looked at Mike, hoping he would speak.

"We ran a check on Smith," O'Kelly said.

"What did you find?" the FBI agent asked.

"Nothing. We think he's probably using a fictitious name."

"Any suggestions?" Parsons asked.

"Be careful," O'Kelly replied. "He has all the signs of a pro—a professional hit man."

The car slowed as we drove through a residential area. Most of the buildings were white frame houses with eighteenth-century architecture. Some of the larger homes had been converted into bed and breakfast inns, identified with quaint signs. I had the definite impression of a summer tourist Mecca, now mostly deserted during the off-season.

We passed the little sign that read "Downtown Truro" and continued north on Highway 6.

"Museum's ahead on the right," the sheriff said.

Parsons found the turnoff and drove about two blocks to a near

245

deserted parking lot with a sign that read "Truro Historical Museum." The Museum consisted of several old houses. It was surrounded by dunes and rolling moors. A stream fringed by tall grasses that merged into the ocean beyond. The lone car in the parking area had a rack of colored lights on top and a hand-painted sign on the door that read "Truro Police." A large woman dressed in uniform stood by the car.

Our four cars parked and the ten of us got out to meet Hank Bozeman, the Truro Police Chief. I guessed her weight at about 300 pounds. Tall, red-faced, short black hair, she wore small pearl earrings to remind us of her gender. Otherwise, her appearance was decidedly masculine. Even her voice had a low range that, while it was physiologically regarded as contralto, could easily be mistaken for a male in the tenor range.

Hank introduced herself to agent Parsons who, in turn, introduced the rest of us.

"During the past hour I've done a little research," Hank said.

"Go," Parsons said. The rest of us gathered around.

"I talked with the manager of the Cape Inn," Hank continued. "That's the largest motel on the west side, one of the few that stays open all year. It's located on the shore of Cape Cod Bay. They also rent houses. They rented one of their houses today—unusual for this time of year."

"Did you get a description of the renters?" Parsons asked.

"My first question "Three men, a woman, and two youngsters.""

"Go on . . ." Parsons said.

"Paid a month's rent in cash," Hank said. "The house is located at 16 Lighthouse Street. It's back down the highway about three-quarters of a mile, on the west side, near the bay."

"I'd like to take a look," Parsons said. "Would it be better to go

COLLUSION

in your car or one of our unmarked cars?"

"My police car," Hank answered. "It's routine for us to drive the streets at sundown every day."

We all looked to the west to see the burnt orange rays of the setting sun. I estimated it would be dark in another thirty minutes.

"I'd like for three of us to go with you," Parsons said. "O'Kelly, Hartman, and me. Rest of you wait here and stay out of sight as much as possible."

"I'll open the museum," she said. "You can build a fire in the fireplace." She and the seven members of our team, who were not going, started carrying firewood.

A few minutes later, Parsons, O'Kelly, and I got in the Truro Police Car with Hank and started down the highway. In a few minutes she turned off on a narrow blacktop street. In the dusk I made out a small sign which read "Lighthouse Street." The houses looked uniformly old, white, and New England. Only one had lights—number sixteen. A white SUV, parked in the driveway, had a Hertz sticker on the back bumper. As we drove by I noticed a small canvas backpack on the porch. It looked like the one Luke carried to school. My gut twisted and I clenched my teeth to stifle my anger. Had my grandson left it there on purpose?

O'Kelly grabbed my arm and squeezed. "Easy," he whispered, "we're gonna get them."

"Want to drive back by the house?" the policewoman asked.

"No," replied Parsons. "We've seen enough."

We drove back to the museum in silence.

CHAPTER 37

The Truro Historical Museum

A fire roared in the fireplace of the big, old, white-frame house, giving welcome warmth to our tense situation. The Historical Society had cleared most of the furniture and converted the downstairs area of the house into a museum-like setting. The dining room, however, still had its large table and a dozen chairs. Parsons asked us to gather around.

"Isolate, contain, negotiate," Parsons said.

"The three precepts of dealing with hostages," O'Kelly confirmed.

The others sat silently—some nodded their agreement. The FBI's principles, I learned later, had been taught in law enforcement seminars since the 1930s, dating back to the Lindbergh kidnapping

"First thing we need to do," Parsons continued, "is to make sure the three hostages are in the house. To do this, we need to organize and get going."

Several of the officers pulled out writing pads and pencils.

"What can I do?" Hank asked.

"We need manpower," Parsons replied. "I can make this a 100%

FBI operation, but I think we'll be more efficient if we use a blend of some local law enforcement agencies. How many officers are you offering, and how soon can you get them here?"

"My two officers can come immediately," she answered. "I'll call Provincetown PD and the Truro County sheriff."

"Ask them to meet me here at the museum and be sure you emphasize the need to come quietly," Parsons said. "No lights. No sirens."

Hank Bozeman went to the other room to make her calls.

"Sheriff, how much help from Barnstable County?" Parsons asked.

"I know I can have three more cars and six additional men here within the hour," the sheriff answered.

"Same thing," Parsons said. "Have them come quietly, and meet me here at the museum for assignment."

The Barnstable sheriff left.

"This room will be our headquarters and communications center," Parsons said. "I'll work here." He turned to O'Kelly. "As you know, there needs to be one person designated as the negotiator. Mike, I'd like you to be our man—the one and only person who communicates with the kidnappers."

"Yes, sir," O'Kelly said.

Hank Bozeman came back to the table. "My two men will be here in the next few minutes," she said. "Provincetown PD will give us two cars, four men. Truro County is sending three cars, six men. They'll be here within the hour."

The Barnstable County sheriff interrupted: "My six men are on the way. Three cars will be here in about an hour."

Parsons wrote down the numbers. "This gives us fifteen cars and twenty-nine men. The FBI is committing thirty agents and fifteen vehicles. We've alerted the national kidnapping task force in Washington. They'll send more as needed." He sketched notes on his diagram, then looked up and made eye contact with each of us sitting around the table. "Here's what I want you to do."

Parsons organized the group quickly and efficiently.

"Mike O'Kelly will take eight officers to the scene to watch the house and determine whether or not Jennifer, Luke, and Melissa are there," Parsons said. "Chris will go with the group and—since he's the only one who can recognize the hostages by sight—have primary responsibility for identification. The Barnstable sheriff will place a car at each end of Lighthouse Street to make sure no one enters or exits the area. Police Chief Bozeman will remain at the museum and assist me with coordination and communication."

Terrified, I climbed into the back seat of one of the FBI cars with Mike O'Kelly and rode back to Lighthouse Street. We parked at the end of the narrow blacktop, left our cars partially hidden in a grove of trees, and crept toward the hostage house. Mike separated us into four groups, one in front, one at the back, and one on each side of the building.

I ended up with two FBI agents at the front. We positioned ourselves across the street, well hidden behind some green junipers by a neighboring house. I could see into the hostage house through a row of large front windows. One of the agents gave me a heavy coat, gloves, and a pair of binoculars. We hunkered down to wait and watch.

Mike O'Kelly left to walk the perimeter and check on the other three groups.

December weather on Cape Cod varies widely. That night, we lucked out with a partly cloudy, moonlit sky, temperature in the mid-thirties, and a light wind blowing in from the Atlantic.

One of the agents took a phone call. He spoke softly. From his whispered conversation I could only distinguish one word. "Pizza."

"What's up?" I asked.

"We've got trouble," he said. "There's a pizza delivery from Provincetown. We have him stopped down at the end of Lighthouse Street. Parsons is trying to figure out how to handle it."

We waited.

In a few minutes, Parsons joined us, breathing hard. I could tell he'd been running.

"We've had a break," he said.

"Pizza delivery?" I asked.

"Yes," he said, "and we've substituted one of our men for the delivery guy. He's on his way now."

We watched as a car with a lighted pizza sign on top, drove up and stopped. A man got out and carried two pizza boxes to the house. I watched with binoculars as he knocked at the front door.

The door opened and I recognized the man. John Smith.

The muscles in my gut tightened at the sight of the thug who was terrorizing my family. I held my breath as he passed a wad of bills to the delivery man, took the pizza boxes, and closed the door. The entire transaction happened so quickly it left me stunned, wanting to see more.

The delivery man hurried back to his car, turned around, and drove away.

"You recognize him?" Parsons asked.

"Damn right, that's John Smith," I answered.

That was all the confirmation O'Kelly needed. "We need to move to the kitchen side of the house," Parsons said.

251

HARRY HAINES

I followed the FBI chief as he hurried to a back alley. In a circuitous route, we crossed to a neighboring back yard where we could look into the kitchen of the hostage house. From a distance about seventy-five yards, I saw three people sitting at a table eating pizza. My heart skipped a beat. I recognized them.

Jennifer, Luke, and Melissa.

CHAPTER 38

The house at 16 Lighthouse Street, Truro

With mixed feelings, I gripped the binoculars and scanned their faces one by one. The children, thankfully, showed no signs of abuse or apprehension. Melissa, especially, appeared to be almost totally focused on her pizza. Luke ate slowly, peering around the room, seemingly more interested in the situation than the food.

Jennifer, on the other hand, looked tense and worried. I studied her face and her body language, trying to evaluate her reaction to the conditions. I thought she projected a high level of poise. Her hands appeared steady For a life-threatening situation, I was amazed at how cool she looked as she nibbled at a slice of pizza, but I knew she was alert to the situation. She had the look of a tigress, ready to fight to the death to protect her children. So much for my worrying about her falling apart. Right then I was so proud of her I could barely contain it.

John Smith walked to the table, and I felt wild, raw, unrestrained rage. I gripped the binoculars until my fingers ached as I watched him lecture my family. Without success, I tried to read his lips. But, while I couldn't grasp his words, I easily understood his body language. He projected a slick, oily persona, smiling as he talked to them, offering more pizza. I imagined his attempts to lie about the circumstances.

"He's trying to use the Stockholm Syndrome," Parsons said, studying the scene through his binoculars.

"What's that?" I asked.

"Back in the 1950s, in a hostage situation in Stockholm, the hostage takers were able to sweet-talk the hostages into believing their cause was laudable and that they, the bad guys, were being persecuted by the police."

"What happened?"

"The hostages felt sorry for the kidnappers and blamed the police for creating the confrontational situation."

"So the hostages switched sides?"

"Yes, and this same scenario has happened repeatedly over the years—in airplane hijackings, in bank holdups, and in a number of other hostage situations."

"You're saying that Smith is trying to convince my family that he and his henchmen are the good guys and we are persecuting them?"

"That's the essence of it."

"Impossible," I said.

"He'll provide your daughter and the kids with food," Parsons continued. "He'll treat them with kindness, and all the while keep talking about how the police are harassing him, accusing him unfairly, depriving him of his constitutional rights."

"Bullshit," I said. "It'll never work."

"What about Ruby Ridge?"

"This is different."

"That's what they said in Stockholm in 1954."

COLLUSION

"What finally happened in Stockholm?"

"Two people were killed, a policeman and one of the kidnappers," Parsons said.

"End of story?" I asked.

"If that were the end, we wouldn't have the legendary syndrome."

"So, how did it end?"

"The hostages testified at the trial—on behalf of the kidnappers," O'Kelly said. "The hostages blamed the two deaths on police tactics."

I shook my head. "What does this have to do with my family?"

"It has to do with John Smith."

"I guess I don't get it."

"He's smart," Parsons said.

"I could have told you that," I answered, pressing the binoculars to my eyes and taking another brief look.

"He's using a highly effective but little-known psychological approach on your family. Not many kidnappers would do that."

I pondered Parsons's words.

"And he started his Stockholm tactics," he looked at his watch, "less than twelve hours into the kidnapping episode."

"Is that significant?"

"In all the cases I've studied, it started much later," Parsons said. "Usually in the fourth or fifth day. Sometimes, not until the second or third week."

My pulse surged in anger and I exploded. "God damn it, Parsons, how long are we going to let these bastards hold my family?"

"Chris, shut up," the FBI chief whispered, yanking on my coat.

I tried to control my rage, kneeling behind a bush.

"Cool it," he said.

"I can't."

"Either you simmer down or I'll send you back to the museum."

"Okay, but, how long are you going to let this go on?"

"As long as it takes."

His words hit me hard. Until that moment I hadn't thought about the length of time my family might have to endure their role as hostages.

"Statistics show that time is on our side," Parsons said. "The longer it lasts, the better our chances of a successful resolution."

That was the last thing I wanted to hear. But as his words sank in, I felt an easing of my emotions. My breathing slowed to a more normal rate and my anger subsided. I thought about Smith, about the evil he had brought into my life. My brain took over.

"You okay?" Parsons asked.

"No."

"Let's get something straight," he said. "No more outbursts."

I nodded.

"Next time you yell, you could get your head blown off."

"Look, I said I'm okay."

"Chris, this guy is smart, maybe even brilliant. We need you to help us outthink him."

"I'm doing my best," I said.

"A moment ago you weren't. Venting your emotions is counter productive."

"What do you suggest?" I had to get Parsons thinking about something other than my behavior.

"Isolate, contain, negotiate."

"We have the kidnappers isolated and contained."

"Yes."

"So, now we negotiate?"

CHAPTER 39

Outside the hostage house at 16 Lighthouse Street, Truro

Fog rolled in from the Atlantic and transformed the neighborhood into a dank, soggy, winter's night that oozed with coldness and wetness. A streetlight a block away was ringed with a misty halo, the lighted windows of the hostage house no longer gave sharp, clear images of the interior. Colors faded into hazy shades of gray and reminded me of a London scene from a 1940's Sherlock Holmes movie.

At midnight, FBI Agent Parsons ordered a shift change and eight new law enforcement officers came to relieve those who had been on duty since the beginning of the surveillance. A new FBI kidnapping expert took over the scene and Parsons went back to the museum for a few hour's sleep.

I rode back with Agent Parsons.

Still on Houston time, I tried to calculate my sleep. Except for a short nap in the Lear Jet on the flight from Texas to Hyannisport, I'd been going strong for almost forty-eight hours. With a massive amount of Adrenaline pumping through my system, I probably couldn't have slept if I'd tried. Now, however, fatigue caught up and gave me trouble walking from the car into the museum.

HARRY HAINES

Chief Henrietta Bozeman showed me upstairs to an old army cot with a pillow and a blanket. I plopped down and promptly fell asleep. The next thing I knew, Mike O'Kelly was shaking my shoulder.

"Chris, they're serving a McDonald's breakfast in the dining room," he said.

I looked at him, trying to remember where I was.

"The FBI chief, Parsons, has asked me to be the official negotiator," O'Kelly said. "In about fifteen minutes I'm going back to the house," "I'd like you to go with me if you're up to it."

When he said "the house," it all came back to me. Still wearing my shoes, I swung my feet to the floor, then looked at my watch and calculated I'd slept about six hours.

"There's an electric razor in the bathroom," O'Kelly said, "I'll wait for you downstairs."

I shaved. And while mowing the two-day-old stubble, I received a visual shock. My image in the mirror looked horrible. Rumpled clothes, uncombed hair, a tired face with sagging dark circles under the eyes—I wished for a motel room, a shower, and clean clothes. Instead, I washed my face, combed my hair with my fingers, and staggered downstairs to find coffee and a Sausage McMuffin.

"You don't have to go with me," O'Kelly said, studying my haggard appearance.

"Wrong," I said. "That's my family. I have to go."

"You don't look so hot."

"Brief me," I said. "What's happening?"

"The kidnappers still don't know we're here," he said. "We're going to break the news to them."

"What's the plan?"

"We've called the phone companies," O'Kelly said. "They've

rigged the phone in the house so that the only number the kidnappers can call is us. And we got their cell phone number from the pizza place. The cellphone company discontinued their service."

"Isolate?"

"Completely. No one can call in, and they can't call out."

"Contain?"

"We've doubled the troops. We now have sixteen men surrounding the house. And we have four snipers—one on each side."

I thought this through. "So now you negotiate?"

"That's the next step," he said. "And we need to do it carefully, with reassurance."

More than anything, I feared for my family. In some ways, O'Kelly's approach scared me. But, my impression was that he knew how to deal with kidnappers.

"Chris, this is going to be a major surprise to Smith and his two henchmen," O'Kelly said. "They're riding high. They think you're in Houston doing their bidding and that no one knows they're here."

"How are you going to put it to them?" I asked.

"Telephone. But first, we're hoping they'll send someone out for breakfast or groceries. If they do, we'll arrest him and that will be one less to deal with at the house."

"Sounds good." I went for another cup of coffee, and we left.

O'Kelly drove and we headed back to Lighthouse Street just as dawn began to lighten the foggy morning. Parking at the end of the street, we walked two blocks to the house and took up surveillance across the street. During the night a significant improvement had occurred. The agents on duty had moved our post from behind the bushes to a warm, comfortable position inside a nearby vacant house. We now had a table with a phone and a row of chairs near the window.

"I'll be back in thirty minutes," O'Kelly said. "I'm going to walk the perimeter and see how the other guys are doing."

I found a chair near a policeman who was looking out the front window, patiently watching the hostage house across the street. Using binoculars, I, too, made a slow, careful study of the house and the surrounding area. Nothing seemed to be happening.

After thirty minutes, O'Kelly returned.

"Any sign of movement in the house?" he asked.

"Nothing," the policeman said.

"There's one man in the kitchen," O'Kelly said. "The guys can see him from the back side of the house."

"What about Jennifer and the children?" I asked.

"We think they're asleep in one of the bedrooms," O'Kelly said. "No one has seen them since this shift began at midnight."

I started to ask him more about my family when the lights came on in the front room of the house. O'Kelly and the policeman immediately picked up their binoculars and started scanning. Two more officers came into the room and joined us. I could feel the tension as all five of us watched for movement. O'Kelly used his cell phone to call the blockade and warn them to be ready in case someone left.

The policeman with the sniper rifle went outside and took a position behind the bushes.

Then it happened.

A man came out of the house and walked to the vehicle closest to the street, one of two Ford Explorers. He stopped, stood by the front left door and looked around. Slowly and deliberately, he got in the car, backed out, and started east toward the highway.

"Here he comes," O'Kelly said, into the cell phone.

We waited, knowing there would be a confrontation, hoping for the best, dreading the worst.

I watched the second hand creep around my watch. O'Kelly held his cell phone to his ear. Just when I was about to give up, he spoke, "Good. I'll be right there."

"What happened?" I asked.

"They took him by surprise. No struggle. No shots fired."

"Any news about my family?"

"I don't know," he said. "You want to come with me while I grill this guy?"

I bundled up and walked with O'Kelly to the end of the street. Police had the suspect handcuffed and shackled. I watched as O'Kelly and others tried to question him. It didn't take long. He clammed up, completely. Not a word—he just stared at the ground. Finally, FBI agents from Boston loaded him into the back seat of an unmarked car and took him away. O'Kelly and I walked back to the observation house.

"What's next?" I asked.

"Negotiate," he said.

"Can you give me details?"

"I've made arrangements for you to listen in."

"Thanks, but I'd like to know what to expect," I said. "How are you going to approach this?"

"Every hostage situation is different," he said, "but at the start, I'll try to stay cool. See if I can get Smith to do the same."

We went back into the house where two men from the telephone company were setting up phones and recording machines. O'Kelly took charge and I moved out of the way. After about fifteen minutes of preparations, we seated ourselves around a folding table near the front window.

HARRY HAINES

O'Kelly had the main phone and took a chair at the end of the table where he could see the rest of us, as well as look out the window to observe any developments at the hostage house. I sat next to him with an earpiece. This allowed me to hear the conversation but prevented me from saying anything. The guys from the phone company manned the recorders. Two other FBI men, wearing headphones, sat on the other side of O'Kelly.

"Everyone set?" O'Kelly asked. He made eye contact with each of us. After receiving go-ahead nods, he turned to the lead phone man.

"Showtime," O'Kelly said. "Dial it."

As I listened to the familiar sound of a phone ringing at regular five-second intervals, I had a sinking feeling in the pit of my stomach.

CHAPTER 40

Inside the house across from 16 Lighthouse Street

The phone rang too many times.

I didn't count, but after several rings I decided Smith wasn't going to answer. Just as I was ready to give up, I heard his familiar voice.

"Who is this?" Smith yelled, angrily.

"Captain Michael O'Kelly, Houston Department of Police." Mike spoke in a calm, slow tone. He let his Texas drawl come full force on the last word. It sounded "Po-leese."

Smith's response astounded me.

His voice went up an octave and he began screaming. Obscenities came in an avalanche of words I could barely understand.

At first, O'Kelly held back and let Smith rant and rave. Then, he tried to interrupt. "John, I want to help you," he said.

"You goddamned pigs. You assholes know I have Hartman's grandkids. You pea-brained motherfuckers don't know who you're dealing with. You bastards better—"

"John, I said I can help you."

Smith hung up. The line went dead.

I sat stunned. Finally, I looked around the table at the others.

Their faces showed worry and concern.

Except one. Mike O'Kelly appeared poised and confident. We all stared at him—waiting for him to speak.

"We'll give him five minutes," O'Kelly said. "He needs a little time to allow reality to register."

"Mike, what if he goes off the deep end?" I asked.

"Give him some slack. Let him see that we're not sending in the SWAT team."

I didn't know what to do or say, so I sat and studied my watch.

Everyone looked at their watches.

At the five-minute mark, O'Kelly nodded to the telephone man. "Dial it," he said.

The phone rang once.

"How do I know you're who you say you are?" Smith asked. This time, his voice sounded nearly normal.

"Go to your front window and check on your tires."

Across the street we could see Smith come to the window and peer out. He couldn't see our sniper in the bushes, but we could.

A shot rang out and the front tire of their Ford Explorer went flat. A second shot hit the back tire and the vehicle leaned.

A few seconds passed. Smith's irate voice came back on the line. "If you assholes think a couple of flat tires is gonna stop me, you've forgotten something. I have a couple of kids and a mother who's not going anywhere, either."

"John, you are totally surrounded," O'Kelly said. "There's no way out."

"And I have three 'get out of jail free' cards," Smith countered.

"John, I think we can work this out."

"Damn right, we can. My way."

COLLUSION

"John, my name's Mike O'Kelly. I'd like us to use first names."

"Hell, I don't care if we use nicknames with middle initials."

"I want to help. What can I do to help?"

"For starters, you could send back Correlli with some food. Where is he?"

"Antonio Correlli has gone. He won't be back."

"Gone? Where to?"

"I'm not sure, but we can get you some food. What would you like?"

"I want Tony Correlli and our breakfast."

"I have a suggestion. Ask each person what they want. We'll get anything you request."

"What is this, a game?"

"No tricks. You have us over a barrel and we'll get whatever you want for breakfast. What would you like?"

Smith didn't say anything.

"Whatever you want," O'Kelly repeated. "Tell us, we'll get it."

"Just a minute."

We waited several minutes. Then Smith came back on the line.

"I have a grocery list. You ready?"

"Go."

"Coffee, hot chocolate, milk, cereal, bread, butter, jelly, and bananas."

"What kind of cereal?"

"God damn it, the kids want cereal. Just get them some cereal. Any kind of cereal."

"How about a Kellogg Variety Pack? Then each person could choose."

I heard a click and the line went dead.

HARRY HAINES

O'Kelly sent a policeman for groceries.

"Why make such a big deal about the cereal?" I asked.

"Did you notice? He quit asking about the other guy, Antonio Correlli?"

"I'd forgotten about him, too."

"One of the rules in hostage negotiation—concentrate on the things you can do for the hostage takers," O'Kelly said.

"And you try not to talk about the things that are nonnegotiable?" I asked.

"You're a quick study. And another rule—keep talking," O'Kelly said. "Let's call him again." He nodded to the guy in charge of the phones.

"What do want?" Smith barked.

"John, this is Mike."

"So, what else is new?"

"I've sent a man into Provincetown for your groceries. He'll be back within the hour."

"God damn it, why're you taking so long?"

"We're moving as fast as we can," O'Kelly said, "and if we can find a doughnut shop, we'll bring you some hot doughnuts."

"You called to tell me this? Asshole."

"It's Mike. And my boss is requiring me to ask you something."

"What the hell does he want?"

"He says that before we can deliver the groceries, I have to speak with each of the hostages."

"No way."

"John, look at it his way," O'Kelly continued. "He just wants to know that everyone's okay and that you're not mistreating the kids."

"Fuck him."

COLLUSION

"John, are you lying to me? Have you injured the children?"

"No, they're fine."

"Then why not let us talk with them? Just a few words, and I can get authorization to send in the food."

I heard the click, and again, the line went dead.

"Give him a few minutes. He's coming around."

"God, I hope so," I answered.

We sat, silently, for a few minutes. Then, O'Kelly picked up his phone and nodded to the telephone man.

"Okay, you can talk to them," Smith said. "Here's the mother."

"Hello," Jennifer said. The sound of her voice was music.

"Mrs. Banks, I'm Michael O'Kelly of the Houston Police. Are you all right?"

"Yes, I'm fine."

"We're going to get you out of there."

"Thank you. I hope it's soon."

I could hear some scuffling and voices in the background.

"Hello, this is Luke Banks," my grandson said.

"Luke, I'm Captain O'Kelly, Houston Police. Are you okay?"

"Yes, sir."

"I need to know, have they mistreated you or your sister?"

"No, I don't think so."

"May I speak to Melissa?"

"Sure, here she is."

"Hello," came the voice of my seven-year-old granddaughter.

"Melissa, are you feeling okay?"

"Yes, sir."

"Do you need anything?"

"I'd like some Fruit Loops, please."

"Fruit Loops?"

"You know, Fruit Loops, the cereal."

"Okay. We'll try to get you some Fruit Loops. But if we don't get them this morning, we'll have them for sure for tomorrow morning."

"How long do we have to stay here?"

"Not long, we hope. And you can take the Fruit Loops with you when—"

I could hear the phone being yanked away and Smith yelling at the kids.

"That's enough. Are you satisfied? Asshole?"

"It's Mike. And the groceries should be here any minute. We'll set them on the front porch and call you."

Smith hung up.

Five minutes later we sent the groceries. A policeman placed them on the front porch. O'Kelly called. We watched as Jennifer came out onto the porch, picked up the sacks, and took them into the house.

I breathed a sigh of relief and eased back into my chair.

"Chris, we've got a problem," O'Kelly said.

CHAPTER 41

Inside the house across from 16 Lighthouse Street

"We don't have an endgame," O'Kelly said.

"You're the hostage expert," I said. "What do you usually do at this point?"

"There is no 'usual' hostage situation. The circumstances are always different."

"But Mike, aren't there some basic structures?" I asked. "Can't you suggest some place for us to start?"

"Okay, let's start with Smith. What does he want?"

"He wants me to write a report absolving TEI corporate officers of any blame. I can't do that."

"Just so I can explain our problem, let's suppose you give in. What happens if you agree to write the report—that you do exactly what Smith is asking?"

"I would hope he'd release my family."

"There are two things wrong with that."

"And they are?"

"Once he releases your family, he has no hold over you. What's to keep you from recanting? You could go to the media with the truth about the TEI bad guys."

"And I would."

"Even worse, Smith knows that once he gives up the hostages, we're going to nab him."

I hadn't thought about that. I'd been so worried about my family it hadn't occurred to me to start thinking about the end-game scenario—what would happen to Smith and his henchman after the release of Jennifer and the kids. Now, as I thought about the possibilities, I could see that the authorities would have to charge these thugs with kidnapping, and probably file charges for the murders of Bryan Banks and Joel Wilson.

"Smith has no motivation to release Jenny and the kids?"

"That's the way I see it," O'Kelly replied.

As always happened when a thorny problem arose, we sat silently, each of us alone with our thoughts.

The fog began to lift and I studied a break in the clouds as a tiny sliver of sunshine lit the house across the street. Leafless trees would normally seem less forbidding without the fog, but the visual improvement now brought a reverse effect. I looked at the hostage house and could see more clearly the hopeless conflict that affected my family.

"We've backed him into a corner," I said.

"Chris, you're a smart guy," O'Kelly said. "What else does Smith want?"

"He wants out."

"Very badly."

"You think, if he wants that so badly, he may be willing to forego his demands about my TEI report."

"Yes, I think he probably will."

COLLUSION

"What other possibilities do you see?"

The police captain stared out the window for several minutes. Then he turned and made eye contact. "None."

I nodded.

"Let's hope we can sell it," he said.

"Hey, you're not going to let Smith and this other guy go?"

"No. Of course not."

"But, you're going to let him think that you might?"

"Chris, he has to have a goal—"

"Something he's shooting for?" I asked.

"Let's not use those words," he said.

"Sorry," I answered. "But you see what I'm talking about. In a hostage situation, there has to be something to negotiate."

"And if this is all we've got, we have to go with it."

"We have the Lear," I said. "It's still parked at the airport."

O'Kelly dropped into his thinking mode. As expected, he looked outside and the familiar, faraway look came over his face. I waited while he considered the ramifications of my reference to the jet.

"Let's use it," he said, finally.

"I'll need to call Powell," I said, "and clear it with him."

"Of course."

"He'll want to know what to expect. How far are we prepared to go with our offer to Smith?"

"Good question."

"Smith has to think the offer is genuine or he won't buy it."

"Ask Powell how far he's willing to let us go with the offer."

"So if Smith wants to fly to South America, you're going to let him go?"

"If that's what it takes to get your daughter and the children—yes."

271

"I don't see how we're going to do this."

"Neither do I," O'Kelly said. "But we have to start with the possibility. Ask Powell if he feels this is a possible scenario?"

I did. And to my great relief, Billy Ray Powell said, "Do whatever you need to do to protect and bring about the safe return of your family." I wanted to hug him. And if he'd been present in the old, white-frame house across from 16 Lighthouse Street, I would've.

We sent out for sandwiches for lunch. The afternoon passed slowly. Then, about sundown, we called for pizza. Every six hours, the police changed their shift. At midnight, I went back to the museum, and after an exhausting, eighteen-hour day, I found my same old army cot and immediately fell asleep. Another day with no progress.

O'Kelly woke me the following morning and we followed the same routine. After one more quick McDonald's breakfast, I rode with him back to Lighthouse Street.

"While you were asleep," he said, "Parsons and I talked about the Lear."

"What about it?" I asked.

"We think it's time to make the offer."

"How're you going to do it?"

"Telephone."

"When?"

"Right after Smith has his breakfast."

"God, Mike, this is scary."

"I know, but we've got to do something."

"Have you thought of any other possibilities?"

"Snipers. Storm the house with a SWAT team. Or, keep on doing what we're doing and play a waiting game."

"None of which sound good."

COLLUSION

"So, we're back to trading a Lear Jet for hostages." He laced his fingers, put his hands over his head in a gesture of frustration, and said, "Chris, we're going to be very careful, but, you have to realize, every alternative has risks."

I nodded, and with great anxiety, watched and listened as O'Kelly turned away and started negotiating, step by step, for the release of my family.

First he convinced Smith to give up any demands about my writing a report to absolve Upton and any of the TEI executives. Then, he started his pitch about the jet. O'Kelly had all the numbers, the model, the speed, the range—everything. The selling of the escape plan took most of the day. Finally, by dinnertime, Smith agreed. The next morning, he would exchange his three hostages for a free ride on a Lear—destination unknown. The exchange would take place at the Hyannisport Airport at ten a.m.

O'Kelly arranged for me go back to Hyannisport, purchase some clothes, and spend the night in a Holiday Inn. At first I felt reluctant to leave the scene, but he convinced me it would be better to get a good night's rest and be at my best for the exchange.

The shower, my first in four days, felt wonderful. The feeling of cleanliness, followed by a bed with pillow, changed my psyche. I expected to be so worried about the hostage exchange that sleep would be difficult, if not impossible. Instead I passed out immediately. And the next morning I felt energized.

I called O'Kelly.

He ordered me to get a good breakfast and meet him at the plane. I wanted to drive back to Lighthouse Street and be present for the arrangements to move the hostages, but he said I'd be in the way and repeated his command to go to the airport. He expected to arrive a few minutes after ten o'clock.

I checked my watch. It was five minutes to eight.

After a huge Holiday Inn buffet-breakfast, I drove to the airport, parked the borrowed FBI car, and walked out to wait by the jet.

Leonard Parsons, still the FBI agent in charge, greeted me and briefed me on the situation.

"We've exchanged pilots," he said. "We have two FBI agents, thoroughly qualified pilots, who will be flying the plane."

"So, you're actually going to fly the kidnappers to South America?"

"Hostage release is the goal. We'll do what we have to do to achieve the goal."

Just hearing his words, I felt better.

"The transfer from the house to the car went well," he said. "They're en route now."

I nodded.

"We expect them in about thirty minutes."

"How are you going to handle this?"

"We have a three-vehicle caravan," Parsons said. "The lead car has O'Kelly and three officers. Next is the hostage car with two kidnappers and three hostages. One of the kidnappers is driving. Your daughter is with him in the front seat. The other kidnapper, Smith, is in the back seat with the two children. They are followed by a third car with four officers."

Parsons walked me to a clear area about twenty yards east of the plane. "We'll lead the caravan to about here," he said. "We have snipers positioned in the control tower, in the terminal building, in those bushes across the way, and in that van." He pointed to a blue van parked about thirty yards beyond the tail of the jet.

"What do you expect?" I asked.

"Plan A is to maneuver the two kidnappers into the jet, and when he releases the hostages, let him take off."

"Is there a Plan B?"

He nodded. "If we get clear shots, we'll take the kidnappers with sniper fire."

I cringed at the thought of gunfire around my family. "Any other plans?"

"Yes, several," he answered.

I waited for him to go on.

"Chris, we've spent hours going over all the possible scenarios." He looked at his watch. "They're going to be here in a few minutes. You need to go to your assigned position and trust us to handle this."

"Okay, where's my spot?"

"Over there, behind that Barnstable County sheriff's car." He pointed to a car about fifty yards back in the parking area. "We want you out of the line of fire so we don't have to worry about you."

As ordered, I walked over and stood behind the car. A deputy handed me his binoculars. I looked at my watch. Ten o'clock.

We waited.

CHAPTER 42

The Hyannisport Airport

The airport swarmed with police. From my position, standing with two deputies behind the Barnstable County sheriff's car, I counted a dozen law enforcement vehicles. Nothing moved. No planes took off or landed. No cars came or went. No one walked—anywhere.

Slowly, three cars came into sight on the other side of the terminal building. They stood out as the only moving objects in an airport under siege. I watched as the procession drove through the security gate and out onto the tarmac toward the isolated Lear Jet. The three-car caravan circled the plane and stopped at exactly the spot Parsons had planned. Through my binoculars, I saw Jenny, Luke, and Melissa in the middle car, sitting where Parsons had told me they would be.

After a few minutes, the front and back cars drove away and parked about twenty yards behind the plane. Then, much to my disappointment, the hostage car moved. It circled and drove over to the plane's stairway, stopping less than five yards away from the stairs. The car's new position effectively blocked any sniper fire between the car and the plane.

Ten minutes passed and nothing happened. Then, O'Kelly got

out of the lead car and jogged over toward me. It took him a long sixty seconds to cover the hundred yards or so that separated us.

"Chris, we've got problems," he said. He carried a small, two-way radio, one that reminded me of a military walkie-talkie.

"What's wrong?" I asked.

"We've told him he can't take any of the hostages on the plane. He says he won't board the plane without a hostage."

"God damn him, he's got the pilots for hostages."

"I want to wait him out," O'Kelly said.

"No way. You're supposed to be getting my family out of there."

"That's what we've been negotiating for the last ten minutes."

"So what are you telling me? What's been decided?"

"So, he's made a new demand."

"What?"

"He wants to speak with you."

"Why me?"

"No telling," O'Kelly said. "But I don't like it."

"What happens if I don't talk?" I asked.

"The usual. He's threatening to shoot someone if we don't let him talk with you."

"I'll talk."

"Chris, this is bad strategy. You shouldn't get involved."

"I'm already involved. Besides, I can always say no."

"What if he threatens a member of your family?"

"He's already doing that."

O'Kelly, paused. I knew he was thinking.

The radio came to life. "Asshole, you still there?" asked the familiar voice.

The voice stirred unpleasant thoughts. The memory of his phone calls in Houston, his threats against Luke and Melissa, and his first admission about killing my son-in-law. Things hadn't changed, and my reaction was the same. Fear. A paralyzing, debilitating fear.

"Yes, I'm here," O'Kelly, answered, into the radio.

"Time's running out," Smith said.

"Let . . . let me speak to him," I said, my voice faltering.

"No. You'll only make matters worse," O'Kelly said.

Before I could respond, Smith came back on the radio. "Okay, we'll play it your way. I'm sending out my buddy, Charlie, with a message for Chris Hartman. Don't shoot. Here he comes."

We looked at the hostage car. Parked about fifty yards away, I could see the driver open his door, stand, look around, then slowly start walking away from the car toward me.

Suddenly, three shots rang out. The guy fell to the ground.

Immediately, I grabbed my binoculars to study the figure lying on the tarmac. I could see blood gushing from his head. Anger gripped me as I blamed some trigger-happy policeman, a sniper whose poor judgment now jeopardized our negotiations.

"That's a warning," the voice on the radio said.

Smith's three-word message jarred me. Why would he say that?

"Parsons, what happened?" O'Kelly asked, speaking into a second radio, a small, police-like, portable, hand-held radio.

"Who fired those shots?" Leonard Parsons's voice commanded.

"Not me," a voice said.

"Nor me," another voice added.

"Wasn't me," a third voice said.

"The shots came from behind," a fourth voice said, "from the car . . . from Smith."

"Why would Smith shoot his own man?" I asked.

COLLUSION

Seconds later, the answer came.

"Asshole, I hope you and Chris Hartman are watching and listening," Smith said.

"I'm here," O'Kelly answered into the walkie-talkie.

"Just wanted you to know that I'm serious," Smith said. "I'll give you two minutes to get Hartman on the line. The mother's next."

I grabbed the walkie-talkie, pushed the button marked "talk."

"I'm here," I said. Anger replaced fear. Hatred took control of my emotions—my body. My voice, which only a few moments ago would hardly work, now rang out with steely resolve.

"Dr. Hartman," Smith said, "I'll trade three hostages for you. Walk over and stand on the bottom step of the jet's stairway and I'll release these three. You've got five minutes."

I took the strap from around my neck and handed the binoculars to O'Kelly along with the walkie-talkie.

"Chris, wait," O'Kelly urged. "Let's discuss this."

"What's to discuss?" I asked.

"If you go to that plane, he'll shoot you or take you to South America. Either way, it's a death warrant."

"And if I don't?"

"Give us some time."

"He said five minutes. You probably only have four left."

"We can rush him."

"You don't have time to plan a rush," I said, and walked away.

Moving toward the jet's stairway, I tried to think of how best to protect my family. Furiously, I searched my brain for ideas. As I came to the jet's stairway, I formed a plan.

CHAPTER 43

The Hyannisport Airport

I placed my hand on the Lear's entrance handrail and stood on the bottom step.

"Jenny, open the car door and stand up," I said. My voice rang out with a commanding presence.

"Wait a minute," Smith said. "I'm giving the orders." His voice betrayed him. It wavered. He hadn't thought out the intricate details of how to conduct the exchange. I had. It gave me a momentary advantage and I took it.

"Jenny, do as I say." I spoke with the same tone of voice I had used thirty years ago. Like a father commanding his three-year-old daughter, I said, "Do it now." She did. She opened the door and stood.

"Hartman," Smith snarled, "Shut up or I'll kill all three of them." He continued to point his gun at me.

"Jenny, open the back door so Melissa can get out and stand with you."

Smith reacted with indecision. He couldn't crouch down in the back seat, restrain a seven-year-old, and keep his pistol trained on me. While he tried to decide what to do, Jenny opened the door and

280

COLLUSION

I kept talking.

"Luke, open your door and get out," I commanded.

"Hartman, for the last time, shut up," Smith shouted.

"John," I said, speaking to him directly, "You need me. They have four snipers trained on you."

As I spoke the two children ran to their mother.

Smith rose slightly from his crouch and turned his gun away from me, toward the three hostages who were now standing on the tarmac, on the other side of the car.

"John, keep down." I said it urgently, loudly, with a ring of command. "The snipers have you in their crosshairs, waiting for a shot."

He ducked.

Jenny and the kids stood still.

"Use me as your shield," I said. "Keep low. Get behind me and back us up into the plane."

He hesitated for a moment.

Then he did it.

I could feel his gun at the base of my neck as we slowly backed up the stairs and into the jet.

Once inside, Smith took charge. I let him.

He told me to take a seat, fasten the seat belt. I did.

He told one of the pilots to close the door, and the other to start the engines. A moment later we taxied out for takeoff.

"Where to?" one of the pilots asked.

"The Caribbean," Smith answered.

"Which island?"

"Just pick one. I'll tell you later where we're going."

I looked out the window to see my family, safely getting into a police car.

Moments later the plane lurched forward, and we headed out over the water in a steep climb. I could hear one of the pilots filing a flight plan to Nassau.

Nothing happened for the next hour. Smith sat in his seat, facing forward, midway back in the cabin. I sat in another, across the aisle and facing him. The two pilots leveled the plane at a high altitude, and using the autopilot, headed south. In a surreal atmosphere, no one spoke, and I had a faint hope that, through some miracle, there might be a way for me to get out of this alive.

Then Smith took the onboard telephone and started making calls. I could overhear bits of the conversation about someone meeting the plane and bringing $100,000. He repeated the figure several times, each repetition in a louder voice. And he wanted the money in small bills, and in a briefcase.

After the phone calls, Smith ordered me to take the rear seat. I did it without objection and buckled up. Then, with pistol drawn, he went forward to confer with the pilots. Shortly thereafter, he came back and flopped into the seat next to me. I felt the engines ease power and sensed the plane headed down.

"Are we landing?" I asked.

Smith shook his head.

I wanted to ask more, but decided it better not to. I watched out the window as the plane flew low over the water. Very low. Then suddenly I saw a beach and we flew over land at treetop level. Smith went forward and stood in the doorway, talking with the pilots and frequently looking back at me. Then, we were in mountains, heading west. I saw a water tower in a small town and tried to read the name. All I could make out were the last two letters—N.C. I surmised we were probably over North Carolina heading west. A few minutes later we started to climb. The climb lasted a long while, and I sensed the plane, once again, leveling off at a cruising altitude. Straining to hear words from the cockpit, one of the pilots seemed to be filing a new flight plan. I could only pick out three words: "Houston Hobby, direct."

Smith returned, took the seat across the aisle, and made another phone call. He didn't seem to care that I could hear his entire conversation. "We'll be at the hangar about one-fifteen," he said.

He listened, briefly.

"Yes, I have Hartman."

Pause.

"You can have him or I'll take him with me," Smith continued. "Your choice."

Another brief pause.

"Right, one-fifteen, with the briefcase." He turned off the phone and replaced it in its wall holder.

I thought of a thousand questions. Instead of asking them, I closed my eyes and sat completely still. The memory of Jenny and my grandchildren getting into a Barnstable County sheriff's car gave me comfort.

The next hour passed without incident.

Then, I felt the engines ease and the plane start a descent.

Smith rose, walked to the front, and stood in the doorway to the cockpit. I could hear him giving orders to the pilots. I looked at my watch—five minutes to one. We came down through the clouds over a huge metropolitan area, which appeared to be Houston. As we dropped lower, I looked to the west and saw the Astrodome and Reliant Stadium. We touched down and began a slow taxi to the general aviation hangars. I recognized the large blue hangar where we had picked up the plane three days ago. We taxied up to the doors and the pilots killed the engines. I could hear one of the pilots talking on his radio to the ground crew.

"Top off the tanks," the pilot ordered. "We'll be taking off again as soon as you can refuel us."

The other pilot came back and opened the hatch.

Smith used his gun to gesture for me to start down the stairway. "Out," he said.

I walked down the small stairway with Smith close behind, his gun pushing against my back.

"Into the hangar," he said.

The tall doors were partially open, allowing us to walk into the huge hangar. No lights were turned on, and the shadows on the sides of the large, cavernous room made it difficult to see clearly. We walked toward a table, which was placed against the far wall. I could make out the figure of a man dressed in a dark suit, holding a tan leather briefcase. I couldn't distinguish his face.

"John, Richard Zimmerman asked me to bring you this briefcase," he said. I recognized the voice. As we came closer I could see his face—Reed Upton.

Smith acted surprised. He stopped. I took an additional two steps and half turned. This left me standing between the two men—the bottom of a u-shaped formation.

With his left hand, Upton held out the briefcase.

Smith took it and started to speak. He said, "Reed—"

A gunshot rang out.

I flinched, afraid I'd been shot.

Smith fell, his face red with blood.

I looked at Upton's right hand and saw the pistol.

CHAPTER 44

Lear Jet Hangar #453, Houston Hobby Airport

"Call 911," Upton said. He knelt to examine Smith.

In shock, I stood there, trying to make sense of what was happening.

"Dr. Hartman," Upton said, "*call* for help." He gestured toward an office.

People came running.

I hurried to the office, picked up a phone, and called for police and an ambulance.

Returning to the scene, I found Smith's body covered with a blanket.

Upton was talking with the two FBI agents, the pilots who had flown us to Houston.

"We've been monitoring Zimmerman's phone calls," Upton said. "About two hours ago Smith called, ordered Zimmerman to bring $100,000 in small bills to this hangar. I called TEI security, placed Zimmerman under house arrest, and came myself with the money."

Upton looked at me. "Dr. Hartman, are you all right?"

"Yes, I'm fine."

"We've been worried about you," Upton said. "Your family called to ask if anyone had any information on your whereabouts."

"Yes, I should call them."

The police came, followed by an ambulance. Amid flashing lights and sirens, I went back to the hangar office to call my family.

I used my credit card to call the cabin in Hyannisport. Agent Leonard Parsons answered.

"Hello," he said.

"This is Chris Hartman," I said.

"Chris! Where are you?"

"Houston Hobby Airport."

"Are you all right? Where's Smith?"

"Smith is dead and I'm fine."

"What happened?"

"I'll tell you in a minute," I said. "How's my family."

"I'll get Jennifer. She can tell you herself."

In a few minutes I heard the most reassuring voice in the world. "Dad?" she asked. "Are you okay? We've been so worried."

"I'm fine, but that's not important. How are you and the kids?"

"We're okay. We've been so worried about Smith and what he might do to you."

"Smith is dead," I told her. "He won't hurt anyone in our family again, ever."

"What happened?"

"It's a long story, so I'll tell you later. How're Luke and Melissa?"

"They're good, Dad. Do you want to speak with them?"

"I'd like nothing better."

In a moment Luke came on the line.

286

COLLUSION

"Hi Grandpa. Where are you?"

"Hey, Luke, I'm in Houston. You okay?"

"Yes, sir. We've been worried about you. Are you all right?"

"Luke, I'm fine. But I want to congratulate you on your message on the Blackberry. If it hadn't been for you, we might not have found you."

Silence.

Like so many kids, Luke didn't know how to accept a compliment. I decided to wait him out. After a few moments he thought of a response.

"I didn't have much time. Only a few seconds."

"Four words were enough."

"You figured it out."

Here was a ten-year-old, complimenting me for reading his clue, the information that saved the day. This kid was going to be something. "Luke," I said, "your quick thinking enabled us to follow the kidnappers. I'm really proud of you."

Silence for a few moments. Then, in a softer voice he said, "Thanks, Grandpa. It means a lot to hear that from you."

"Let me say it again. I'm really, really proud of you." In the background I could hear someone whispering, "Hurry up." "Grandpa, Melissa's here and she thinks I'm hogging the phone."

"Well, we wouldn't want her to think that, would we?"

"It's okay. She's worse than I am about sharing the phone."

In the background, I could hear a loud disclaimer. "I am not."

"Luke, may I speak to Melissa?"

"Sure. Here she is."

"Hi Grandpa." The cheery voice of this seven-year-old warmed me like no other.

"Melissa, how're you doing?"

"Fine, but Mama's crying."

"What's the matter?"

"I think she's just happy that you called us."

"When we get through talking, will you give her a hug for me?"

"Sure."

"And ask Luke to give her a hug, too."

"He already is."

"Good. Now, may I speak with your mother?

Jenny wanted me to come, to be with her and the kids. Nothing would have pleased me more, but I knew I had to finish the damn report—to complete my contract with TEI. I tried to explain.

Jenny tried to understand.

We ended with a truce. I promised to end things quickly. She said she understood, but when she said it, it pulled at my heartstrings. I held the phone until I heard the line go dead. Then I called Elizabeth. No answer at her office. I tried her home and got her.

"Hi, how're you doing?" I asked.

"That's not the question," she said.

"Oh?"

"The question is, how are *you* doing?

"I'm okay."

"Where are you?"

"Hobby Airport. Hangar 345. It's where Powell keeps his Lear."

"What happened?" she asked.

"A lot. May I tell you later?"

"When is later?"

"How about dinner? I can pick you up—" I looked at my watch, surprised to see that it was almost five o'clock. "About seven?"

COLLUSION

"How about I fix dinner for us at my place?" she suggested.

"I'd love it, but I don't know where you live."

"It's 11345 Westheimer. About a half-mile west of the Macaroni Grill—where we had dinner."

"Got it. What time?"

"Anytime. This is Saturday. Come as soon as you can."

I had lost track of the days of the week. "Okay, see you as soon as I can, probably a couple of hours."

We hung up and I went back into the hangar, to the scene of the shooting. I found Reed Upton with two policemen who were taking statements. Upton seemed glad to see me.

"This is Dr. Christopher Hartman," Upton said. "He's a witness. He saw everything."

I gave a complete report to the two policemen. I related the whole story: the kidnapping of my family, the scene at the Hyannisport Airport, Smith's cold-blooded murder of his assistant, his kidnapping and bringing me to Hobby, and finally, Upton's rescue.

Then a couple of homicide detectives came and they wanted the entire story again.

By this time the media had gathered and they insisted on interviews with Upton and with me. I tried to be cooperative.

Finally, I made my way to my parked Toyota and drove to Elizabeth's apartment. Fighting the late afternoon Saturday traffic, I made it by six-fifteen.

It seemed natural for us to embrace. The perfume, which I had always thought pleasant, held special meaning. I inhaled it and pulled her tighter.

CHAPTER 45

Elizabeth's Apartment

I hadn't been sure what to expect when Elizabeth answered the door. There had been little time to talk. I'd been through hell the past few days but she'd been the one waiting, not knowing what was going on. From the tear on her cheeks I guessed the waiting hadn't been easy.

The kiss, the embrace, the welcome—all turned out to be more than I expected. I think our passion surprised Elizabeth, too. For a while we just stood silently, our arms wrapped around each other, each of us waiting for the other to let go. Finally, I made the first move.

Relaxing my embrace, I shifted to hold both her hands and brought them to my lips for a light kiss. "Sure is nice to be welcomed home," I said.

"I wasn't convinced I'd ever see you again."

"Accountants are indestructible. You can't get rid of us."

Then she surprised me. With her fist, she hit me in the stomach, just above the belt buckle. She meant it to be a light, playful tap, a gesture to scold me for downplaying the danger of the past few days and the worry I'd caused her. But she misjudged. She knocked the wind out of me. I doubled over, struggling to breathe.

Immediately, she tried to make amends. "Oh, Chris, I'm sorry. Are you all right?" She grabbed my left arm and started patting me on the back.

I gasped for breath. Holding my abdomen with both hands, I made wheezing sounds and staggered over to lean against the wall. I poured it on—thick, especially the gasping.

Elizabeth bought it. Hook, line, and sinker, she reacted with apprehension and concern. "Chris, I didn't mean to."

I continued to grope for air.

"What can I do? Would you like a drink of water?"

Abruptly, I stopped acting, gave her a big smile, and said, "No, but a glass of orange juice would be nice."

Realizing she had been duped, she hit me again, in exactly the same place, and harder.

This time I was ready. I tightened my stomach muscles and her punch landed on a hardened knot of flesh.

"Ouch," she said, wringing her hand.

"Come here," I said, taking her into my arms.

I guess we both had thought about the possibility. We were adults, free, and not without experience. But when the possibility turned to reality, it came as a surprise to me, and I think, to her.

We made love, not like strangers but as if we had spent years together. A natural and satisfying union.

The next morning I awoke in her bed to the aroma of fried bacon, toasted bagels, and fresh coffee.

Breakfast was followed by more explorations of our mutual tastes, then more soft and satisfying lovemaking.

We spent the entire morning in bed.

I recounted the kidnapping.

She listened intently, to detail after detail.

When we came to the scene in the hangar, she asked me to retell it . . . several times. During the third recanting, she began to ask questions.

"Do you think Zimmerman is behind it all?" she asked.

"A week ago, I would've said no," I answered. "Absolutely, positively, no."

"And now?"

"Now, I'm not so sure."

A questioning look crossed her face, so I explained.

"If Zimmerman hired Smith, plotted the tactics of pressuring my family, and schemed to force me into falsifying the TEI report, it undermines my entire case against Upton."

"Knowing Zimmerman, it's hard for me to picture him in that role," she said.

"I agree."

She continued, "What about all of the details about the SPEs, the financial statement fraud, the money laundering?"

"Upton did it. I have the facts."

"So?"

"So, did Zimmerman orchestrate it? Did he set up Upton to be the fall guy?"

"Is that possible?" Elizabeth asked.

"Like I said. A week ago I would have said no." I thought about it a few moments. "In fact, I would have said, hell, no!"

"What are you going to do?"

"Check the facts, again," I said.

"Back to square one?" she asked.

"Not exactly. The world's largest energy corporation is in bankruptcy, and we know the specifics of how it happened."

"So, you'll be shifting from accountant to detective?"

"In forensic accounting, there's always a certain amount of detective work."

"Chris, you keep dodging the issue," she said. Her voice showed the edge of impatience. "Are you going to release the damned report or not?"

"Yes, but—"

"But what?"

"But I want to go over the motivations behind the major decisions," I said. "I want to satisfy myself that the hubris behind all of this came from Upton."

"Seems obvious to me."

"And to me."

"Chris, if it's so obvious, why not go ahead and release the report?"

"Because Upton saved my life."

CHAPTER 46

44 Leisure Cove, The Woodlands

That afternoon I drove to Jennifer's house. Five days of news-papers lay strewn on the front lawn, a sign to the neighborhood that no one was home. I gathered them up and walked into the house to the sound of a ringing telephone. "Hello," I said.

"Chris, where've you been?" I recognized the voice of Captain Michael O'Kelly, Houston PD. "We've been trying to contact you."

"I spent the night with a friend." I felt more than a little resent-ment. It wasn't any of his business who I was sleeping with.

"Have you read this morning's paper?"

"No, not yet."

"You need to," he said. "The Smith shooting is the lead story."

"Should that surprise me?"

"Upton's making this a major strike against Zimmerman."

As he talked I sorted through the stack of papers and found the cur-rent issue. Pulling the plastic wrapper off, I dumped it on the kitchen table. The front page flopped open. I read the headline: "Zimmerman Accused of Hiring Hit Man." Directly below the big, two-inch head-ing were three photographs—Zimmerman, Upton, and me.

COLLUSION

"Wow. The *Chronicle* didn't waste any time, did they?"

"Anything connected with TEI is news."

"Of course."

"A killing like this just makes the story bigger. The most sensational case of the decade is now more juicy than ever."

"Houston PD feeling a little pressure?"

"A little?"

"What do you want from me?" I asked.

"Information," he said.

"I've told you everything I know."

He paused and I sensed he didn't agree.

"You want to talk about this?" I asked.

"Yeah," he said, "we need to get together."

"Fine," I answered, "Where? When?"

"Chris, my ass is on the line. I'm under terrific pressure to make an arrest."

"Can you arrest both Zimmerman and Upton?"

"With the information I have now, one of them is guilty, the other's innocent."

I didn't respond for a few moments. This time I was the one doing the thinking. He waited.

Finally, I said, "Before you and I flew to Hyannisport, I left ten copies of my TEI report in the Houston PD evidence room."

"I remember."

"Pick up those copies and meet me for dinner tonight."

"Where?" O'Kelly asked.

"Many moons ago, when Smith made the first threat against my family, Joel suggested we meet at the Wyndham Greenspoint to talk over all the possibilities."

"I know that hotel. The one with all the trees."

"Seven o'clock?"

"I'll meet you there with the copies."

"And Mike," I added, "it'll help if you can look over the report."

"Is this an assignment for class, Dr. Hartman?"

"You said you wanted information," I reminded him.

"How many pages are we talking here?"

"About three hundred and fifty."

"Jesus, Chris."

"At least read the executive summary. It's only five pages."

O'Kelly signed off and left me with a couple of hours to think about his problem. Actually it was *my* problem as much as his. I couldn't do anything about releasing the TEI report until the Zimmerman versus Upton question resolved itself. It seemed obvious that the criminal and civil issues linked themselves at the source. Find the person responsible for one and it solved the other.

I decided to put TEI on the back burner and called to check on Jennifer and the kids. Today was Sunday but, tomorrow, she planned to send them to school. A return to routine would help settle her life. I promised to join her as soon as possible.

Next, I called Billy Ray Powell. Thanking him profusely for the use of his Lear, I assured him I would have the TEI report ready very soon. I withheld my doubts about Upton and left him thinking we would proceed as before.

Running down my list of things to do, I tried to call my three CPA associates. As per my instructions, they had all disappeared. I left messages, asking that they call me at the office, and make immediate plans to return to Houston.

I looked forward to dinner, and at the same time dreaded the implications of our conversation. But, the restaurant's festive atmosphere lifted my spirits. This was ten days before Christmas, and the Greenspoint went all out for the holiday season. The huge greenhouse-like lobby, with its dozens of indoor trees, now glittered with thousands of Christmas lights. Tiny, white lights sparkled throughout the indoor forest, giving a spectacular tinsel-town effect. I found O'Kelly seated at a relatively secluded corner table in the coffee shop, an open copy of my report on the table before him.

"How much have you read?" I asked.

He looked at his watch. "Almost two hours worth," he replied.

I chuckled. "Most people respond in pages, not hours."

"Chris, all this stuff about SPEs—the Special Purpose Entities, hiding debt, and financial statement fraud—is out of my league."

"Ironically, I think it's shifted to something else. Something that's in your line of work."

"What do you mean?"

"If we could find out who hired Smith, that would probably be the number one clue to who was behind all the financial crime."

"Upton hired Smith. He admits it."

"According to this morning's *Houston Chronicle,* Upton says he hired Smith at Zimmerman's insistence."

"Which means, Upton is saying that Zimmerman set him up."

"What do you think?"

"I guess I'm leaning in that direction," Mike said.

"You've read enough of my report to understand where that puts me?"

"Yeah. You're going to have to rewrite your report."

"Which, I don't mind doing, if—"

"If Zimmerman masterminded this mess, plotted the murders,

and sent Smith to kidnap your family."

"Let's order. I hate to talk about this on an empty stomach."

We both ordered the same—roast prime rib, baked potato, and a house salad. He ordered a glass of Merlot. I would have loved to. For the first time in several days, I thought about alcohol. I pulled out my chip and did the calculations: one year, four months, three weeks, and three days.

The waiter brought Mike's glass of wine.

"Sure you won't join me?" he asked.

"Thanks, I'm fine."

"So, are you going to rewrite your 350-page tome?"

"Not until you can convince me Zimmerman is, in fact, the heavy."

"Suppose I arrest him. Will that convince you?"

"No."

"What'll it take?"

"Let me ask you a question," I responded. "Are you ready to arrest Zimmerman?"

"Could happen tomorrow."

"Based on Upton's accusations?"

"Plus, he shot Smith."

"True."

"And he saved your life."

"Yes, he did."

"His statement that Zimmerman framed him, sounds plausible," O'Kelly said.

I shook my head. "I question that."

"You aren't absolutely certain he didn't, though."

"Well, no."

COLLUSION

"Public pressure is pushing us to make an arrest."

"So, what're you going to do?"

The waiter brought our salads. O'Kelly appeared to welcome the interruption.

"I guess we'll rework the Upton/Smith connection. Check again to see how the contact was made, and especially look for clues about Zimmerman's involvement."

"Sounds good."

"And we'll watch you."

"Me?"

"If you decide to rewrite your report and name Zimmerman as the person behind the fall of TEI, that would be enough. We'd follow your lead and file criminal charges against him for the Smith murders and kidnapping."

"And if I don't?"

"If you name Upton, I don't know what we'll do."

We picked at our salads.

They brought our steaks.

The big, beautiful prime rib looked medium rare, just the way I like it. It came with horseradish and the aroma was superb. The baked potato was loaded with butter, sour cream, bacon bits, and chives. I've never seen one that looked better. I tried my best to eat this big, tantalizing meal.

I managed a couple of bites and quit.

O'Kelly finished his. We walked out together.

"You okay?" he asked.

"My stomach's tied in knots," I replied."

"You'll get over it," he answered.

CHAPTER 47

44 Leisure Cove

In my bathrobe and slippers, I went out to get the Monday morning edition of the *Houston Chronicle,* expecting that TEI would continue to be front-page news. I wasn't disappointed.

The headline read: "Still No Indictments at TEI." The newspaper ran different photographs of the same three people—Zimmerman, Upton, and me. I took the paper into the kitchen and read it carefully while downing cereal, milk, and coffee.

The *Chronicle* left no doubt in their depiction of the "good guys" and the "bad guys." The story reported that Upton, their quintessential man in the white hat, was working night and day to try to save the corporation, save jobs, recoup losses, and, in general, justify his status as the hero of TEI. The highlight of his superman image was his rescue of me and his killing of the hit man, Smith. Zimmerman, on the other hand, was berated by the press and saddled with all of TEI's problems. The CEO ordered those who worked for him to create the SPEs, to hide debt, and to commit the illegal acts that brought about the fall of the corporation. Frequently, he was cited as the person who had selected Smith and authorized his employment.

COLLUSION

I could see that unless I changed my report, I was going to have an uphill battle with my characterization of Upton.

But I charged ahead, oblivious of the trend taken by the press. I needed some additional information, and called the office of the Chief Financial Officer of Texas Energy, Incorporated.

"Reed Upton's Office," the secretary said. Her familiar voice conveyed the usual frosty, unwelcome response.

"This is Christopher Hartman. May I speak to Reed Upton?"

"Mr. Upton is extremely busy," she answered. "I'll take your number and see if we can have someone call you."

I gave her two numbers—home and office.

"What is this regarding?"

"My report to the TEI Board of Directors," I said. "Maybe you should contact Mr. Upton. I think he'll want to talk to me."

"I have my instructions," she replied.

"I don't mind holding while you ask."

She responded with a sigh of exasperation.

Before she could answer, I jumped in. "Upton is the central figure in this report, which will be soon released to all of the media. He may be disappointed to learn you declined my offer to let him review it."

During the long pause that ensued, I could almost hear her thinking about my words, "you declined."

Finally, she responded. "Just a moment, please."

Five seconds later, I heard the familiar voice.

"Dr. Hartman, how are you?"

"Alive. Thanks to you."

"We'll never know for sure what John Smith had in mind, will we?"

"Having witnessed Smith's cold-blooded murder of his coworker at the Hyannisport Airport, I think I could see what he had in mind for me."

"All's well that ends well, I always say."

"Well, thank you for saving my life."

"You're entirely welcome."

"But I still have to make a report to the Powell Committee."

"Yes, I know."

"Unfortunately the report, as it is now written, will not portray your CFO work in favorable terms."

"I figured as much."

"I'm calling to offer to you a chance to review the report and to meet with you privately in case you want to respond to any of the material before it's released."

"Chris, I appreciate your offer. And yes, I'd like to do that."

"I'll send it to your office this morning," I said.

"How much time can I have?"

"How about two days?"

"That would be fine," he answered. "I'm assuming it will be to my advantage to meet with you, so, can we set up a meeting for ten o'clock Wednesday morning?"

I agreed to meet him and we said our goodbyes.

I dressed carefully, my first time in a week to wear a coat and tie, and joined the rush hour, slow march into downtown Houston. Caitlin was there, cleaning the office.

"Hey, I just called you yesterday afternoon," I said.

"Yeah, my folks gave me the message," Caitlin said.

"You were supposed to be safe, hiding out somewhere in New England."

COLLUSION

"I figured that's what the bad guys would think."

"So, where were you?"

"Hiding out here in Houston at a friend's house."

"Caitlin!"

"I've been very careful."

"Well, the good news is that Smith's gone."

"I know, it's been in the *Houston Chronicle.* I was expecting your call."

"I could use a little help."

"Ready to go. What can I do?"

I gave her a copy of the report. "Run this up to Reed Upton. His office is on the fiftieth floor."

"Is this what I think it is?"

"The completed report—the final document."

"You're giving it to Upton?" She rolled her eyes.

"You need to do this quickly, Caitlin. They're waiting for it."

Reluctantly, she took it and hurried out the door.

The phone rang and I made a mistake—I answered it. A reporter from *U.S. News and World Report* wanted a telephone interview. I tried to answer her questions, yet maintain a noncommittal position. She didn't like "neutral," and rephrased her questions repeatedly, trying to maneuver me into taking a stand. All the while, the other phones continued to ring. I begged off and hung up.

Caitlin retuned and we programmed the answering machine to take calls.

"How'd it go at the CFO office?" I asked.

"Mission accomplished," she said. "I gave the report to Reed Upton himself."

"Any reaction?"

"He seemed pleased to get it."

"Why do you think that?"

"Well, he said it at least three times, and he walked me to the door."

"Any other feedback?"

"He said he's going to meet with you at ten o'clock Wednesday morning."

I nodded.

"What's going on?" she asked.

"Caitlin, did you know Upton saved my life?"

"Not really," she said as she shook her head. "All I know is what I've read in the papers."

"Smith was all set to take me as a hostage to some out-island in the Caribbean, and that would probably have been the last you'd ever have heard from me."

She looked stricken. "I read in the *Chronicle* that Upton killed Smith," she said, cautiously.

"I was there. I saw it."

"Oh, wow. Of all the people who might come to your rescue, Upton is the last person I'd have expected."

"Yeah, me too."

"Why would he take such a risk? Am I missing something?"

"Exactly what I've been asking myself."

"Didn't he regard you as the enemy?"

"When he reads that report you just gave him, he won't have any doubt I'm the enemy."

"He won't?"

"No, he'll *know* it. In spades."

She heaved a sigh, shook her head, and stared at the floor. Caitlin was one of the most organized people I knew. She didn't like confusion and it showed in her reaction.

"I'd like you to do some research for me," I said, attempting to coax her out of her temporary funk.

She looked up. "Okay, sure."

"We need information on John Smith."

"Not exactly my favorite person," she said.

"Nor mine, but we need to find out more about him."

"Any suggestions about where to look?"

"Start with TEI's personnel department. You might get some help from Houston PD. And, there's always the Internet."

"Anything special to look for?" she asked.

"Yes," I answered. "Search for contacts with Zimmerman and/or with Upton."

Caitlin went back to her desk and started working.

Soon after, Bart and Jack arrived. After a short greeting and update on the situation, Caitlin took them undertow, and the three of them divided the search for information about Smith.

I called Elizabeth and arranged to meet her for dinner at her apartment. She asked me to stop by the Macaroni Grill and bring take-out pasta. And she offered to furnish the wine. I started to ask about a Diet Coke, but didn't get the chance.

At six o'clock, we met at her house.

"What'cha got?" she asked as I handed her the sacks of food.

"Lasagna and caesar salad,"

"Smells heavenly," she said, leading me into the kitchen. I have a Robert Mondovi Merlot that should be perfect with the lasagna." She handed a bottle to me with a corkscrew.

I started to explain about my non-alcohol status, but it didn't seem like the right time. Instead, I said, "I'll open the wine while you dish up the food." I wondered how I could gracefully ask for something nonalcoholic to drink.

"What, no lovey-dovey?" She smiled, mischievously.

"I was hoping we'd get to that after dinner."

"The most important things, like food and wine, come first?" The smile was ear to ear.

"Was it Einstein who said, 'It's all relative'?"

"Professor, you'll have to do better than that."

"How about Socrates?"

"Socrates?"

"Socrates said, 'Moderation in all things.'"

"I believe Socrates said that when he was drunk."

I punched her in the tummy, exactly as she had hit me on Saturday evening. It took her completely by surprise and my light punch knocked the wind out of her. She staggered back, holding her abdomen with both hands, and making gasping sounds. I put my arm around her and started patting her on the back.

"You okay?" I asked.

"No," she whispered, between gasps.

"Relax, I have experience with this condition."

"So, is this payback time?"

"I hadn't intended it."

"Sir, what are your intensions?"

"Honorable, ma'am, I assure you."

"Well, shucks."

"Well, how about some dinner and then we'll negotiate." I held out my arms and she came to me. We embraced. We kissed, slow lingering kisses.

COLLUSION

She surprised me. "Dinner's getting cold."

"Damn."

"You're the one who's been insisting we eat."

"That was before you enticed me."

"Open the wine." She released me and started dishing up the salad and lasagna.

I opened the bottle, poured one glass of Merlot, one glass of water, and joined her at the table. We had a toast and then started in on dinner. Dinner tasted wonderful. Elizabeth watched as I scarfed down my half of the meal and then finished what was left of hers.

"You were really hungry," she commented wryly as I swallowed one last bite of lasagna.

"No lunch," I admitted.

"I noticed you skipped the wine."

"Yeah, there are some things you don't know about me."

"Want to tell me?" She placed her hand on mine.

"I'm what is known as a recovering alcoholic."

"I didn't know. Sorry about the Merlot." She squeezed my hand.

"That's okay. Happens all the time."

"I'm here to listen if you want to tell me about it."

"Not right now. I'd rather talk about the Zimmerman/Upton dilemma."

"I may have some inside information," she said.

"Really?"

"These last couple of months, since TEI's stock cratered, I've grown closer to Upton's secretary."

"Ms. Congeniality? I had a run-in with her today. It wasn't pleasant."

"It's all front," said Elizabeth. "Her name is Joella Jordan, and

307

underneath that icy exterior is a very thoughtful, hard-working person. Like a lot of us, she's running scared, afraid she's about to lose a high-paying job."

"She has her bluff in on me."

"Plus, she's the personnel secretary for everyone who works on the 50th floor."

"She processes the paperwork for everyone who's hired or fired?"

"On the corporate level."

"Would Joella have the details of how John Smith was hired?"

"More than any other person at TEI."

I thought for a few moments. "How loyal is she to Upton?"

"I'm not sure, but I think she's more scared of losing her job than being loyal to anyone in particular."

"Really?"

"Really. Guess what? Joella and I are having lunch tomorrow."

"Ma'am, ah had no i-dee y'all Texas ladies were so devious."

"Let's wait and see what I can find before you start passing out compliments."

I stood, took her in my arms. Eventually, we ended up in her bed.

Tuesday I slugged away at the office. The feeling that the walls were closing in—that the time for me to finalize the report, to name names—motivated me to review every scrap of information. Elizabeth called and we talked about me spending the night at her place again. I wanted to, but I knew that for my meeting with Upton, I needed a good night's rest and an early start tomorrow morning. She sounded disappointed.

I hated it. But duty calls at the most inopportune time.

CHAPTER 48

44 Leisure Cove

I should have spent the night at Elizabeth's. Try as I might, restful slumber eluded me. I tossed, turned, dozed, and finally got up just before the alarm went off. My normal routine of shaving, showering, and a McDonald's breakfast eaten in the car, put me into a foul mood to tackle rush-hour traffic into downtown Houston.

After a brief stop at my office, and the long ride up to the fiftieth floor in an express elevator, I arrived at the office of the Chief Financial Officer. Before walking in the door I checked my watch to find the only good news of the morning—five minutes until ten. Better to be early than late for a meeting that was sure to be confrontational.

"Mr. Upton's expecting you," Joella, the secretary said. "It'll be just a moment. May I get you a cup of coffee?" She didn't smile, exactly, but her greeting was certainly a step up from the usual, frosty brush-off I'd encountered in previous visits.

"No thanks." I took a seat and wondered if her semi-friendly welcome was, in any way, the result of her luncheon with Elizabeth.

Almost immediately, Upton came out of his office and gave me his full treatment. I stood as he grabbed my hand.

"Dr. Hartman. Good to see you this morning. How's your family?"

"Fine, thank you."

"Are the children back in school?"

"Just started back today."

"And your daughter, Jennifer, how's she doing?"

"Just fine. Thank you for asking."

"Will they be moving back to the Houston area? Is there anything I can do to make their adjustment easier?"

"We've not decided about their location. But it's good of you to offer your help. Thank you."

"Bryan was one of our brightest and best. If there is any way we can assist his family, please don't hesitate to ask."

"Thank you," I said. "Have you had a chance to look over my report?" A rhetorical question, I was sure he had studied it with a microscope. I steeled myself for his reaction.

Surprise.

He reacted calmly. In a normal tone of voice, he answered with a question.

"Have you considered the possibility that you're wrong?" He said it so nonchalantly, so casually, it seemed surreal. I could picture him asking about the weather and suggesting that the forecaster might be wrong.

I didn't know what to do, what to say, or how to react. So I played along. "Yes, I've considered that. In this business there is always that possibility." I waited for him to make the next move.

"At first it might appear that we are on opposite sides," he said. "That you are accusing me of a number of illegal acts and some poor financial judgment that brought about the fall of the corporation." He

COLLUSION

paused. "And that I am fighting back, denying your allegations."

"I think you have summarized the circumstances well," I answered.

"Actually," he said, "for the big picture, I think we're on the same side."

How could that be, I thought. But I said, "Go ahead."

"We both want to find those persons who brought about the fall of TEI."

I didn't say anything. And I wondered where this was going.

"Certainly," he continued, "we both want to see that all illegal acts are uncovered and that those responsible are punished."

"That's my job," I answered.

"I want to help you," he said. And he said it with a straight face.

"Even if the investigation points to you?"

"*Especially* if any information points to me."

For the next few moments we sat there, eyeball to eyeball, waiting to see who would blink first. In the deathly stillness I could hear a copy machine in the next room. I was so aware, I think I could have heard dust settling.

Finally, I looked down. Reaching for my briefcase, I pulled out a yellow pad, took a pen from my pocket, and got ready to take notes. "As you know, the report has a great deal of material that points to you. If you'd like, we can take it point by point?"

"I'd like that very much But may I make a suggestion?"

"Go ahead."

"Why don't we move to the boardroom and use the big table? And if you don't mind, I'd like to ask our comptroller, Larry Norton to join us."

"I don't mind at all. Lead the way."

We moved down the hall where Larry was waiting for us. He had the table loaded with documents. The big room, the huge table, the stacks of material, and the appearance of Norton, gave the impression that I was in for a lengthy dog and pony show.

"Where should we start?" Upton asked.

"Your choice," I answered.

"Let's take the Special Purpose Entities, first. On page twenty-one you cite—as an example—the Cayman Energy Limited, a partnership corporation we call CEL"

"Yes." I was proud of the documentation. It listed Upton as president, included photocopies of the charter signed by him, and cited insider trading which acknowledged payments to him in the amount of slightly more than thirty million dollars. It was one of our best examples of Upton's wrongdoing and would be sure to make headlines when the report was released. As one of the leading illustrations of Upton's blatant involvement in TEI's downfall, I looked forward to hearing what he would have to say in defense of the case I had made.

"I was acting on instructions of our CEO, Richard Zimmerman," Upton said. He produced a stack of letters and memos. I read the first three carefully, and scanned the next six. Time after time, Zimmerman spelled out directives for Upton. One memo even covered the sale of CEL stock, the most egregious example of Upton's wrongdoing. Zimmerman had written to Upton, specifically ordering Upton to sell it.

"CEL's charter was illegal," I said. "You used TEI stock to collateralize it."

"Yes, I know," Upton replied.

"The SEC strictly forbids this when forming a partnership corporation. It has to be new money and the capital has to be at risk."

COLLUSION

"Larry has a memo from Dennis Johnston, our chief auditor with Stephen Svensen." Upton nodded and Larry Norton handed it to me.

I scanned the two-page document and read where Dennis Johnston instructed Norton and Upton to sign the charter application. Dennis, the auditor, acknowledged the SEC rule but gave his reasons for going ahead. In his last paragraph, Dennis stated that he and Zimmerman had gone over the potential for being cited by the government for illegal action. I read the sentence slowly and carefully:

The SEC rarely examines this aspect of a charter application, and if they do, Texas Energy, Incorporated *can claim 'Scribner's Error,' a clerical mistake. Zimmerman has ordered me to prepare the charter for you to sign. If you object to doing so, you'll have to clear it with him.*

The gist of Upton's response was that the charter infraction was minor and that— acting on the advice of the chief auditor and orders from his CEO—he was caught in a corporate squeeze. If he'd done something wrong, perhaps even technically illegal, the blame should rest with those who were advising and ordering him to do it. It sounded plausible. I decided to go on to other infractions, of which there were many.

"Let's put CEL aside," I suggested.

"Sure," Upton said. He smiled the smile of a winner. "Why don't you pick the topics you want to discuss?"

We started down the list. I had a total of seventy-three others to pick from. I chose the ones I thought were the most blatant.

We took infraction after infraction. Money laundering, financial statement fraud, illegal wire transfers—the gamut of white-collar crime. Upton had prepared well. He had an answer for everything. Most of the time he had something in writing to document his position, to explain that it was either accidental or it was someone else's fault. When he didn't have it in writing, he just said, "No, it was verbal, but you can ask so-and-so."

Finally, we came to money. I pushed hard to nail him on insider trading. I had the facts. He had sold shares at high prices before the stock fell. He answered me with two questions.

"What was the date of that transaction?" he asked.

"September 30," I answered.

"Was that the same date Bryan Banks sold 75,000 shares at $41.23?"

His two questions stopped me cold. If my own son-in-law had sold shares, how could I hold Upton's feet to the fire? I changed to the one topic I thought most incriminating—his relationship with the hit man.

"Apparently, you had a hand in employing John Smith," I said.

"I was, and still am, in charge of TEI security."

"So you chose him, employed him—he worked for you?"

"That's only partly right," Upton said. "Zimmerman picked him out. On Zimmerman's orders, I employed Smith. He reported to me for his official TEI security duties, as do all security officers."

"Houston police say Smith murdered both Bryan and a police detective named Joel Wilson."

Upton looked at me silently, nodding his head in agreement.

"Smith kidnapped my family and tried to force me to rewrite this report."

"Didn't work, did it?"

"Obviously."

COLLUSION

"Chris, you need to give me credit for minimal intelligence. If Smith worked for me, the last thing I would do is send him to threaten your family, a flawed scheme that was doomed to fail."

His reasoning—viewed after the fact—made sense. In fact, it sounded so reasonable I couldn't think of a response.

"And why would I kill Smith? If Smith worked for me, all I had to do was give him the money and let him take you away."

Upton had my attention, and his words zeroed in on my emotions. Brilliantly, he had now pinpointed exactly my expectations on that Saturday afternoon at Hobby Airport. I couldn't argue.

We sat there quietly for a few moments and I felt like a heel. Here was the man who had saved my life and I was trying to cut him down. My report, if approved by the government, would mean certain prison for civil indictments. And even worse, possible criminal charges for his involvement with Smith, for kidnapping, and for at least two counts of murder.

I looked at my watch, surprised to find that we'd been going for almost three hours. "I think that's enough for today," I said.

"Chris, I appreciate this opportunity to respond to your report."

"Certainly. It's the least I could do."

"I hope I've convinced you to make some changes."

"You've certainly given me a great deal to think about."

"I've prepared a written response." He handed me a big, impressive-looking document, almost as thick as my 350-page report. I scanned the title page: *A response to the Christopher Hartman TEI Report" by Reed Upton*. "Most of what we've talked about this morning is included—with documentation."

"Look, Reed, I'm not out to get you," I said.

"Would you say that again?" he asked.

"I'm not out to get you."

"Just to be sure I understand, would you say it again, slower?"

"I'm . . . not . . . out . . . to . . . get . . . you." I said with emphasis.

"Thank you," Upton responded. "However this turns out, I know your motives are honest and sincere." He rose, and held out his hand.

I shook it and left.

In the elevator on the way down, I felt a sense of unrelenting turmoil. Frustration consumed me. I stomped into the office, went directly to my room, and slammed the door.

After months of backbreaking, bone-crushing labor, I knew what caused the TEI debacle. I could tell the world in great detail about the illegal acts, the specific details of white-collar crime, and the loss of trillions. In most cases I could cite names, acts, and dollars.

However, it now appeared the one thing I couldn't do was what the country wanted most—provide the name of the person who'd led this disaster.

With hands in my pockets I paced. And I felt the chip. Dismayed, thwarted, and miserable, I took the chip and hurled it at the wastebasket. It hit with such force it made a sharp clang. I walked out of the office.

"Where are you going?" Caitlin asked. "Are you coming back?"

I didn't reply.

Outside, on the street, I searched for a bar. Two blocks away I found one. The lunch crowd was gone and it was too early for happy hour. I took the last stool away from the entrance.

The bartender gave me a look of welcome. "Yes, sir?"

"Double Scotch, on the rocks," I said.

"You're Dr. Hartman, the TEI investigator?"

COLLUSION

"Yes, that would be me."

"I've seen your picture on the front page these last few days," he said with obvious admiration. "You're gonna nail the guys who took all our money, right?"

"Just an accountant, trying to do my job." Actually, I was annoyed that he wasn't getting my drink.

He shook his head as he moved down the bar and splashed a generous amount of Scotch into a big shiny highball glass. "Us folks here in Houston are sick of these shysters who are stealing millions and getting away with it," he said, adding ice.

He set the drink on a paper napkin in front of me.

I stared at it.

The pale, gold color was as beautiful as a cloud-filled sunset on a summer day.

"A black kid can steal fifty dollars from the convenience store on the corner and our criminal justice system sends him to Huntsville for ten years. These big shots at TEI steal billions and get away with it." He smiled at me as he went on talking to a near-empty bar. "Dr. Hartman, I'm sure glad we've got people like you to hunt 'em down."

I looked again at the beautiful glass of Scotch, and then up at him. He grinned back at me with a look of unbridled admiration.

And I made a decision. In my heart of hearts I believed Upton to be the individual whose pride, greed, and arrogance had led to the downfall of Texas Energy, Incorporated. I couldn't prove it conclusively, but I decided to stick my neck out and go with my gut feeling.

I got up and left a ten-spot on the bar.

"Hey, your drink," he called after me.

I walked out the door.

Back in the office, I called Billy Ray Powell.

"Billy Ray, I want to release the TEI report," I said. "I'd like to call a press conference for ten o'clock tomorrow morning."

"Okay," he said. He responded with much less enthusiasm than when I'd called him the first time. "I've been following the articles in the *Chronicle*. They're saying that Zimmerman is the man behind all our troubles."

"I think they're wrong," I said.

"You think it's Upton?"

"Yes."

"God, Chris, I hope you're right."

"You want to be a part of this press conference in the morning?"

He didn't say anything.

"Billy Ray, if you want to pass, I'll handle it by myself."

"If you don't mind, Chris, I think it best for me to sit this one out."

"Sure, I understand."

We said an awkward goodbye.

I phoned the TV stations and the newspapers.

Elizabeth called and invited me to come by. I told her about the news conference and asked for a rain check so that I could spend the evening getting ready for the morning's presentation.

"After you get your press release ready, you could come over and spend the night."

"What, you think I'm easy?"

"There have been rumors."

We talked some more and I asked about her search for information about Smith. She said she'd lunch with Upton's secretary, Joella Jordan, and that she might have something. If so, we'd have to give it a few days because Joella was really scared.

COLLUSION

As I hung up, I reached down into the wastebasket and retrieved my chip. Taking a moment to calculate the days—one year, four months, three weeks, and six days—I thought about trying to find a meeting.

Instead, I picked up my car, drove north to Jennifer's house, ordered pizza, popped open a Diet Coke, and settled in at Bryan's computer to write the mother of all press releases. Then I noticed the blinking light on the telephone's voice mail.

I pushed the button and listened to the recording, "You have one new message." Then the voice of James Wright, one of the three TEI board members who served on the investigation committee, came on.

"Chris, I've learned that you have called a press conference for ten o'clock tomorrow morning and that you are going to try to nail Reed Upton. I think you're making a terrible mistake. Upton's a good man. He's a strong leader, and if TEI has any chance to survive this mess we're in, he's the person we need to support. I hope you'll reconsider."

The machine made a beeping sound, and blinked its little red light.

It was all I could do to keep from grabbing the phone and throwing it out the window.

CHAPTER 49

The Investigation Office, TEI Building

Thursday before Christmas, my next-to-last day in this office. At least I hoped it would be. With a bit of luck, I could soon pack and take a flight to Boston to be with my family for the holidays.

Arriving at the office early, I busied myself making final corrections to my press release. Caitlin, Jack, and Bart soon appeared and kept the photocopy machines humming. By nine-thirty we had fifty copies of both the TEI report and the handout. My assistants found three, two-wheel dollies and we loaded our stacks of paper for the trip to the fiftieth floor. I packed my prepared speech in a briefcase and held the door for the others to roll our materials down the hall toward the express elevators.

Just as the last dolly rolled out the door, a surprise visitor appeared—Larry Norton, the comptroller.

"May I visit with you for a moment?" he asked.

I looked at my watch—nine-thirty-five. "Larry, I have a press conference in the boardroom in a few minutes. I could talk with you after that."

"Then it will be too late." He handed me a document.

COLLUSION

I glanced at it. It had the name of a bank in Zurich, Switzerland in the letterhead. "Larry, I have to go. People are waiting."

From down the hallway, about fifty feet away, Caitlin called, "Dr. Hartman, the elevator is here, do you want us to go on?"

"Yes," Norton answered for me. "He'll be there shortly."

I resented Norton's intrusion, and I started to yell for Caitlin to wait. But before I could get the words out, Norton whispered urgently, "This will only take a minute and it may be the most important decision of your life." He held the door open and gestured for me to step back inside the office.

Reluctantly, I did. "Make this quick," I said. And I said it with anger and in a tone of voice that left no doubt about my antipathy.

"Take just a minute to look over those papers."

I looked at the document again but without comprehension. I could see someone had listed my name. And in the middle of the first page—in big letters, set off from the narrative—was the following:

$30,000,000.00 (Thirty Million in U.S. Dollars)

"What is this?" I asked.

"It's a Swiss Bank Account in your name in the amount of $30-million," Norton said.

"What . . . a bribe?"

"It's something my friends and I want to do to help Reed."

"No way."

"You don't even know what we're asking."

"It's obvious, isn't it?"

"Chris, don't be a fool. How many times in your life have you had an opportunity for money like this?"

"I won't dignify that question with an answer."

"The money's there. You don't have to do anything illegal to get it."

"You and I have different definitions for the word illegal."

"No one has to know."

"Larry, that may be true except for one important exception."

"What's that?" he asked.

"*I would know.*"

He looked stunned.

I handed the papers to him. "I have to go." And I hurried down the hall to the express elevators and pressed the button.

On the fiftieth floor, at the boardroom, I found what could easily be described as a lynch mob. TEI was definitely the news of the day and it attracted a mix of newspaper people, magazine writers, free-lancers, and an overabundance of radio and television crews. In a sense they reminded me of the barbarians sweeping into Europe, looting and savaging. Only in this case they weren't looking for worldly goods, but for news, for any tiny scrap of information that would fill their needs for a slant or unique angle into history's top financial story.

I fought to bring order into chaos by insisting on making an opening statement. It worked. Gradually, my summary, which I read, brought the unruly assembly into a modicum of order.

My speech lasted ten minutes. Roughly paralleling the five-page executive summary, which I had written for the report, I spelled out the principal causes for the downfall of Texas Energy, Inc. Of the seventy-four illegal actions cited in the report, I chose the fifteen most serious and gave a brief summary of each.

News people need headliners—tiny little news bites that will capture readers, listeners, and viewers. I knew this and I gave them some. The best one, in my opinion, was a number—one point three trillion in loss of shareholder equity.

Repeatedly, I used the name Reed Upton. His signature was on the CEL charter as president. He'd organized five other SPEs, which were used to hide debt and accounted for a majority of the illegal wire transfers. As CFO, he had primary responsibility for interacting with Stephen Svensen Accounting, and, therefore, shared accountability for the lapses in TEI audits.

On purpose, I deliberately avoided two specific topics: Richard Zimmerman and criminal indictments.

By omission, Zimmerman came across as a benign bumbler. While I didn't use the term, the inference was certainly there. I hoped Zimmerman would have the good sense to recognize the favor I had done for him.

The omission of accountability for two murders and a kidnapping was justified, in my opinion, by the nature of forensic accounting. These criminal actions, no matter how involved and/or intertwined with finances and accounting, remained the province of law enforcement agencies.

Then I took questions.

At first the crowd shouted and chaos returned.

I started pointing, like the president does at news conferences. That was something news people understood, and soon a measure of order returned. I tried to pick people I knew or those who represented reputable news agencies, reporters who wouldn't try to nail me to the cross.

I won some and I lost some. Overall I thought I came out ahead. Even Lisa Tegmeyer, head reporter for the *Houston Chronicle,* and a leader in current thinking that Zimmerman was the "root of all evil," gave me a degree of respect, and with her line of questioning, indicated some latitude in the *Chronicle's* current editorial position.

After an hour of grueling questions, I thanked them for their kind attention and suggested they refer to the report itself for further answers. They didn't like that and some of them followed me to the elevator. With Caitlin, Bart, and Jack, we beat them back and managed to take an elevator, by ourselves, for an escape to our fourth-floor office.

I thought some might be waiting for me but they weren't.

My three associates were full of compliments. Together we found chairs at our conference table and prepared to meet for what I thought would be our last time together.

"Dr. Hartman, did you see what Upton's people were distributing?" Bart asked. He handed me a one-page memo.

MEMORANDUM

From:	*TEI Public Relations*
To:	*All Area Media*
Re:	*Special News Release*

Tomorrow, Friday, December 20, TEI's Chief Financial Officer, Reed Upton, will hold a special news conference to present his "insider information" about the cause of the corporation's recent financial problems.

He will, in particular, give factual information that refutes the statements recently distributed to the press by the Christopher Hartman report.

This news conference will be held in Room 5005 of the TEI Building at 10:00 a.m.

"Didn't take him long, did it?" I said it with a smile. And I expected some laughter, or at least a chuckle in response. Instead, what I got from my three assistants were worried looks.

"Dr. Hartman, he's out to discredit our report," Jack said.

"And you," Bart added.

"What did you expect? Upton is fighting for his life. He has to go on the attack."

"An attack is his best defense," Caitlin said. As usual, she zeroed in to the bottom line.

"Troops, you've done your job," I said. "And you've done it well. Time now to call it quits and head for home."

"Aren't we going to fight this?" Bart asked.

"No. "We've done our work. Our report is out there for the whole world to evaluate. It's good, solid, forensic accounting. And, most importantly, it's honest. It'll do just fine. You'll see."

My pep talk helped. It didn't "carry the day" as I would have hoped, but it quelled the discussion and any ideas about further work by our team.

They packed. And by the end of the day everyone was gone except me. I continued to pack and was just about to wind it up when Elizabeth called.

"Congratulations on your presentation this morning."

"Were you there?"

"Back in the corner."

"I didn't see you."

"Good. I was trying not to be noticed."

"Worried about losing your job?"

"The minute Upton and his bunch become aware that I'm on your side, that's the end of my employment at TEI."

"I have a suggestion."

"Okay. I'll take whatever you've got."

I hummed a few bars of the famous song by Johnny Paycheck.

"That a clue?" She laughed.

"Come on, you know the song."

"So, we're playing 'Name That Tune'?"

"The name of the song is 'Take This Job and Shove It.'"

She chuckled. "I have to admit, I've thought about it."

"Elizabeth, I've been thinking about this a lot. I'd like you to come to Boston with me."

"Would I qualify for housing at the Hartman Home for Unemployed?"

"Or the Salvation Army, your choice."

"No strings at the Salvation Army."

"Nor at the Hartman Home."

"Maybe I should look into this?"

"Quit your job. Move to Boston with me. Start a new life."

"How about easing into this decision? Give me a little space so that I can meditate about what I'm getting into."

"God, you're a hard sell."

"Someone was making jokes about me recently because they thought I was easy."

"Elizabeth, I'm serious. I want you to move in with me."

An awkward pause lasting too long fell between us. I struggled to think of what to say. Before I could form the words, she responded.

"Okay," she said.

CHAPTER 50

The Investigation Office, TEI Building

The next morning, after spending the night at Elizabeth's apartment, I went back to the office to finish packing and close up shop. About midmorning, a delegation of two reporters and a photographer from the *Houston Chronicle* came into the office. I recognized Lisa Tegmeyer, their leading investigative reporter on the TEI story. Lisa had helped me over the past several months when I needed access to newspaper files.

"Good morning," she said.

"Hi, Lisa, guess I know where you're headed." I looked at my watch to see that it was 9:30, only a half hour until Upton's press conference.

"Yeah, we stopped by to invite you to go with us," Lisa said.

I laughed out loud. I didn't think about it, it just popped out. And the amazing thing was that the three of them laughed, too. Then something infectious grew out of the situation. We started laughing at each other. Lisa took a Kleenex and wiped her eyes. Finally, after a long five minutes of uncontrolled mirth, the laughter subsided and we each regained a semblance of control.

"Whew, I didn't know the TEI war could be that funny," I said, wiping the tears from my eyes.

"All the more reason you need to come with us," Lisa said.

"An Upton press conference is the last place on earth where I would be welcome."

"You can stand in the back corner with Jonesy." She nodded to her colleague, a 300-pound giant of man who looked more like a tackle for the Houston Texans than a reporter. "He plans to place himself in the back and write about the reaction of others."

When I first learned of the press conference, I had quietly thought about how interesting it would be to hear what Upton had to say. And I facetiously entertained ideas of trying to sneak in to the boardroom, to be a "fly on the wall," so to speak. But I dismissed it as wishful thinking.

Now, here were some people offering me the chance.

I took it.

And as we boarded the elevator, I studied my companion. His name was Herbert Eugene Jones, Junior. Lisa called him "Jonesy." Everyone else called him "The Refrigerator," because of his physical resemblance to the famous tackle who played for the Chicago Bears in the 1990s.

When we exited the elevator, I walked close, ducked my head, and let Refrigerator shield me. As we headed into the boardroom to take our places in the back corner of the room, opposite from the huge glass wall and as far away as possible from the big conference table and the speaker's lectern, I hunkered down into his shadow. Well hidden, I searched the room for Reed Upton.

The CFO was nowhere to be seen.

COLLUSION

The crowd, composed of mostly the same people as the day before, appeared to be less feisty.

At exactly ten o'clock, Larry Norton and Reed Upton came into the room. Norton walked to the microphone.

"Thank you for coming," he said. "I'm Larry Norton, and I am the comptroller for Texas Energy, Incorporated. We have a hand-out." He held up a big, thick document, which I supposed was the same material Upton had given to me on Wednesday morning. "Does everyone have a text?" A few did not. TEI secretaries quickly distributed copies to those who wanted them.

"It's my pleasure to introduce to you my friend and colleague, the Chief Financial Officer of TEI, Reed Upton." Norton backed away from the mike and clapped. A surprise to me, everyone in the room followed suit. clapping along with him. The difference in the reception given to me yesterday morning and what was happening now, for Upton, astounded me.

I could see that I needed to take a few lessons from Reed Upton in how to work the press. He was off to a much better start. An uneasy feeling came over me as I thought about the implications of things to come.

Upton began by recounting his accomplishments, of which there were many. He was the CFO of the nineties when TEI changed from a small gas pipeline company to become the largest energy corporation in the world. He presented chart after chart on a big easel in the front of the room. Most of these accomplishments were familiar to me, but the striking presentation made them seem far more impressive. To those assembled in the room, it must have been dazzling.

After establishing his credentials for building the company, he started his defense of my attack. He didn't mention my name, always referring to me as "his detractors" or "outsiders who are quick to criticize." Point by point, he always had an answer. And in simplistic terms, his answers had the ring of credibility. Here was the CFO of the company, the man whose middle name was "finance," giving expert testimony.

It was a brilliant presentation. Slick, polished, and convincing. I could see that he was winning the hearts and minds of the press.

Then he took questions.

And the tenor of the queries confirmed my suspicions. Hardly any question addressed the TEI problems. Instead, person after person asked about the accusations against him. One openly asked if he planned to sue for defamation of character.

Upton responded with elegance.

"I hold no grudge against those who malign me," he said. By taking the high road, he adroitly avoided criticizing me. That placed me in the role of an unsavory critic, a person who was destroying his reputation, denigrating his accomplishments of the past, and impeding his ability to save the corporation.

This went on for almost an hour and then Upton turned the mike back to Norton.

Upton left the room with heavy applause.

Norton addressed the group. "I have one last bit of evidence to show you the type of mudslinging that's going on. Wednesday morning Reed Upton met with Christopher Hartman, the man heading the TEI investigation. I have a tape recording of a part of that meeting I'd like to play for you so that you can hear for yourselves the nature of the intimidation to which we are being subjected."

Then he played the tape.

Two voices, Upton's and mine, were immediately recognizable.

COLLUSION

Upton: "Chris, I appreciate this opportunity to respond to your report."

Me: "Certainly. It's the least I could do."

Upton: "I think we're on the same side. We both want to find those persons who brought about the fall of TEI."

Me: "Go ahead."

Upton: "I want to help you."

Me: "Lead the way."

Upton: "Let's take the SPEs. On page twenty-one you cite CEL.

Me: "Yes, CEL's charter was illegal."

Upton: "I was acting on instructions of our CEO, Richard Zimmerman."

Me: "But the SEC strictly forbids this when forming a partnership corporation."

Upton: "Larry has a memo from Dennis Johnston, our chief auditor with Stephen Svensen. Let me read it. 'The SEC rarely examines this aspect of a charter application. Zimmerman has ordered me to prepare the charter and for you to sign. If you object to doing so, you'll have to clear it with him.'"

Me: "Let's put CEL aside."

Upton: Like I said, I want to help you clear this up."

Me: "Apparently, you had a hand in employing John Smith. You chose him, employed him—he worked for you."

Upton: "That's only partly right. Zimmerman picked him. On Zimmerman's orders, I employed Smith."

Me: "Look, Reed, I'm out to get you."

Upton: "Would you say that again?"

Me: "I'm . . . out . . . to . . . get . . . you."

At that point, Norton stopped the tape. The room was so quiet the "click" came at us like a rifle shot. For a moment no one moved or said a word. I wanted to yell, to say to the room, "He doctored the tape." But I didn't. Instead, I pointed toward the door, a signal to Refrigerator that we should leave. He nodded and together we sneaked out, the first ones through the door. As we left I could hear a few bits of conversation.

"Wow."

"Hartman is sure trying to do a number on Upton."

"He won't get away with it."

"Character assassination."

"It's sure to backfire."

"Yeah, big time."

I left Refrigerator at the elevator and walked down the hall to the CFO's office.

"What do you want?" Joella asked, her frosty persona now back at full force.

I didn't respond. Instead, I walked past her desk toward the door to Upton's office.

"Stop. You can't go in there," she yelled, rising to her feet.

I turned the knob and walked in to find Upton standing by the window, a highball glass in his hand. Joella was right on my heels. "That's okay," he said to his secretary. "I'd like to visit with Dr. Hartman."

She stood there, nonplussed.

"Joella, please close the door behind you," he said.

"You sneaky son-of-a-bitch," I said. "You doctored the tape."

"No, we just rearranged the conversation." He smiled. "And left out a couple of words."

"It'll never fly," I said. "Eventually, the truth will come out."

"Chris, want to see what I was looking at?" He gestured with his glass at an object outside the window.

"No."

"Come here, you'll find this interesting. If you'll look at this tanker for a minute, I'll make a deal with you." He smiled. It was a slick, oily smile, the kind one kid gives to another when he has something he knows you want. "I'll tell you about Smith."

Reluctantly, I walked halfway, close enough that I could see the tanker he was pointing toward. It was huge.

"That's the Exxon Galleon, sister ship to the Exxon Valdez. It's for sale."

"Tell me about Smith."

"And I have a secret, like the spiral staircase, a feature of this building that not many people know about."

His comment about the spiral staircase caught me off guard. I wondered how many people knew about it, or realized its implications in Bryan's death?

"It's a hidden balcony." He turned to his right a few steps, pulled back the drapes, and opened a door. He disappeared through the door.

Forgetting for the moment about the staircase, I walked over and cautiously looked outside. The small balcony was about three feet wide and fifteen feet long. Upton, with his drink in his hand, stood at the far end and motioned for me to come closer.

I didn't want to do it. A cool December day in Houston was no time to go out on a balcony, especially one that was fifty floors above street level.

"I want to tell you about John Smith," he said. His words were slurred.

HARRY HAINES

I'm an expert on drunks. I was one. I'd bet the drink he held was at least his third. If so, I knew I'd better talk to him now before he passed out, or worse yet, fell over the railing.

"Come on," he said, again.

I didn't want to do it. And when I took the first step it scared the shit out of me. But I walked out on the balcony and cautiously inched halfway down its fifteen-foot length. "Tell me what you know about Smith."

"He was a cold-blooded bastard." Upton took one last drink to empty his glass. Then he threw it. He hurled it like a football, a big strong throw that sailed it out away from the building. It caused him to loose his balance and he teetered back and forth at the the railing.

I grabbed him and kept him from falling.

"We'd better go inside," I said.

"Wha'sa matter? You scared?"

It was obvious to me that his state of inebriation was rapidly growing worse. I took one of his arms, hooked it around my neck, and used my other arm to loop around his back and grasp his belt. Then, mustering all my strength, I started dragging him down the length of the balcony toward the door.

Upton, the drunk, didn't want to go.

"You said you wanted to hear about Smitt . . . 'bout Schmidt."

"Yes, inside."

"I'm only gonna tell you out here on the balcony."

"You can tell me inside." I inched us a little closer to the door.

"Outside." He yelled it and his demeanor changed.

Some drunks are playful. Up to that point, Upton had been.

Some drunks are vicious. It appeared to me that Upton was now changing into one of the most vicious drunks I had ever encountered.

COLLUSION

"Outside!" He kicked and screamed.

I looked at the door. So close, but with Upton on a rampage, I didn't know if we could make it. I pulled. He jerked my head and we almost went over the rail together. I slipped my head out of his grasp and used both hands to get a grip on his arm. We gained a few inches and I thought for a moment I could force him to the door.

Then he really became furious. He put his foot up against my thigh and kicked, all the while yanking to free himself. I couldn't hold him, and when we came apart, he fell back against the railing. The force of his separation from my grasp pulled him away with such momentum he couldn't stop.

He went over the railing.

Fifty floors down.

To his death.

CHAPTER 51

The Fiftieth Floor Balcony, Outside Upton's Office

Halfway in the door, halfway out on the balcony, I stood panting. Horrified. I didn't want to look, but I did.

I forced myself to the railing to peer down at the tiny figure sprawled below. People gathered around. Some looked up. Traffic stopped.

I staggered back into the office and slumped into the first chair I saw.

For a few moments I sat and did nothing. My heart pounded and I felt nauseated. With trembling hands, I found a tissue and wiped the perspiration from my brow. Gradually my breathing and pulse slowed. I rose, steadied myself on my feet, and slowly made my way to the outside office.

Leaning against the doorway, I spoke to Joella. "Call 911."

"What for?" she asked. Her voice quivered, an indication that she was scared of me and of anything I wanted.

"Upton, fell," I said, weakly. "Call the police."

"Fell. Where?" she asked.

"From the balcony," was all I could say. I looked for another place to sit.

She jumped up from her desk and hurried into Upton's office. Moments later she screamed.

In response to her scream, the other two people in the room ran into Upton's office.

I took a big breath, got up, walked over to Joella's desk, and dialed 911. In slow, careful words, I asked for the police and an ambulance. Then I gave a brief explanation of what happened.

The next two hours were the longest of my life.

It started with a couple of uniformed policemen. They took my statement, and asked me to wait in Upton's office.

In what seemed like hours, but in fact were only a few minutes, Mike O'Kelly arrived.

"Tell me what happened," he said, pulling up a chair beside mine and flipping open his notebook.

I recounted the situation and gave him the conversation, as best I could, word for word.

"You want a lawyer?" he asked.

"No."

"Might not be a bad idea," he cautioned.

"I've done nothing wrong."

"The press is after you," he said. "They smell a story."

"Fine. I'll talk to the press. There's nothing to hide."

"Chris, I've seen situations like this before. These people are after blood. If you don't give it to them, they manufacture it."

"I'll give them the truth. If they print something else, I'll sue them."

"I wish it could be that simple."

"Truth will win out. I told that to Upton less than an hour ago."

"See, *that*'s what I mean," O'Kelly said.

"What's *that*?" I asked.

"Invoking the name of the deceased."

"So help me, Mike, it's the truth."

"So you say."

"You don't believe me?" I asked.

"Of course I believe you, but I know you. News people don't know you. They won't believe you. They want to believe Upton— it's the best story."

"Mike, I've dealt with the press."

"From the viewpoint of a person who is suspected of killing someone?"

"Well, no."

"Take it from me, you're in a new ball game."

I said it again. "Truth will win out. That's the creed I've followed throughout my life and it always works."

"Truth in this situation is dull, uninteresting. These people hope you're lying. They want a cover-up, something that sells news."

"Sorry to disappoint them."

"They won't take 'no' for an answer."

"How about drunkenness?"

"Upton was drinking?"

"Skunk drunk," I said. "Have your medical examiner check his blood alcohol."

"Hmm." O'Kelly gave me his faraway look—the *thinking* look.

I waited, too exhausted to do otherwise.

"Drunkenness helps, but it doesn't absolve you. You could have pushed him—drunk or sober."

"Are you accusing me?"

"No, just trying to do my job."

"How can I prove my innocence?"

"I don't know that you can."

"What happened to 'innocent until proven guilty'?"

"It's still there, one of the foundations of the American judicial system."

"Well?"

"In this case, you've been heavily involved, publicly, in a dispute against Reed Upton."

"So?"

"He could have died of a heart attack in the middle of Times Square with a thousand witnesses, and some people would say you caused it."

I thought about what my friend was trying to tell me. Neither of us spoke for the next few moments.

"I think I'm getting through to you," he said.

"You think I'm a suspect for murder?"

"Personally, no. But as an official from Houston PD, I'll be the one who has to arrest you."

"Guess I'd better take your advice and call a lawyer."

"There's the phone." He pointed.

"Problem is, I don't know who to call."

"How about Billy Ray Powell? He's a partner in one of the biggest law firms in Texas."

I called Billy Ray. And he came to the TEI Building with one of his young, hotshot criminal law partners. Together we went with O'Kelly to police headquarters where I was released after questioning.

I called Elizabeth to ask if I could "hide" at her apartment.

A cab took me there, unobserved.

HARRY HAINES

I spent the night.

The next morning she fixed a big breakfast—bacon, eggs, toast, orange juice, and coffee. It smelled wonderful and tasted great. As a result I felt a bit of starch coming back into my persona.

"Feel like talking?" Elizabeth asked.

"Sure. I always feel like talking to you."

"Last night you didn't."

"Yesterday was a trying day."

"I guess being questioned as a murder suspect qualifies as a trying day," she said.

"But today I'm ready to talk." I tried to give her a smile of encouragement—a forced smile. "What's up?"

"Joella Jordan."

The smile quickly faded. "Upton's secretary?"

"Yes, I went to lunch with her on Wednesday."

"I remember. How'd it go?"

"She let something slip."

"Oh?"

"She said to be careful in Upton's office. He tapes conversations."

"Yeah, I know. He doctored the tape of our Wednesday meeting and had Norton play it at the Friday morning press conference."

"Joella called me Friday afternoon."

"After Upton's death?"

"Yes."

"And?"

"She knows where the tapes are. She said for me to call her if you want to listen to them."

"What tapes?"

"*All* the tapes."

340

COLLUSION

"Say that again."

"All the tapes. Every word that was ever spoken in Upton's office. They go back for years."

I smiled. And I didn't have to force it. It was a real, big, natural smile that filled my face.

Elizabeth smiled back at me.

We called Joella Jordon and asked her to meet us at Upton's office at ten o'clock. Then we called Mike O'Kelly, told him about the tapes, and he agreed to meet us at the same time and bring a crew of HPD recording experts.

Elizabeth and I drove to the TEI building. We didn't know what to expect.

First, we found that Upton did not have years and years of tapes. He only had about fifty of the big fifteen-inch reels, which, the HPD recording guys said would go back about ten or eleven months— less than a year. Apparently, Upton used the tapes over and over, erasing the previous material. But, for our purposes, ten months was enough. It gave us information about the fall of TEI and the role Upton played in the financial dealings.

We started with the most recent tape, a recording of two men talking. I recognized the voices as Upton and Norton.

Upton: Did Wright call him?

Norton: Last night, Wright called the house and left a message.

Upton: Any result?

Norton: Apparently not. He's going ahead with the press conference this morning at ten o'clock.

Upton: "Did you prepare the Swiss Bank letter?"

Norton: "Yes I have it here." (*Sound of paper rattling.*)

Upton: "Looks authentic. Larry, you do good work."

Norton: "What'll we do if he calls to check this out?"

Upton: "Have him call the bank and talk to Franz Schmidt. Schmidt is my banker. He'll cover for us."

Norton: "What if he tries to withdraw funds?"

Upton: "I've instructed Schmidt to transfer anything up to one mil. If Hartman gets greedy and tries to withdraw the entire thirty, we'll have to go to plan B."

Norton: "Without Smith, how can we do plan B?"

Upton: "You or I will have to do the dirty work."

Norton: "Reed, I don't think I can handle a plan B assignment."

Upton: "Relax, we're a long way from that." (*Pause.*) "It's after nine. You'd better get down to Hartman's office and get ready to make the offer."

(Sound of paper rattling. Sound of door closing.)

Machine recording: "Thursday, December 19, 9:03 a.m."

"The recording is voice activated," O'Kelly explained. "Whenever there's conversation, it turns on. When conversation ends, it stops and the machine cues it with date and time."

Then we heard a click and the machine started again.

Upton: "How'd it go?"

Norton: "He turned it down."

Upton: "He *what*?"

Norton: "He turned it down."

Upton: "Did he suspect it wasn't a bona fide offer?"

Norton: "No, he bought it."

Upton: "I don't understand. What happened?"

Norton: "Reed, he saw it as a bribe and he turned it down."

COLLUSION

Upton: "Even a dumb ass doesn't turn down thirty million."

Norton: "Well, Hartman just did. I couldn't believe it."

Upton: "Thirty million!"

Norton: "It wouldn't matter how much."

(Pause, sounds of people moving.)

Norton: "You'll have to think of some other way."

Upton: "Well, if he's really a Boy Scout, I know how we can get to him."

Norton: "How's that?"

Upton: "We'll outshine him with purity and goodness."

(Laughter.)

Upton: "Call a press conference for ten o'clock tomorrow morning. Get the girls to run-off an announcement and pass it out to the news people at Hartman's meeting in the boardroom. Better hurry."

(Sounds of quick movements and door closing.)

Machine recording: "Thursday, December 19, 10:21 a.m."

"Thank god," I said, almost numb with relief. Upton's hubris had just saved my life. If he hadn't installed the tape recorder—

"And we now know, that's exactly how it happened," Elizabeth said, flashing me a huge, encouraging smile.

"We'll take the tapes and make a complete transcript," O'Kelly said, standing to leave.

"It's going to take some time to do all fifty tapes," I said.

"Whatever it takes," O'Kelly answered, "we'll do it."

"I have a suggestion," I said. "Start with late September and see if there's any information about how Smith was hired."

"Good idea," Elizabeth said, "Smith came to work the first week in October."

The police left with the tapes.

Elizabeth and I faced Joella. I wasn't sure how to handle our new relationship.

Elizabeth embraced her and said, "Thanks." That helped.

I took her hand and held it with both of mine. "I don't know how I can thank you."

Joella smiled. The first time I'd seen her without a frown. "I'm just glad it's over," she said.

Then Elizabeth and I drove to Galveston. We found a little seafood restaurant and pigged out on boiled shrimp. It was a pleasant afternoon and we talked about us.

She wanted to quit her job. There didn't seem to be any future at TEI, and she wanted to come with me back to Boston—but only on a temporary basis. No long-range commitments. We'd live together for a short time and see how it went. Christmas on Cape Cod with my family would be the first test.

When we got back to her apartment that evening, we found a message on her answering machine. Elizabeth pushed the button:

"Elizabeth, this is Mike O'Kelly. I assume you're in touch with Chris since I can't seem to find him. Tell him we have a transcript of the tapes for the last week in September. Upton had ties to the mob. He used his contacts to find a hit man by the name of Giovanni Lucero. When Lucero came to work at TEI, he used the name John Smith. We've traced him through FBI files and found that he has a rap sheet as long as my arm. Incidentally, the name Smith was suggested by Upton. We have it on tape. And there is absolutely no doubt that Smith was hired by Upton to murder Bryan Banks. Tell Chris he's no longer under suspicion. Merry Christmas."

CHAPTER 52

11345 Westheimer Road

The biggest problem in getting Elizabeth to come to Boston turned out to be logistics. She couldn't decide what to pack.

A single woman with a high-paying job at a Fortune 500 corporation had to have something to spend her money on. After a few days in her apartment I figured out what it was.

Clothes.

She showed me her closets and I almost went into shock. Closets—plural. Two for clothes and one for shoes. I will never understand what any woman would want with a hundred and thirty-seven pairs of shoes.

From the first day I met her, I realized she dressed beautifully. Always elegant, immaculately groomed, stylishly coiffured. What I didn't know was that Elizabeth Garcia was the biggest clotheshorse in the history of women's fashion.

But I didn't push it. Instead, I went with her to a luggage store where we purchased two huge suitcases to go with the four she already had packed. I warned her that my condo in Cambridge had limited closet space. She defended herself, saying I lived there and

345

she was moving. Therefore, she had to bring extra.

When we reached the airline ticket counter at George Bush International, we checked seven bags—six for her, one for me.

The guy at the Continental counter just smiled.

At the airport in Boston, I found a minivan taxi. Even then, we had trouble getting seven suitcases on board. At each step of the way we had a good laugh. In fact, that's the way I would describe life with Ms. Garcia . . . a barrel of laughs. But I kept my stomach muscles ready for the punch—just in case.

As soon as we had suitcases in the door, I called Jennifer and arranged to drive out to the Cape the next day.

That night and into the next morning it snowed—big, fluffy flakes that turned everything white. When we got to the beach house we found Luke and Melissa outside throwing snowballs. Kids in Houston rarely experience snow. These two new residents of Massachusetts thought it was wonderful.

Luke and I carried in wood and we made a roaring fire in the fireplace.

Jennifer and Elizabeth shared a common thread with Bryan. He had been the focus of each of their lives, one personal and at home, the other professional and at work. They didn't talk about it—but I sensed the mutual concern and the empathy it brought to their rapport.

After a while, Melissa sidled up to me with a deck of cards. "Grandpa, wanna play 'Go Fish'?"

"Sure," I replied. Together we sat at the kitchen table where I expected we would play our usual two-handed game.

"Could we ask Elizabeth to play, too?" Melissa asked.

"How about it?" I asked Elizabeth.

COLLUSION

"You'll have to explain the rules," Elizabeth answered as she pulled out a chair.

We had a great game while Jennifer prepared dinner and Luke programmed the VCRs to record the evening news.

At the cabin we had two TVs—one in the family room and one in the back bedroom. So when the national news came on at 6:30, we watched CBS and taped ABC and NBC.

We sat by the fire, watching all three newscasts, one after another.

As expected, the lead story on each was TEI. They used film clips from my press conference, photos of Upton and Zimmerman, and a live interview with the federal prosecutor in Houston. A federal judge quoted my report saying that indictments were being prepared against all those persons named.

Mike O'Kelly and an FBI Agent were shown. They confirmed that John Smith, A.K.A. Giovanni Lucero, murdered three men and kidnapped my family.

And finally, Reed Upton was identified as the person behind it all. He'd caused the downfall of the world's largest energy corporation, the greatest loss, up to that date, of shareholder equity, and he, personally, had hired the murderer.

Each of the networks gave a short tribute to the "Hartman Report." It was held up as a testimonial against wrongdoing of all kinds. I liked the words the commentator used.

He said, "Truth will win out."

Luke turned off the VCR and we had a moment of closure, of family happiness. Jennifer came over and gave me a hug. It seemed the perfect time to hand my daughter her big surprise.

I gave her the Prudential Insurance Policy.

"What's this for?" she asked.

"Now that Bryan's death is no longer ruled a suicide," I said, "you can collect on his policy."

Her face flushed, and her eyes grew larger as she tried to ferret out the implications of what I had just said. "Say that again?"

"You'll have to sign some papers, and it'll take about a month, but you've got a big check coming."

"A million dollars?"

"No," I said.

"No?"

Then I paused, trying to heighten the tension, and I gave her my best father-to-daughter smile. "*Two* million," I answered. "The policy has a double indemnity clause."

For a moment I thought she was going to cry again. But instead she laughed. It was a laugh that bordered on hysteria.

Melissa and Luke wrapped their arms around Jennifer's waist.

"Momma, what's so funny?" Melissa wanted to know.

"Mom, are you all right?" Luke asked.

Jennifer pulled up a kitchen chair, sat down, and hugged her two children. "Kids we're rich." She beamed—the biggest, brightest, glow I'd seen since Bryan's death. "We can save the house. Everything."

For the next few moments I just watched. Melissa climbed up on her mother's lap and kissed her. Jennifer pulled Luke close and squeezed him.

In the quietness of the cabin we could hear the Atlantic, the waves pounding the shore in rhythmic repetition. A full moon now filled the horizon with a brightness that illuminated the shoreline and the white foam that covered the harsh blue of a wintertime ocean in full attack. The fire crackled. And the cozy shelter of our little house enveloped our world.

COLLUSION

Elizabeth came over and put her arms around me. "So tell me about the hero business," she said. "What's it feel like?"

CREDITS

A published novel is always the result of collaboration. I'd like readers to know a short list of those to whom I am indebted.

The first thing people notice about any book is the cover. I'm lucky to have a good friend and colleague who is a very talented artist. Steve Mayes worked tirelessly with multiple designs to produce the cover for this novel (and covers for my other two novels). He and I met for coffee every Monday morning to kick around ideas. And together, we want to thank Pat Hickman and the Happy State Bank (of Canyon, Texas) for allowing us to "borrow" the $100 bills that you see photographed in the cover's background.

Doris Wenzel, my publisher, also likes the artwork that Steve Mayes produces. She chose the cover and made all the final decisions about publication. If you like the layout, thank Doris.

Paula Silici (of Pro-edits in Denver, Colorado) who I believe to be the world's best book editor, went through the manuscript and made hundreds of suggestions. The fact that this manuscript is 99.9% free of errors is due mainly to Paula and her blue pencil.

There's a lot of Harvard University in the story and I have Jim Aisner, Director of Media Relations for the Harvard Business School, to thank for all the authentic details.

Garret VonNetzer, former publisher of the *Amarillo Globe-News*, called his friends at the *Houston Chronicle* and made appointments for me. Garret's newspaper buddies welcomed me and briefed me about SPEs, CELs, and all the intricacies that can cause a major energy corporation to go belly-up.

What would a thriller be without a kidnapping and several murders? Well, thanks to Joel Richardson, Randall County's award-winning Sheriff, Collusion has stuff like "The Stockholm Syndrome" and authentic FBI procedures such as "Isolate, Contain, Negotiate." Thanks, Joel, I couldn't have done it without you.

Good critique groups are hard to find and I was lucky to have two that helped with this novel. Janda Raker, Joan Sikes, Diane Neal, and Caron Guillo met at the church on Thursday afternoons. We read our stories aloud, and learned from each other. Wednesdays at noon, I had lunch with Betty Deckard, Scott Williams, and Jodi Thomas. We took each other's writing home and worked hard to make the stories better.

And again, I feel obligated to quote Fred Harris—former US Senator from Oklahoma, now living and writing novels in Albuquerque—who says that the two most boring human activities are studying and writing. Since I don't do much studying, I'm not sure about that, but Fred is dead right with his theory that "writing requires powerful stimulus to get it done." I've found that I do it best in a restaurant, early in the morning, sitting alone in a booth, with white noise to block out aural distractions and the pleasant aroma of food to create a comfort zone.

Collusion was mostly written in Denny's Restaurant on I-40 in Amarillo. Those nice folks always welcomed me and never once talked about charging me rent. And finally, special thanks to Diane McGinnis, the world's best waitress, who brought at least 1,000 cups of coffee to keep me writing.

—Harry Haines, August, 2010

Novels by Harry Haines

Orphan

Texas Panic

Collusion